KARL MARX

and the LOST CALIFORNIA MANIFESTO

a novel

SCOTT D. CARLSON

Chucklehead Press

For Kathy—for everything.

Contents

JOAQUIN
MURRIETTA

1

A Most Desperate Character

August 14, 1879, San Francisco

I DON'T FREQUENT SALOONS, BUT A GENTLEMAN ASKED TO meet me in one of this city's finer ones for some business, and I wanted to oblige him. I didn't know where else to meet, having just returned here after thirty years away; the town's change is such that I hardly believe what I see. When I left here it wasn't much more than a large camp, and now it's one of the biggest cities in the country. The people have changed too. Back then, in the gold rush, this place was mostly open to anyone from anywhere; not all of California was open to people like me, but this town was, to all comers. Today, I wasn't sure I would be served or even allowed in the "finer" saloon, but the gentleman I met was a regular, and there was no problem. One or two might have looked my way, but that was all.

As we were leaving the saloon, I overheard a red-haired man in a nearby booth telling his friends he'd seen the head of Joaquin Murrieta "pickled" in a jar. Hearing this, it was all I could do to keep calm until we were outside and I could ask the gentleman I'd done business with if he, as someone who went there often, knew the red-haired man. He did, and I asked if, as a favor, he would go ask the man where he had seen Murrieta's head. He did so, and when he came back, he seemed a little embarrassed.

"Dr. Jordan's museum," he said, "on Pine Street, close by."

I had never heard of the place, but then again, I'm more or less still a stranger here and don't know much about museums. Doctor Jordan's was only a short walk away. Under the sign on the street front that read "Dr. Jordan's Pacific Museum of Anatomy and Science" was another that said "Gentlemen Only." At the door, I paid a young man twenty-five cents to get in, and he gave me a little handbook titled *The Philosophy of Marriage and Catalogue of the Museum*. I was curious to read what the "philosophy" was all about, but the first room I entered commanded immediate attention. The room had its own name: the Pathological Room. On several tables were parts of bodies—heads, feet, hands, inner parts, even private parts—that looked pretty real, but as there was no odor in the room other than burning oil lamps, I soon realized they were colored paraffin or wax. By lamplight, I read about some of the "models":

> "892—Head of a young man, illustrating general appearance arising from the filthy habit of self-abuse. The look of imbecility and languor accompanying the features are highly indicative of consumption and general debility. This party died from excessive exhaustion and decay."

> "958—Very fine dissection of the Neck and Head, showing the brain, etc. The emaciated appearance of the face, and general look of imbecility, is the result of the pernicious habit of self-pollution."

> "989—Very fine model of a young man who died from Syphilis, in New York. The ulcerations on his person are as truthful and natural as the art of the artist can design."

According to the catalogue, these specimens were supposed to "inculcate in the minds of visitors the lessons of virtue, wisdom, and morality," as were many other examples of male and female private parts in stages of disease and rot, brought on by the sins of their owners. Some of these owners had been lucky patients of Dr. Jordan, who had "successfully treated" them. There was no "philosophy of marriage" expounded in the handbook after all. I guess the whole display of "eruptions," "chancres," "ulcerations," and "buboes" caused by loose living was meant to spell it out for you.

Two samples that were of some personal interest to me seemed out of place in the "pathological" room, as they were no fault of their owners. One was the foot of a Danish man with nine toes on it; his other foot, not there, was said to have the same number. Next to his was his sister's foot, with eight toes. They both also had, according to the handbook, five fingers plus a thumb on each of their hands. I knew about extra toes but had never seen, or heard of, quite that many. Why, I wondered, nine for the brother but only eight for the sister? And how many did the parents have all together?

I was thinking it was a little strange that I was the only person in the museum when a short, bald man appeared in the doorway to the next room. He was wearing thick spectacles and a crisp bowtie.

"William Smiltberg," he said.

"I'm Harry Sexton," I said.

"Pleased to meet you, Mr. Sexton. I am Dr. Louis Jordan. Smiltberg was the Dane. His sister was six feet four inches tall. He was more than seven feet tall. A giant. You have an interest in polydactyly?"

"Polly who?"

"Polydactyly—having more than the normal number of digits. Fingers or toes."

"Oh, yes. A passing one."

The doctor smiled and nodded. He looked to be at least eighty years old but still quick and spry.

"And of the other specimens here? Your impressions?"

"To be honest, frightening."

"Then you are a wise man, Mr. Sexton. Some men think of themselves as gods. Or godlike, immune to the shocks that flesh is heir to.

My impression is you may be just the kind of man, Mr. Sexton, who would be interested in my service."

I asked, with a general idea of where the good doctor might be heading, "What service is that, doctor?"

"I have devised a highly accurate test of male urine. Once the test is applied, I can see, in a sample under a fine microscope, the elements of venereal blight—minute particles of the brain and drops of vital seminal fluid invisible to the eye. For only ten dollars, you may learn if you need to seek further treatment. I have successfully treated many difficult cases. Treatment is, I must say, at an additional cost—but your good health is priceless, yes?"

"Well," I said, "yes, but thank you—my health is fine. I am married."

"I have had many patients who were married men, Mr. Sexton."

"Thank you, doctor, I will keep your service in mind. Today I'm most interested in seeing the head of Joaquin Murrieta."

"Very well, then. I hope you will commend my service to any of your acquaintances who are in need. Murrieta—this way."

I followed the doctor through another, larger room not as "pathological" as the other—hands showing bones and veins, lungs, an extra-large tongue, skulls human and animal, a lobster—then into a smaller, end room with only a few things in it. On a shelf on the back wall I saw, floating in a clear liquid, a head. Dr. Jordan led me to it, reciting word for word the handbook description.

> "563—Head of Joaquin Murrieta, a celebrated bandit and murderer, well known in California in early days as a most desperate character and terror of the country. He was shot in 1853 by Captain Harry Love, who secured a State reward of $5,000 by his capture."

"There are many stories about Murrieta," the doctor said. "One is that Murrieta appeared nightly to Love and said, 'I am Joaquin Murrieta, and I want my head back.' I bought it by private sale.

Actually, the owner—not Mr. Love—pawned it to me and never redeemed it. What is your interest in it, Mr. Sexton?"

"I saw him once—a long time ago."

"You must have been very young at the time."

"I was, yes."

"Well," said Dr. Jordan, "enjoy your visit, Mr. Sexton. Stay as long as you please."

I thanked him, and when he left the room, I went closer to the jar so I was face-to-face with the head. It seemed to be real, not wax like most of the rest of the things in the museum. Maybe a bit puffy but well-preserved. The black hair and bristly mustache were floating a little in the liquid. One eye was closed, as if it were winking at me. I winked back at the poor soul, whoever he was. He wasn't Joaquin Murrieta. I had more than just "once seen" Murrieta—I knew him very well.

From Karl to Jenny

April 1, 1849

Aboard the ship *Fanny*

Mein Liebling Jenny,

We are now only a day or two before Acapulco, Mexico, out on the great Pacific Ocean. Even though we have come far from New York, I am sorry to say I have still not found my sea stomach, and I am often "paying tribute to Neptune," as the Americans on board say. The molasses and vinegar water they give to the seasick— "switchel"—is a cure worse than the malady. However, at times I am intoxicated by the winds and freedom of the sea—*Die Luft der Freiheit weht!* So unlike the dread I was feeling in London!

Our ship's miserable food hasn't changed since New York. The cook dishes up monstrous hashes that are easily offered up to Neptune—the alternating *plats du jour* are "scouse," a vile mash of salt pork, potato, and hard bread, and "hashmagundy," an even more bilious paste of turnips, parsnips, and fish parts. Breakfast brings "dandy funk," more hardtack cooked with molasses and raisins and cinnamon. They tried to give us moldy cheese, but several of us revolted and threw the barrels overboard. Our bread is full of weevils; if they make the coffee hot enough, you can soak the bread in it and cook the weevils. Some of us demanded that the captain take on fresh supplies at Rio de Janeiro, but he refused. A churl, he scoffed and said he's eaten this "cuisine"—slop—his whole life. We pressed the issue, but he said the ship could not take on any more weight. However, just as we were leaving Brazil, he brought on two women of questionable character and has housed them in his cabin. Don't be alarmed by these women—you know there are many poor souls like them in London.

I try to read or write much of the day, but it is hard to fight off the boredom. We sometimes have music. An American with a "fiddle" entertains us with folk songs and quaint ditties. One of his creations sums things up pretty well:

> We live like hogs penned up to fat our vessel is so small
> We have a duff but once a week and twice a day a squall
> A meeting now and then is held which kicks up quite a stink
> The Captain damns us fore and aft and wishes the box
>   would sink

But truly, Jenny, things are not so bad. I have hope now, which I had little of in London. If the reports about the gold in California are only half true, I am confident I will be coming home to you and the girls as a new man, able to pay our debts and erase the shame of poverty. I am sorry that we didn't have more time to make this decision together, but my—our—choices were limited. I had to leave soon or be thrown into prison for my debts. You, of course, did not want me to go, leaving you and the children. But where else was there to go? France and Germany will not allow me; even if all of us were to cross a border successfully, we would have to live a secret life. Sweden, maybe, but Sweden is a country without balls (and I'm not referring to fancy dances), not an actor in history anymore but a spectator. And Prussian agents would easily find me there. Indeed, where in Europe would they not find and hound me? Even now there are two men on the ship who I suspect are Prussian secret police. One of them is a mutton-headed giant who every night gives us all a tremendous nasal serenade. A Spaniard began calling him "Tenerife" because when he lay flat his huge nose resembled a mountain peak on the Canary Islands. The other is a fat dumpling with such flatulence that the Americans in the bunks threatened to throw him overboard, so he now sleeps on deck. His partner lashes him to the poop deck every night to keep him from being pitched into the sea. Why they are following me to America is a mystery, other than to report to their Master that I am not in Germany. Not even a dog can live in Prussia without the police spying on it.

Our journey has, it seems, been either doldrums or *Sturm und Drang*. Near the equator in the Atlantic Ocean, a calm of several days set in, so hot that the tar on the ship's mast and sides melted like caramel. To pass the time, many of us improvised fishing poles. I caught a shark! One of the crew helped me haul it in, then cut its heart out, and that organ lay on the deck for several hours, still beating, and jumped when I touched it! Then we were tossed about by several storms before, during, and after Cape Horn. Most of us lashed ourselves in our bunks to avoid being tossed out. More than once waves came over the deck and washed into our compartments, making us miserably wet. A silver lining of the storms was that they kept off the Patagonian Indians, who, some on board averred, are cannibals.

Still, for all the trials, I am healthy, while many on board are not. We have slid more than one shroud-wrapped corpse into the sea. They had been afflicted with the cholera, and the meager remedies of mustard plaster, massage, and doses of camphor or laudanum laced with pepper or ammonia were useless.

Ah, Jenny: I realize now that I am melancholic proof of my own ideas—I, too, at least for the time being, am dominated by the lust for money. There are too few men on earth who are not. At times I wonder if any. The men on board this ship are mad with gold fever, it is almost all they talk about. But one day, I, and these others, will be free of that domination, and we will unite with the workers of the world to live in freedom!

Your loving Karl

2

Sixto (Harry Sexton)

1849, Yerba Buena

*T*HWACK!

That was the sound of my stick—*THWACK!* One more dead rat for my bag. I'd throw it in, and already Domingo would be off chasing another one. I'd hear him run between the big stacks, then growl, and the rat squeal. In the dark I'd follow the sounds, between the stacks and then along the edge of the dock. I had to be careful not to trip, or I'd fall into the cold water, and there was no one around to fish me out. At that time of night, anybody trying to help was going to be drunk and would fall in himself, and then two of us might drown. I'd see Domingo, the rat in his teeth, shaking it. I'd raise my stick, and Domingo would drop him. Stunned from the shaking, it was too dizzy to run, and it would look at me, its beady little eyes glowing.

THWACK!

I'd pick it up and say to myself a quick word of prayer, because that was the way the padres at the mission taught me, to respect the dead. Maybe even rats have souls, I thought, only God knows. My gunnysacks for the dead rats were big, but the rats were big too—rats from all over the world, fat from months of eating in the holds of ships. White, pink-eyed rice rats from China, as big as alley cats; fearless jungle rats all the way from the Amazon. Domingo never backed down from one of them. After I left Yerba Buena, I heard that ten thousand dollars was offered to anyone who could clear the town of rats; someone tried poison, and the rats went mad with thirst and dove into the drinking wells.

Every day there were new ships coming into Yerba Buena, bringing more men and more stacks of everything—calico and silks, wood, bricks, tools, tables and chairs, shoes, whiskey, nails, tobacco, paper. The whiskey didn't stay long on the dock, but everything else piled up in stacks until there was no more room. The captains from the ships said the stacks were supposed to be picked up by men in San Francisco—that's what the Americans had started to call Yerba Buena—but there weren't enough wagons or men to move them because every able man was dropping everything and hurrying off to the mountains to dig for gold. That's all they wanted to do, dig and drink and fight. I was seventeen and knew only a few things about Americans then, but one was that they could be kind of queer. I knew because when I was eleven years old, I went to live with a family of them.

One day, Padre Arturo, like one of those angels that delivers a surprise message from God, came to tell me he was going back to Mexico. After the Mexican government had, years before, taken the mission's lands, he and Padre Tomas had stayed to keep the church open. But now a new priest had come, and the padres had to leave. The new priest said I must go, too, that I could not live there anymore, the only home I had ever known. I was, Padre Arturo said, old enough to go and work like a man.

I thought that meant he was going to take me to a *rancho* and I would get to do what I had always dreamed of: become a *vaquero*, a cowboy. But Padre Arturo had a different idea for me. He took me over to the coast, to Monterey, to live with an American family, the Morgans. At that time, there were very few Americans living in Monterey. That was going to be the best thing for me, he said. He and the other padres had taught me to read and write in Spanish, and the Americans had promised they would keep teaching me—in English. Someday, Padre Arturo said again, just before saying goodbye, you will understand why this is the best for you. I see now he may not have had much choice. He didn't want me to live with the Ohlones—the *Indios*—and none of the *Californio* families—the ranchers of Mexican descent who had long lived in California—would have wanted me.

Mr. Morgan was an agent for a New England trading company that bought cowhides from the Californios. In return, they bought from him everything from boots to buttons to bullets. Mrs. Morgan, his wife, let me call her Sarah, even though Mr. Morgan did not like that; and they had a daughter, Dolores, who was two years older than I was. It was Dolores who gave me the name I eventually came to use, Sixto. The padres had named me Sextus—Sextus Rodrigo Jesus Serra. *Serra* because of Padre Junipero Serra, the first padre to come to California; *Jesus* because of Jesus; *Rodrigo* because that was one of Padre Arturo's names; and *Sextus* because I was born on the sixth day of the month. And another reason—I had, and still have, a sixth toe on my left foot. So the padres were either having a little fun or they thought my foot was a sign from God, one clear enough to fix on me my name. I believe I owe my names mainly to Padre Arturo, who pulled me from my *Indio* mother. I was born, too, with one loose eye—until I was about ten years old, this eye, my right one, would, especially when I got nervous, turn in toward my nose, as though to say "I'm tired now and have seen enough." But my name—why could Padre Arturo not have named me after one of the saints, such as Diego or Jose? Why instead *Sextus*, which at the mission became *Sexto*, and then in Dolores's teasing ridicule became *Six Toes* and finally *Sixto*? Maybe I should be grateful the padres were kind and did not later tack on me another name such as *Strabismus*.

At the Morgans I did not become a vaquero but instead a stable boy, taking care of their horses. Padre Arturo had taught me to do that. In the stable, too, is where I lived. My other work was helping Mr. Morgan when the Californios brought the hides to town. To trade with the ships from Boston, vaqueros from *ranchos* far and wide around Monterey drove their wagons full of stiff and heavy hides down to the beach. I could carry only ten or so at a time, but the vaqueros carried bundles of forty or fifty. We had to be careful to keep them dry, loading them into small boats that took them out to the ship anchored in the bay. The first time I saw the ocean, I was with Mr. Morgan. I was walking behind him and stopped to take it all in, and I was so awed that I completely forgot where we were going and why. He went on walking and then got angry with me when he saw how far behind him I was. I had known that, once in a great while, a padre went to or from Mexico in a big ship, and I heard them talk about the trip in a way they often talked about things—you could have your own hopes, but in the end, everything was in God's hands. And when I saw the ocean in a winter storm, I understood that on the ship, as big as it was, the ocean was much more powerful and you were in God's hands indeed.

Dolores's hair was like the fur of a red fox, even brighter. This was another thing new to me, that color, and at first I thought she was ill. I also thought she was beautiful, even more so when I learned she wasn't ill at all. It wasn't long before I loved her, and she knew it. But she would tease me, not just about my toes but about almost everything—my English, my not having a mother or father, the way I walked "like an Indian." My mother was an Indian, I told her, so why should I not walk like one? She wasn't truly cruel; she just liked to tease. It was one of her ways of playing. Her father didn't want her to speak to me at all, but he was often gone to ranchos, and she was lonely. The Californio families in Monterey didn't want their sons or daughters to mix with her—or even speak to her—and kept them away. Although the Morgans were required, under the colonial law, to convert to Catholicism to even live in Monterey, many believed—and rightly so—that at heart they were still Protestant. In the locals' eyes, Dolores was also a little wild, and, with her flaming red hair, maybe even a witch of some kind. But I was right there in the stable for her, someone to talk to other than her mother, who wasn't very happy.

Mrs. Morgan seemed never to smile, but she was kind to me. She taught me how to read and write English, mostly by reading the Bible—a Protestant one—and often told me she was sorry I had to sleep and eat in the stable. At other times she told me things that were different from what I had learned at the mission—there were no saints to be honored, I did not have to confess my sins to a priest, and I could make myself right with God all on my own.

Padre Arturo himself had told me there were Christians other than *catolicos*, and about the *alcalde* of Monterey making the Morgans convert. He said the Morgans, though possibly not true *catolicos*, worshipped the same God and that I should listen to them, but if I had any doubt, in my soul and secret self I should remember his and the other padres' teachings and I would be safe.

I had never known anyone like Dolores. When her father was away and her mother turned a blind eye, we played her games. She liked adventure and liked to pretend we were spearing whales on a ship at sea, or hunting grizzly bears in the wild, that she was the Queen of Spain and I was a conquistador giving her the head of an Aztec chief, or we were explorers in a canoe in a jungle. Dolores and Padre Arturo were the only people in the world I could say I loved and, at least in Padre Arturo's case, I believed loved me. She is the only girl I have ever kissed. Or rather, it was the other way around—she kissed me. She came to the stable one day, wanting to play, and said we should have a knife fight, like Indians. I said I didn't know what that was. What kind of Indian was I, she said, who didn't know how to knife fight? She said we had to tie a rope to my wrist and the other end to hers. For knives we would each have a fistful of stiff, fresh straw. It would be, she said, a fight to the death, just like the Indians do. I'd never heard of Indians fighting like that, but she didn't want to hear that; she said they did it all the time. So I tied a rope to her wrist, and she tied the other end to mine. Then we went around in a circle and lunged at each other a couple of times with our knives. I tripped and fell on my back. Dolores was quick as a cat and strong, and she pounced on top of me and pinned my arms. I expected her to start stabbing me, but she just sat up there, breathing hard, looking down at me. I could see she had something in mind, and she did— she leaned over and kissed me right on the mouth! One moment she was Dolores, my play friend, and in the next she was the sharp-pointed end of a feeling, like a rattlesnake bite only sweet, that I had never felt before. It was, I was sure, what heaven must be like. I had other thoughts, too, not so heavenly. And maybe that was a sin, thinking that way, and I had to pay for it. Because in the next moment, Dolores's father pulled her off me and then jerked me to my feet. He had never beaten me, but I thought he was going to then. He sent Dolores away, and, more calmly than I expected, told me to never touch, speak or even look at Dolores again. The next day, before dawn, Mr. Morgan woke me and told me to sit back in the wagon full of his wares, and we left Monterey. I didn't know the full why or the where-fore. We passed by San Juan Bautista, a pang in my heart. That night, we arrived in Santa Cruz, where I slept in a stable, in the still-loaded wagon. In the morning, Mr. Morgan sold a few odd things to a man I'd come to know as *El Loco*, and that man and I set off in his wagon northbound on the El Camino Real. Late that night, we arrived at El Loco's rancho. I was fourteen years old.

El Loco came from England. He was a *marinero*, one of the yan-kees or others who jumped their ships and stayed in California. But El Loco's ship had jumped him—it sank in a storm off the coast near Monterey, and all aboard had drowned except him. Everyone in the valley of his rancho called him El Loco, though not to his face; I had to call him *Señor* Smith. The *Indios* who lived near the rancho thought he was a *diablo* because he had drowned and come back from the dead, but I knew he wasn't one because he could bleed, and *diablos* didn't bleed. Once when he was out hunting, a grizzly bear tore off one of his ears, and he brought it back and made me sew it back on. He said that I'd put it on crooked, and he beat me for that. It was crooked, but it was the best I could do. That ear rotted until Loco pulled it off one day and tossed it into the bush for the coyotes to eat.

El Loco's rancho was in the hills above the old Mission Santa Clara de Asís, in a small valley. Going up from the rancho farther into the hills, you could see the bay. He went out hunting up there, alone, and always came back with something. There was a small *Indio* village not too far from the rancho, and sometimes he would pass through it on his way back from his hunting, with deer antlers hanging on his back, or rabbits on his belt, or a bobcat slung over his shoulder. If he took a mule with him, he carried back a whole deer or bear on it. The *Indios* were afraid of him and said he had powers, that he could kill an animal just by looking at it. To keep them afraid, I think, he often wore a string of skulls, small ones of squirrels and gophers, that hung low from his neck. That was mostly what he ate, meat from his hunting; and he mostly drank *aguardiente* and wine, water hardly ever.

When I first saw El Loco, I was so frightened that I wanted to run. He looked like a very big condor. He had a large, kind of gourd-shaped head, and it had no hair except a thin row in back and around the sides. He almost never washed, so this hair was always stiff and stuck out from his head like feathers. His nose was curved, like a beak that could sink into your flesh. What scared me most of all were his eyes—black stones that shifted from side to side when they followed you, like you were a rabbit he was going to swoop down on and clutch with his claws.

Mr. Morgan had told me, just before ordering me onto El Loco's wagon, that if I did my work, "Mr. Smith" would treat me well. Maybe he thought that was going to be true, but he was wrong. El Loco beat me when he was drunk, which was most of the time, and when he was sober. I don't know if booze made him crazy or crazy made him booze. He bought *aguardiente* and wine by the barrels, many at a time. He drank any time of the day, but at night was the worst. I lived in the stable, and at any hour of the night he'd shout for me to come to his *adobe* and tell me to get firewood or clean up the guts and bones of the animals he skinned, or to fetch another barrel. He made me keep the stable clean, in "Bristol fashion" he called it, but his own adobe was a pigsty. It was just two rooms, and in the back room was where he gutted the animals and threw pieces of them out back to his dogs. What they didn't finish off was what I had to clean up. The chore I hated most was cutting his toenails. His toenails were so thick they were like hooves, and he made me cut them with a sharp knife. I was scared to death that I might cut off a toe—and, he said, if I did, "Boy, I'll cut your throat with that very same knife."

In Monterey I'd had Dolores, but at Loco's I had no one except Domingo and a *burro* I named Arturo. It was not long after I went to Loco's that I found Domingo under an oak tree, dying. He was an Indian dog, part coyote, and he'd been in a fight with some thing or things that tore him up. He let me take him to the stable, and he lived. I named him for the day I'd found him, a Sunday. Loco had his dogs, two just as mean as he was, but Domingo became mine and never forgot that I saved his life. Day or night, he would follow me wherever I went and would stare down both of Loco's dogs at the same time if they so much as crossed their eyes at me. He had a great hatred of snakes and would go after them, and once a rattlesnake bit him in the face and I found it still stuck in there, his face all swollen up. He got through that, and it didn't stop him from going at snakes, though he never got bit again.

Arturo was El Loco's burro and had come to the rancho just before I did. El Loco had never wanted a burro. He won Arturo in a card game with a vaquero who had nothing more to bet, and even though Arturo carried his barrels of *aguardiente* and his hunting carcasses, El Loco had no respect for him. I believe a burro, and a horse as well, takes a like or dislike to a man at their very first meeting and will never work with a man it does not like. And Arturo did not like El Loco. He would not let El Loco put the *cabezon*—the yankees call it a hackamore—on him, and sometimes while moving along, he'd come to a dead stop for no seeming reason other than to vex El Loco. El Loco would whip him with a stick, but Arturo wouldn't budge until he was ready. It got so that El Loco swore that one day he was going to eat Arturo.

I named him, of course, for the man who named me. Not naming him was part of El Loco's disrespect. El Loco's horse, a stallion called

King, got much better treatment even though he was skittish and gave El Loco almost as much trouble as Arturo did. King and I usually worked things out, but Arturo was a friend. He could sleep standing up, but in the stable with me he felt safe enough to lie down, and on cold winter nights he slept next to me and kept me warm. Once in a great while, Loco let me take him out for a ride into the hills. Domingo would come along, and the three of us seemed almost like a family, able to understand each other without saying much at all.

When Loco would call for me in the night, he usually wanted me to do something for him, but sometimes he just wanted to talk. Many times he told me the story of his shipwreck. Too many times he would say, "Boy,"—*boy* or *half-breed* was what he always called me, never by my name —"do you know what the bottom of the sea looks like?" Then he would grab me from behind, put a hand over my eyes, and say, "*That's what it's like! Dark as night!*" And then, "And do you know what it's like on the way down there?" I knew, because he'd shown me before, but that didn't matter. With one hand still over my eyes, he'd put the other over my mouth and nose until I kicked and screamed for air. Other times he made me go out at night with him, walking around the rancho in the dark. There was nothing but rocks and bushes around, but all of a sudden he was on the big ship again, and he'd point to something and scream, "Bloody rocks to starboard! Hard over! Hard over!" or "Heave ho! Heave and raise the dead!" Even with all that, I guess I never knew if he was really crazy or not. Once, he told me, "I know what they call me around here, boy. They think I'm nickey in the noggin. That's because I'm a hard customer, you hear? A hard customer. But there was a treasure that went down with that ship. And one day I'm finding a way to get it."

In his adobe El Loco threatened many a time to beat me but never did. But if he had a certain look in his eye when he was coming to the stable, I knew I was in for trouble. He'd already decided to beat me for some reason—the smallest piece of horse dung left on the floor, or for no reason at all. He used what he called "the cat," a short stick with nine long leather strips at one end, each strip stinging my back like a hornet. The small mercy he showed me was that I could keep my shirt on; and, I must say, he rarely went at me in full fury. The cat stayed in the stable, hanging on the wall, and he warned me never to touch it. On the ship, he said, they had to take their whippings like a man. He said I had to also, and I always did. I never once gave him the satisfaction of crying.

Then one day, he came out and said he was going to have my hide. I knew why—I had taken King out to graze, and he'd got away from me. I knew, and I believe Loco knew, that King would come back, but Loco was mad as the devil. He never tied me up when he did this; there was no need to, because there was no use in running. He started in on me—full fury this time—and I heard him curse and try to hit Domingo too, who ran around barking at him. He gave me more lashes than usual. During other beatings I sometimes thought of Jesus and how they whipped him, and that helped me take it. But this time Jesus wasn't helping quite enough, and I thought I might just give in to the pain and die.

But then, all of a sudden, it stopped, and there was only Domingo barking. I waited until I dared to turn around and look, and I saw El Loco down, flat on his back, dead or knocked out, the cat still in his hand. And I saw what must have happened: Going after Domingo, maybe, he'd got too close behind Arturo. Maybe he spooked Arturo, although Arturo didn't spook easily. I like to think Arturo knew what he was doing and gave it good to El Loco, with two-legged gusto.

As bad as things were at El Loco's, I had never really thought of running away. It just wasn't something that I imagined possible—how to do it and where to go. But right then, without even knowing where I was going, I threw a saddle and *cabezon* on Arturo and rode away. Domingo followed us. It was late in the day, the sun already getting low. I thought of going to Monterey, though I wasn't sure how to, and thought that El Loco, if he was alive, might think of that too. I had heard of Yerba Buena but didn't know how far it was, only that it was to the north and that the El Camino Real would take me there. I hoped I could find the Camino, and I did, and went north on it all night, and the next day and night, without eating, stopping only for a few hours of sleep. At sunrise I was on top of a hill, looking at Yerba Buena and the bay spreading wide around it. From the hilltop, Yerba Buena seemed no bigger than the pueblo of San Juan Bautista, and I was surprised and puzzled by all the ships near it in the bay.

By the water just below Yerba Buena, I found a tumbled-down adobe hut that I patched with brush and muddy clay. I made the door high enough for Arturo to enter, so the coyotes could not come at night for him. It was a minor *milagro* that this hut didn't fall in on us. It was big enough for all of us to sleep in, with a fire to keep us warm. I was proud of how much it shut out the cold west wind that blew in from the sea almost every day and brought the fog. It was a peaceful spot, far enough away from the village, which I found out quickly was not so peaceful. Every day, new ships were arriving, bringing strange men from strange places. Their ships sat out on the water, empty. With their bare masts and booms they looked like naked trees in the winter. The weather was strange to me too—in the afternoon a strong, cold wind blew in from the sea and brought fog sometimes so thick that from the dock I couldn't see the village. I'd seen fog in Monterey but not with so much cold wind.

I called it a village then, but Yerba Buena—San Francisco—was changing quickly. It was becoming something else, bigger than Monterey and much wilder. I went into town to see the ships up close, and a ship captain saw Domingo catch a rat on the dock in broad day-light. He told me he would give me a small bag of beans and corn for every big bag of dead rats I gave him. I needed food—I had nothing to hunt with, and besides, there were few animals left to eat around there. So, every night, I went to the dock with Domingo. It wasn't hard to fill a bag, and many nights we filled two. In the early morning the captain would come and tie the tops of the bags and then throw them into the water. He wanted to sail back to Boston, he said, but couldn't muster a crew.

Every night on that dock, late into the night, I could hear the ruckus of the Americans and others in Yerba Buena, and in the big camp of tents right by the village, that they called Happy Valley. The racket in the camp was like the bellow of a herd of cattle in the *matanza*, the time of slaughter at the ranchos. Some nights a hard wind blew campfires out of control, and many tents and whole buildings went up in flames.

I mostly stayed away from the town itself, as I was more than a little frightened by it. I went in once and thought I might die. A drunk man staggered down the street, firing his pistol. There were touts in front of many houses, rattling off the odd names of the games inside—faro, monte, roulette, thimble rig, rondo. At the time, I didn't know what these were or a thing about gambling. I looked inside the houses, and they were full of tables, men standing around them, giving, it looked to me, their money away. I also saw some large paintings on the wall—forgive me Jesus!—of ladies without any clothes.

From the dock I saw other queer things too. Men in small boats went silently in the night, going from ship to ship, stripping from them whatever they could. Twice I saw a dead man floating in the bay. Once a deserted ship broke anchor and drifted off like a ghost into the fog.

Down the shore from the dock was a house that I thought very curious. There was lamplight in it almost all night, but it was not loud like the houses with the cards and paintings. One morning I asked the captain about it, and he said, "That is a special place. It's the house of the ladies of the night."

"Ladies of the Night," I said. "Is that like one of the houses just for holy sisters that Padre Arturo told me about, in Mexico, like the Sisters of Notre Dame?"

He laughed and said I should go there for a visit sometime and see for myself.

I thought: The Sisters of Notre Dame—in the same village with paintings of women without any clothes! Yes, Americans are queer, very queer indeed.

From Lt. Junger and Lt. Fischel to King Frederick William IV

April 23, 1849

To: His Excellency King of Prussia Frederick William IV
Re: Herr Karl Marx

To our most high King, the greatest sovereign in all of Europe—*Ja* in all the world! We have arrived in the village of San Francisco on the western coast of North America. The village is, if your Excellency will please pardon the expression, a miserable little shithole of a settlement. When it rains, the "streets" are worse than a Polish barnyard. Men and animals risk sinking in the quagmire. Rats are numberless and are minded no more than chickens. When it is dry, the wind blows sand and dust through the settlement as in an Arabian desert sandstorm. Most in the village live in tents like Bedouins and suffer the elements. Fleas and lice are, if your Excellency will pardon the expression, King here. They rule without mercy (unlike your Highness) every man in the village. In the line of duty your servants are living in a large tent full of rabble from every corner of the world. They all purport to be gold miners, but they are of such low character that we would not be surprised if some are communistic conspirators, possibly in league with Marx.

During our voyage, Herr Marx was a leader among those flummoxing the American captain of our ship. His insubordination rubbed that man to exasperation, so much so that we overheard the captain say to the first mate that he ought to put Marx ashore among the cannibals of Patagonia. However, he did not, and Marx is now in San Francisco.

We arrived in San Francisco two days ago, at dawn. Upon anchoring, we were greeted by a longboat full of unsavory-looking men who rowed out to our ship. They demanded to know if we had any "professional" women on board. Our captain told them to wait, then brought up onto the deck two women whose character (and only that, we swear) had been known to us since they joined the ship in Brazil. The captain then asked the men what they would be willing to pay there and then to have these "pretty dames, fresh from Rio de Janeiro, grace your place of business?"

An auction then broke out, each man bidding vigorously. However, during the auction Herr Marx appeared on deck in a singular costume. On our voyage he had dressed more or less like a London dandy (a bankrupt one) but was now wearing what he apparently supposed to be the dress of a gold miner—tight-fitting trousers tucked into high riding boots, a white blouse and short blue jacket, and a blue shepherd's cap. A satchel was strapped around one shoulder, and in his other hand he held a large iron frying pan which he had brought with him from London, and which he now brandished as if a sword. He uttered a kind of war cry, stopping the auction and engaging the captain. Marx protested that while he rued their virtue, the women, if they so chose, should be allowed to use their talents in whatever labor they wished, but he would not stand silently by and watch petty capitalists exploit them. The captain and the longboat men would have none of it. The captain ordered the first mate and another crewman to pitch Herr Marx overboard, which they promptly did, frying pan and all, followed by his trunk. The trunk began floating away with the tide. It was all Herr Marx could do, still clutching his fry pan and trying to keep the satchel afloat, to thrash his way toward the shore. The men in the longboat jeered at him and would gladly have watched him drown.

The captain and crew also called him some names that were very unkind to Germans generally. Somehow, Herr Marx made it to where he could stand in the water. However, because of the outgoing tide, he was still some distance from the shoreline, and he could move no closer, as he was stuck in the harbor's muddy bottom. He stood there, his feet cemented in the muck, holding his frying pan overhead to keep his balance and avoid falling and re-submersing. His shepherd's cap was of course gone. Waist deep in the water, his thick beard dripping, he resembled a cross between Poseidon and a short-order cook. Chastened, he did not renew a verbal assault on the longboat men. By this time, the men had taken the professional women on their boat and were almost ashore. Your servants were in a dilemma—should we pursue the floating trunk, as it maybe contained the Communistic screed Marx is thought to be preparing? Or did the satchel contain it? We had tried to search both during the voyage, but the trunk was locked, and Marx kept the satchel on his person at all times.

Our pulling Herr Marx from the muck might give away our identities and expose our mission. On the other hand, by chasing the trunk, Marx would remain stuck and perhaps re-submerse and drown. The disappearance of Marx's screed would be no loss, but if he and the satchel were to disappear, we might lose the opportunity to learn from letters or a journal who his co-conspirators are here and in Europe.

Our dilemma was solved by a brown-skinned *Junge*, apparently a North American Indian, who was at the end of the dock. He threw a loop of rope a remarkable distance out to Herr Marx and tied it to a donkey. With no small effort, the donkey managed to pull Marx through the water and the muck to the shore. Because of the early hour and no other apparent reason for his presence, the *Junge's* willingness to rescue Marx must mean he was waiting for him and that he is a co-conspirator.

Seeing that Marx and his satchel would not drown, your servants used a rowboat to retrieve his trunk. Unfortunately, we found no manuscript in it, only numerous pitiful *tchotchkes*, a broken tea service, London dandy clothes, and a small library of freethinking rubbish. These we all dumped into the sea. At a distance from the rowboat, we were able to see Marx and the *Junge* go off in a direction away from the settlement. We are confident we can track them.

Your servants,
Lt. Ernst Junger
Lt. Franz Fischel

3
Don Karl and the Duke of Wellington

AT THE MISSION I WAS THE ONLY CHILD LIVING WITH THE padres. The *Indio* children—children of Christian Indians, or "*Christianos*"—lived with their families in the adobes around the mission, and there were a few Californio children in the pueblo nearby. I worked hard at the mission, sweeping the courtyard and carrying water and helping with the horses and cows, and in return the padres were mostly good to me and taught me to read and write. Sometimes the Californio children came for the lessons, but not the Christiano children—the padres read to them but did not teach them how to read. The Californio children were often cruel to me. They called me an *Indio* and threw stones at me. They said I had the *mal ojo*—the evil eye—and that my father was a *diablo* who had feet like an animal and eyes that spun in his head, that it was he who gave me my foot and my wild eye because that's what *diablos* do—they make trouble for people, even their own children. They teased me about the broken seashell, a small piece of purple spiral, that I wore around my neck on a leather string—the only thing, Padre Arturo said, that my mother left behind when she went away. They said I was just like the shell, only half of something, a thing nobody wants. The *Indios* considered me to be either a Californio or a little padre to be, and so the mothers told their children to stay away, and they did.

I did not know myself what I was. There was no looking glass at the mission, but I'd seen myself in a pool of water, and saw that I looked like the Ohlones and did not look like them. My skin was much lighter than theirs, and my eyes were rounder. But my cheekbones were high like theirs, and I had a short, flat nose like they had. My mother was an *Indio*, Padre Arturo said, but he said she was not an Ohlone. He did not understand any of the little she said, and the vaquero who found her and brought her to the mission said her language sounded like one he had heard in the mountains. Padre Arturo told me that when I was angry my eyes were like hers, fierce like a trapped mountain lion. As for my father, I knew nothing. Once when I was very young, I asked Padre Arturo who he was, and he said only that God was my father. That might have satisfied me then, but as I grew older, both my mother and my father became something both distant and near—not quite ghosts or people in a dream but something else, figures of my imagination that could change their forms and faces.

I was thus very lonely at the mission, even though I knew that in some ways I was lucky to live with the padres. Padre Arturo was my only real friend. He said the other children were maybe jealous that I lived where I did and I should try to understand and forgive them. Padre Arturo was different from the other padres, younger and kinder. If I made mistakes in my reading and writing lessons, the others would punish me by making me work extra or by locking me in my room without food, but Padre Arturo didn't do these things. He would only say I must do better if I wanted to please God. I was more fortunate than the Californio children; they were sometimes whipped, not always lightly, if they failed a lesson twice.

Padre Arturo had his own special horse, a copper stallion, and on fiesta days he put a red silk hood on its head and neck and a gold blanket around his saddle. For himself, he too wore red silk, a sash under his robe. He liked to go riding with the vaqueros from the ranchos nearby when they went chasing deer in the night, or hunting for grizzly bears. The vaqueros hung a cut of fresh cow meat on the trunk of a big oak tree, then hid and waited. When the bear came to eat, they charged at him on their horses and lassoed him with their *reatas*, very strong lassos made from cowhide. They then rode fast in short circles around the tree, tying the bear to it. Sometimes they killed the bear right away and took its meat; other times they brought it back to the pueblo to use it in a fight with a bull. I, too, wanted to be a vaquero, to play the guitar and dance in *fandangos*, to ride my horse and win in the riding games they played. The padres sometimes let me walk out to a rancho near the mission to watch the vaqueros herd the cattle into the corrals and, if it was the time of the *matanza*, throw their reatas around the ones to be killed.

One day a vaquero gave me my own reata, a very good one. The best reatas, he said, come from the hide of steers that were drying up, from sickness or hunger, even before they died. Long strips are cut from the hide in the winter when it is wetter, then braided together and hung to dry and turn black. If good, the vaquero said, your reata "has eyes," and he showed me how to use it. Every day, I worked long at throwing it until I could easily rope a stray dog or one of the Californio boys who threw stones at me. After that, they left me alone.

Padre Arturo taught me that a good Christian must be kind and do whatever he can to help other people in need. So when I saw them throw a man off a big ship and into the bay, and that he was stuck in the mud and they meant to leave him there to drown, I knew I must do something. I always had two reatas with me, one around my belt, the other on Arturo's saddle. I tied the two together to make one long one, and after a couple of tries I got this around the man, then took my end back down the dock as far as I could and tied it to a post. Arturo didn't want to go out into the shallow water and mud, but I tugged at him and finally got him as far as the post. I had to stand on Arturo's saddle to reach the reata, but once I got it, I tied it to his saddle, and together we pulled the stuck man to the shore. Our legs were black with the mud, and the man, from being dragged through it, was smothered with it like an old log in a swamp. He was still holding a frying pan in one hand, and with his other he had a kind of saddlebag pressed tight against his body.

At first I was afraid he might be dead, that the reata had squeezed him too tight, or that he'd choked on mud, because he seemed not to be breathing, but after I cleared the mud from his nose and mouth he made a little sound like a sick dog when it is sleeping, and said "Yenny." I thought that might be his name. He was a short man with some muscle thickness to him; he wasn't old or young in years, but in the middle somewhere, with a beard like a tumbleweed bush and a head of wild curly hair, both matted with mud. It wouldn't have been right to just leave him there, so I tried to clean him some more, then managed to slump him across Arturo's saddle. I thought about throwing the frying pan into the bay, but I kept it because it must have been pretty important to him.

My adobe was not what you'd call spacious. Arturo and I sometimes scraped our heads on the roof branches. We had enough room for a fire, and for me and Arturo and Domingo to sleep together in a heap if needed. After catching rats I would sleep during the day, and Arturo could stay outside, as the coyotes would not come for him then. At my adobe, I made a fire to dry the man's clothes and then wrapped him in a blanket like a piece of *pollo* in a tortilla and put him by the fire too. His coat was very heavy, not just from being wet—on the inside I found many gold coins sewn into the lining. Inside his saddlebag were some papers that were wet but not muddy. Once the mud was off him, I saw his skin was like that of some Californios, darker than a yankee's but not as dark as an *Indio's*. And something I hadn't noticed before—around his neck, a thin chain with a little silver medallion that said "Jenny." A couple of times he woke me up, rolling in his sleep and saying "Yenny" again and again. I moved him away from the fire so that he wouldn't roll into it, and saw that his face was wet with sweat. When I moved him I touched his leg, and that was wet and hot too, and I knew it wasn't just the fire but that he had a fever. I had heard there were many on the ships dying from fever before they got to Yerba Buena, and they were dropped into the sea. At Yerba Buena the ship captains would sometimes put the sick in a separate boat and send them straight to a doctor's tent if there was one, but the doctors didn't save them. So if he was going to die, I thought, just as well he do it in my adobe.

Still, maybe there was something I could do to help. The padres had learned from the *Indios* how to make a fever medicine they called *kisin*, from a plant with long, thin leaves that are green on top and silver underneath. They boiled the leaves and drank it. I got on Arturo and rode very far, almost half the way to the ocean, until we found a kisin bush. I picked some leaves, brought them back, and boiled them to make a tea.

Although he didn't want to, and said things I couldn't understand but was pretty sure were cursing, I made the man drink it twice and then let him sleep, because I had to sleep, before the night. When night came, I had to leave him alone to go to the docks. I made a fire, big enough to last most of the night, but not so big it would burn down the adobe. I knew there was a good chance that in the morning he was going to be dead, and I was afraid of having to deal with that.

When Arturo and Domingo and I came back in the morning, he wasn't dead at all. He was lying awake, so weak he couldn't unwrap himself from the blanket. For several more days I gave him the kisin tea, until I had no more. All that time he was quiet, too weak to speak to me or even to curse anymore. Then one morning there was fresh smoke leaking out from the adobe, and he was standing outside it, looking across the bay. When he saw me he smiled and held out his arms.

"Young man, I believe I am in your debt," he said. "I will find a way to return your kindness. What is your name?"

I told him, and he made a bow and said, "Mr. Sixto, it is my good fortune to meet you. You may call me Karl."

"Then you are not Yenny?"

"Yenny? Oh Yenny!" he said and laughed. He had a slight, odd accent, a little like El Loco's but one I'd never heard before. "No, Yenny—or Jenny—is my wife, in England."

"England!" I said. "El Loco is from England!"

"Who?"

"El Loco—Mr. Smith. Do you know him?"

"If he is here, no. You, my friend, are the only person I know here. Who is Mr. Smith?"

I told him a little about El Loco and what I did there, and he said it was a pleasure to meet a "Master of the Stalls." I didn't tell him I'd run away. I wasn't sure I could trust him—how many people were there in England, after all, and how could he not know someone like El Loco? So I wasn't taking a chance, and told him Loco had died. But he asked me more questions, and soon I could tell he was *simpático*, something El Loco never was or would be. He wanted to know how I knew English, so I told him about Monterey and the Morgans, and that before them I'd lived at the mission. Geography was not something I learned there, or at the Morgans, even though ships came to Monterey from many places, so I asked him where England was, and with a stick he drew a large circle in the dirt.

"This is the earth. Here is California," he said, making an X on one side of the circle. "And here," he said, marking the middle of the circle, "is England."

"And Mexico?"

"Not as far but still far away. Down here."

"How far?"

"A thousand miles? Or more?" he said.

"When I am standing by the sea," I said, "and I see where the sky and the sea come together—how far is that?"

"I don't know exactly—twenty miles? Twenty-five or fifty? Here— in Europe—is my first home, Germany."

I asked him if they had many ranchos there, and then had to tell him what a rancho was.

"There are farms there, yes," he said. "But also a lot of cities. Ones much bigger than Mexico City. They are places where you can find the best and worst of mankind."

He went on to tell me more—that I lived in what was called the "New World," that he was from the "Old." He said the old was like a field—it once had a great possibility to grow things, but now the field was rotting away. He then said something else I didn't understand; it sounded like he was trying to cough out a fish bone stuck in his throat.

"Are you all right, Don Karl?" I asked.

He laughed and said yes. He was, he said, speaking the language they spoke in Germany. "An unmelodious but efficient language. I said that I am so hungry right now I would eat the pope's communion. And you must not address me by that Spanish 'Don.' That comes from the Latin *dominus*, meaning lord or master, and I am neither one of those. Please, just call me Karl."

I only meant, I said, respect.

In my adobe, several pieces of paper with writing on them were spread out to dry on the blanket I'd given Karl. On hands and knees, Karl looked over the papers as I warmed up tortillas over the fire and took out some of my last *carne seca*. I then offered him some food and went to sit down on the blanket. To make room, I picked up one of the papers, and Karl lunged at me so quickly I dropped my tortilla in the dirt.

"Please don't touch!" he said. "I'm sorry about your bread, but please."

I tossed the tortilla outside to Domingo.

The papers, Karl said, were very valuable. He carefully picked one up by a corner and said, "This. This is the key to the lock of history. It is the king's and the capitalist's nemesis. Someday it will stand as the runestone of truth."

I didn't understand how a piece of paper could be a lock or the other things he said it was, and I guess he could tell I didn't.

"I am writing a manifesto. You might call it a message—a kind of letter to people."

"To what people?"

"To all of mankind," he said. "All of humanity."

"You are writing one letter to all the people in the world?"

"Yes, exactly."

"Ah, maybe I see," I said. "It is like the letters that San Pablo wrote? I have read those in the Bible."

"San Pablo?"

"In English he is called Paul."

"Ah, Saint Paul, of course. Well, kind of like those, I suppose. But then very different."

I wondered if that meant he, too, might be some kind of saint in the making, and if so, what it was he wanted to say to everyone, but he was busy eating and reading the paper he'd picked up, and I was hungry. We finished eating without more talking, and then my adobe started filling up with smoke. It had no real chimney at the top, just a small hole that often didn't work very well. We went outside where Domingo and Arturo were playing. Domingo was running circles around Arturo, going one way, then stopping and going back the other. Arturo was chewing on a wad of grass he'd found and pretending not to notice, but I saw him looking out of the corner of his eye as he waited for Domingo to come around the other way. It was a warm morning, before the start of the cold afternoon wind that sometimes blew sand so hard off the hills that it stung your skin and filled your eyes.

Karl said he wanted to "take a constitutional" and have a look around. We went toward the sea, over a couple of the low sandy hills, then stopped on top of one when Karl said he was feeling tired. The hill wasn't high enough for us to see the sea, but off in that direction there was the old mission, and in the other direction, the one we'd come from, we could see much of the bay and Yerba Buena and the islands in the bay. On the other side of the bay were high hills, round and bald *colinas*, gold and green. Karl pointed at them and said, "So that is the way to the mountains. And gold. The Spanish fetish." He said he would be going to the mountains as soon as he was a little stronger. I thought he seemed sad when he said this, not like the yankees who went off in a big, excited hurry, singing and shooting guns into the air when their boats left the dock.

For the next ten days or so, there was hardly a time when one of us wasn't sleeping. Karl slept a lot and slowly got stronger. At night I went to the dock, and during the day while I slept, he wrote his letter to the world or went out walking. Eventually he started sleeping less, and we spent more time together, and I learned that he liked to speak his mind. One night before I went to the dock, we were beside a fire outside. It was a clear night, without fog, and I saw a bright light streak across the sky in the east.

"Look," I said, "an angel just came from heaven. To help someone in need."

"An angel!" Karl said. "Come to earth. Tell me, have you ever seen one of these creatures?"

I said, "We just saw one!"

"Indeed. But have you ever seen the apparition itself?"

"The what?"

"The image—the person, if you will . . . the vision that looks like a person."

"No," I had to admit, "I have not. Many times I have wished for one, but one has never come."

"If you haven't seen the actual image of one, how can you be sure that there are angels?"

That, I thought, was simple to answer. "An angel came to an *Indio* woman at the mission." I remembered this woman; she would sit under an oak all day and mutter prayers and chants. "She was sick and prayed, and in the night, the angel came to her. In the morning, she could walk. Padre Arturo said the angel might have been the Virgin of Guadalupe."

"What—or who—is the Virgin of Guadalupe?"

I could hardly believe this. "You do not know the Virgin of Guadalupe? She is the mother of Jesus!"

"Maybe the angel that the woman saw," Karl said, "was the Virgin's sister. Her sister's name was Mary too. I've sometimes wondered how their parents could name them both Mary. They might look alike. Or maybe all angels look the same, I don't know."

"I did not know the Virgin had a sister!"

"And what would you say," he said, "if someone told you that angels don't exist?"

"I would say he is like the judges in the Bible," I said, "who had their heads in the sand. And I would say, how does he know they don't?"

"That light in the sky—some people think it is a star falling, burning out. Only that."

By this time, I was getting a bit worked up. "How can a star fall? And where does it go? There are many stars, but if they have been falling for so many years, there would be none left in the sky! There are new angels all the time. It is sad when a child dies, but it becomes an angel. That is why there are always enough angels."

Karl went quiet, and I felt I had made my point. Still, I had never heard anyone say such things as he did.

Karl grew stronger. A couple days later, he woke me up in the afternoon and said he needed to go into Yerba Buena and wanted me to "accompany" him. I wanted to sleep more, but I knew he wasn't completely strong yet, and so I went with him. He thought he might buy some of the things he would need to go to the diggings, but first he wanted to go to the post office by the plaza to see if there were any letters there for him. You could also put in a "forward" at the post office there, which he meant to do, to Sacramento.

The plaza was full of people crowding around three or four big, dirty tents that had been joined together. In front of the tents were two men, one with a sad face and a raccoon skin cap with eagle feathers sticking up out of it. He was holding a pole with a large sign that said:

TWO LIVE BOAR CONSTRICTERS
Mail and femail

Also!!!!!
A striped ALGEBRA–STUFT

Besides!!!!!
A pair of SHUTTLECOCKS
and one SHUTTLEHEN–alive!

The!
SWORD WHICH GENERAL WELLINGTON
FIT WITH THE BATTEL OF WATERLOO!

Whom is six feet long
and broad in proporshun

With!!!!
A ENORMUS RATTLETAIL SNAKE–
A REGLAR WOPPER!

And!!!!
THE TUSHES OF A HIPPOTENUSE!

Together with!!!!
A FINGAL TIGER: SPOTTED LEPROSY!

The other man stood high up on a box and was wearing a black stovepipe hat, the tallest I'd ever seen.

"Come and see 'em!" he was shouting, waving his arms. "Come and see 'em! Some of the greatest spectacles west of the Mississippi! There ain't nothin' like 'em! Two days only!"

Now, I had never seen any of these things except a snake with a rattle tail, and some of them I'd never even heard of. So I was certain I had to see them. I had two silver coins with me that I'd found on the dock, and I was willing to part with one of them. Karl said I shouldn't waste my money, but I said I was going to see the tiger and all the rest. He could see I'd set my mind on this and said he'd meet me out in front of the post office when I came out.

The tents were lit inside with lamps, and each was like a separate room, with a hole between them that was covered with a flap. The snakes were in the first one. Inside a wood box with high sides, the rattlesnake was sleeping—or maybe dead, as it was mostly covered with flies. In another box were the two "boar constricters," looking suspiciously like the harmless fat garter snakes we used to kill in the bean fields at the mission. In the next room was the algebra. This looked a lot like a big yellow dog, but it had black stripes running up and down its body and in circles around its legs. It was dead and stuffed full of wood chips that were poking out of a hole on top of its back. People didn't seem to care that it was dead or falling apart; they walked around goggling and pointing at it like it was an old mummy.

The next tent had General Wellington's sword. I didn't know who he was, but I thought he must have been pretty important to have a sword that was almost as long as I was. It was hanging straight down from the top of the tent by a piece of thin string tied around the handle. On the ground, a ring of roped stakes made a wide circle around the sword so folks couldn't reach out and touch it. It was a sight hanging in the air like that, its blade maybe three fingers wide, its handle covered with colored stones that looked like precious jewels. A small crowd and I were all standing around the circle gazing at it—until I looked across and saw El Loco, and then right away, he saw me.

"Thief!" he screamed.

I'd already started running. Out that tent, through the others, and I kept running, through the crowd and, without a word, right past Karl. Only then did I look over my shoulder and see El Loco coming after me, through the parting crowd, with General Wellington's sword. The sword was heavy, and El Loco ran like a bear. That is, he wasn't quick, but once he got going he could cover a lot of ground, so I had to get away early or get caught. My adobe was too far, and even if I could outrun him I didn't want to lead him that way.

I decided to head for the dock and hide in the stacks there; if I got trapped, I could jump into the water. I wasn't much of a swimmer, but I wouldn't drown. I could either hang onto one of the pilings or thrash my way out to one of the ships close by. El Loco did not like water at all. He never bathed. And that sword would surely sink anyone.

I ran around a corner and then suddenly got what I thought was a better idea. Straight ahead of me was the house of the Ladies of the Night. I could try to hide there, and even if he followed me, the holy sisters would surely protect me. It was true I was a thief and had sinned, but didn't a thief die on the cross at the same time Jesus did and so deserved his mercy as much as any other soul? And even El Loco, I hoped, would respect a house of the sisters. The door was closed, and on the run I prayed it wasn't locked. It wasn't, and I rushed through, not knowing if El Loco had turned the corner and seen me go in. I slammed it shut and ran up the stairs. At the top I turned and ran down a hall all the way to the end. There was a closed door there too, but I went through it and swung it shut behind me. And then what I saw was as marvelous as any vision—Dolores! Older, like I was, and yet the same, and right there before me! She was sitting on the bed in that small room, looking just as surprised as I must have. I nearly let out a yell, but that would have been the end of me right there and then, because I heard El Loco snarling downstairs, followed by a woman scolding him and then more snarling. As far as I knew, no one but Dolores had seen me come in. My finger to my lips told Dolores to be quiet, and I dived under her bed. From there I heard—felt too, the floor shaking—El Loco stomping down the hall, opening doors and slamming them shut. Dolores's door flew open, and I saw El Loco's boots. He stabbed the tip of the Wellington into the wood floor.

"Where is he?"

Dolores kept calm. "Sir?"

"The thief! The half-breed!"

"Sir?" Dolores said. "May I help you?"

I watched El Loco's boots go to the far wall, to a window there, then he turned and went out the door, leaving it open. Two women met him in the hall and told him in some surprising, not-sister-like words that he had to leave the house.

"I'll go," El Loco growled, "when I'm good and ready!" I heard him bang around some more, then go downstairs and slam doors there. The house shook and rumbled like it was in a long earthquake, then suddenly it was quiet.

Dolores closed her door. She whispered that to be sure it was safe, I should stay under the bed for a while. When I did come out, I sat on the floor so no one could see me through the window.

"We have to whisper," Dolores said. "He went out the back door. I don't think anyone else knows you're here."

Dolores seemed to have changed, but I couldn't tell right off what it was that was different. She seemed a little sad and shy, maybe not as happy to see me as I was to see her. She was wearing a fancy red and white dress, like she was going to a fiesta. I thought this was strange, but I guessed it might be the special clothes that she and her sisters wore, just as the padres at the mission wore their gray robes.

"I'm not a thief," I said. "Not a real one." In a few words I tried to explain who El Loco was and why I'd had to run away, and that I took a simple burro, not a horse like a real thief would have. It felt a little like I was confessing my sins to a padre. I expected her, like one of them, to be forgiving, and she was.

"You did what you had to," she said. "We all do sometimes. But he'll be looking for you. He's very angry."

I told her then how I caught rats at night on the docks, that from there I could see her house, and that a captain told me it was for the Ladies of the Night. "Like the houses for the holy sisters in Mexico."

"The holy sisters?"

"Padre Arturo said you are like the padres. You wear special clothes and do good things."

"I see."

"That's why I came here—I thought the sisters would protect me. And you are!"

There were no crosses on the walls of Dolores's room, or pictures of the Virgin. Other than the bed, the only thing in the room was a trunk in the corner. I knew the padres didn't have many things either, though Padre Arturo had his horse. I peeked out the window to see if I could see El Loco anywhere. I didn't see him, but I could see the dock. Every night, I'd been looking at Dolores's house!

"Are your mother and father in Yerba Buena too?"

"No, Sixto," she said slowly, "they're gone." Fighting back tears, she told me that right before the last Christmas, they had been invited by a captain to dinner on board his ship. The ship was far out in Monterey harbor, and sailors rowed them to it. During the dinner a storm came in, but rather than stay the night on the ship, they tried to get back to shore, and the rowboat went under. They and the sailors all drowned. She was supposed to go to Boston to live with an aunt she had never met, but instead ran away, like me, to Yerba Buena.

"I am sorry, Dolores," I said. I was sorry for her, even though her father had not always been kind to me. I didn't know what else to say, and for a while we were quiet and I looked out the window. I heard the squawking gulls that pecked away at the mounds of food in sacks on the docks, and the men shouting there. I was sad about Dolores's mother and father, but at the same time I could feel something soft and good surround my heart, something I had lost but now knew again as a thing that only Dolores had ever put there.

"Where do you live, Sixto?" she said.

I told her where my adobe was and that she should come to see it soon. "I will bring Arturo and give you a ride there," I said.

"I don't know, Sixto," she said. "We'll see. What about that man?"

I asked her if I could stay at the house for a few days, until El Loco would go back to his rancho, but she said that wasn't possible. The mother of the house was strict, she said, about guests.

"That's why you have to go soon," she said.

"I'll come back to visit," I said. "At night, before I go to the docks."

"No, wait until I come to see you. I can find you."

I said I would wait. Dolores put her head out the window to look for El Loco, then listened at her door. "You will have to go out the window," she said.

I tied my reatas together to make one long one, then tied one end to her bed and put the other out the window.

Then, without a word, Dolores came to me, took my head in her hands, and kissed my forehead. "Goodbye, Sixto," she said, still whispering. "I'll come to see you someday. But don't come here."

Though I was saying goodbye to her, I was glad with the hope from a kiss and of seeing her again soon. Dolores braced her bed so it wouldn't slide and make noise. I went out the window and down the wall. I knew I should get going *pronto*, but I looked up, hoping Dolores would be there one more time and she might say something a little happier and more hopeful than she had. But only the end of the reata came out of the window and fell at my feet.

To get back to my adobe I went along the shore, looking out for El Loco the whole time. All the way I could think only of him and Dolores. If I saw him, I was ready to jump into the bay and hope for the best. Dangerous as it was not to keep a steady mind and eye for El Loco, I thought of Dolores even more—things happened because God wanted them to, and why else would He bring her my way now other than so we could help each other? I had no one else other than Arturo and Domingo; she had no one else other than some sisters who were not really her sisters, and a faraway aunt she didn't know.

From a distance, I saw Karl outside my adobe. He was making little hops forward in one direction while holding one hand out in front of his body and the other behind his back. Then, without turning around, he hopped and shuffled straight back in the opposite direction—back and forth again and again. I was worried he was sick again and was like a crazy dog that chases its tail. I got even more worried when I got closer and saw he was waving around a long iron rod and poking it at something invisible.

When he saw me, he stopped and didn't seem crazy at all. "My friend," he said, "I've been waiting for you!"

He said El Loco had come back to the plaza, pulled the man in the stovepipe hat off his high box, got up on it, and declared to everyone that I was a thief and he would pay fifty dollars to anyone who handed me over to him.

"And then I spoke to those people too," Karl said. "I said he was a scoundrel and that he had defamed you."

"He did what?"

Karl explained that "defamed" was when someone told someone else something about you that was not true and put you in a bad light.

"But how," I asked, "can I be defamed when I am not even famed? And besides, it is true—I am a thief."

"Strictly speaking, yes, you are. But he didn't reveal all the circumstances and hence the truth. He didn't tell those people that he used to beat you. And so you were justified in running away. And to run away you needed Arturo."

Trying to refame me wasn't enough, I guess, because Karl said my honor also needed to be defended. And to do this, he had challenged El Loco to a duel. With "sabers." At sunrise the next morning. And El Loco had accepted. It would be, he said, "*a la morte*,"—which, he explained, meant "to the death."

"A duel? To the death?" I said. "For me?"

"Yes. You are an honorable person. You came to my aid," Karl said, then turned and shuffled a little and fiercely poked his iron stick at nothing. "It is all in the footwork, you see."

"And that is your saber?"

It would have to do, he said. He'd looked for a "saber" in Yerba Buena but couldn't find a single one. Then he'd come across a broken-down wagon and taken the iron rod off it. He was very proud of it and showed me how he could slash and defend with it.

"You," he said, "will be my second."

I asked what that meant, and he said I would carry his "sword" and "attend to the proper ceremony."

"I hope you will excuse me," I said, "but I think this is not a good idea. El Loco is a very dangerous man. They say he has killed men."

Karl said he wasn't afraid, that he had fought duels in Germany, at a university there. "Look," he said, and showed me scars on his arms. "First, we would drink great amounts of beer. After that, you don't care about a few cuts."

But this duel with El Loco won't be just a few cuts, I told him. He'd said it himself—it would be to the death. What about his wife, Jenny, and his letter to the world? Who would write it if he died?

"History," he said, "is writing the letter. I am just the secretary."

What I didn't tell Karl then was that I knew where there was a real sword—if the yankees hadn't stolen it yet. There was one up at the mission close by, the San Francisco de Asís. The sword was an old Mexican one hanging on a wall in one of the huts behind the church, in the most crumbled corner of the mission. I had gone there looking for anything I could find to use for my adobe, until a drunk yankee saw me and threatened to shoot me. I wasn't going to tell Karl about the sword unless things came down to brass tacks. There was still time, I thought, to convince him not to fight.

Until it got dark, Karl practiced his sword skills with his iron rod. When he came inside I made us some food. Before we ate, I put my hands together for a silent prayer, just as I had the few times we'd eaten together.

"You are talking to God?" he said.

"*Seguro*," I said. "Yes."

"And does he speak to you?"

I did not answer this, as I did not want to admit that I had never heard such a voice.

"That is something I have wondered," Karl said. "Why doesn't God just speak to everyone in the whole world at once? He could, yes?"

"Maybe he knows that not everyone would listen," I said.

"You mean to say that if a voice boomed out that everyone in the world could hear, they wouldn't listen?"

"He gave us the ten commandments," I said. "He spoke to us that way."

"That is not quite the same thing, is it?"

"The padres told me that God speaks to us in mysterious ways. Sometimes we don't even hear it."

We were both hungry and started to eat. While we ate I tried to talk Karl out of fighting the duel. I said I didn't care about my honor; that his iron stick would hardly be any use against a real sword like the Wellington, if that was what El Loco would be using, and he would die; that he was brave but he was still too weak to fight his best. But I couldn't say anything to change his mind; I could see he was set on doing it. Karl was very smart, I guess, but he was also a lot like a burro—once it makes up its mind about something, *buena suerte* getting it to do something else. So after we ate, I told him I had to take Arturo out to graze, and I headed up toward the mission.

Even though I was fond of that mission's other name—they called it Mission Dolores after a creek nearby—I did not like going there at any time, and especially at night. The padres had all gone back to Mexico. The buildings, the old church, and the many adobe huts around it were crumbling like dry tortillas, some more than others. Gold diggers had moved in, mostly yankees who didn't have tents or some other way to live in the village. At the Mission San Juan Bautista there had been many fruit trees—lemons, olives, and figs—and it looked like there once had been many at Mission Dolores, but now they had all been cut down for fires. I had seen the stumps. Yankees gambled in the old church, and one of them had even started making steam beer in one of the huts. Every night, it seemed, they burned a big fire in the middle of the courtyard and had a yankee fandango, drinking *aguardiente* and beer and dancing to fiddle music. *Indios* will do wild things when they drink *aguardiente*, but the yankees were worse because they had pistols and would use them. For the Californios, a fandango was for a special occasion. When you have one every night, it is no longer a fandango; it is just wildness, like animals.

At San Juan Bautista we had a *calaveras*, a place of the skulls, where the Indian butchers killed the cattle and sheep; all the filth from the butchering was kept inside the walls. At Mission Dolores the yankees lived like animals, throwing bones everywhere and doing their toilet wherever they wanted. They did not care about their filth, as they were soon leaving for the mountains.

That night, I saw from a ways off the yankee fire and heard the fandango already going full bore. So as not to be seen, Arturo and I swung wide and went around the outer wall of the whole mission to where there was a large hole in it, near the adobe with the sword. I led Arturo through a hole in the wall and tied him to an old well post. There was a foul smell in the adobe from the yankees making their night soil in there. In the dark I had trouble finding the sword, but it was still there on the wall. The yankees must have thought it was worthless, and for all I knew, it was.

I quickly made my way back to Arturo, then remembered what Karl had said about beer—and thought that if I could get him some, maybe it would help to make him brave or at least a little happier before he died. My luck had it that the beer adobe was close by and I didn't have to get near the fandango. Two yankees were there, not yet mean drunk but happy, and I gave them my last silver coin for a bucket of beer. It wasn't easy holding a full bucket and a sword in one hand while getting onto Arturo and then riding in the dark, but I made it without spilling much, so there was plenty of beer left when I got back to my adobe.

Karl liked the sword and loved the bucket. He downed a few long pulls from it as he looked over the sword. "We shall call it the Cortez," he said. "One thing the Spanish knew how to do is make sabers."

In the light of our fire, the Cortez did not look so good to me. It was little longer than my arm, about half as long as the Wellington, and had large patches of rust up and down the blade. But Karl said it had a good handle, and he tugged on a little pinch of his beard and cut it with the Cortez to show me the blade could still cut something.

I had meant the beer to be for the morning, not that night. I told Karl he shouldn't drink any more or else his head would be full of spiderwebs in the morning, but that didn't stop him. And, I thought, if it was making him happy, why not? I did ask him again why I must go to the duel; if he was set on doing it I couldn't talk him out of it, but why should I have to go?

"If you lose the duel," I said, "and I pray you don't—then I will lose too. I will have to go back to the rancho with El Loco."

Karl considered this—he was a considerate man—and said this is the way it must be done. There must be a second in the duel.

"I defended you in the plaza," he said, "and now I am asking you to accompany me. You won't be fighting. I only need an aide."

He went on to tell me what it was I was supposed to do as his second. El Loco's second—I had to wonder who that would be, as El Loco had never had a "second" for anything—and I were to negotiate a number of things, such as the length of the duel and what would end it, though that had been conveniently decided already by "*a la morte.*" It was also a second's duty, he said, to make an effort to "avert bloodshed" once we got on "the field of honor." All this didn't make much sense to me—beginning with why I had to be "defended"—but I didn't argue with him as I could see he was dead set, so to speak, on it. If he was willing to die, then the least I could do is go with him, do my "second" duties as well as I could and say a prayer at the end.

I didn't go to the dock that night; I saw no use in going. Karl had no trouble falling asleep—helped by the beer, I suppose—but I stayed awake for a long time, sorry for him and sorry that I would be going back to El Loco's rancho. When I finally got to sleep, I had an odd dream: I was out on the dock in the middle of the day, and all of Yerba Buena was like a ghost town; I couldn't see or hear a single other person anywhere. Then I saw El Loco come on to the dock, and I hid behind a stack, and when I looked again, it wasn't El Loco but a grizzly bear coming. The grizzly came close and stood up, showing its fangs and claws, then all of a sudden a white hawk came from out of nowhere, swirling and diving around the grizzly's head, driving it crazy. The grizzly swiped at it so hard that he fell off the dock into the water. It was a strange dream, but maybe the strangest part of it all is that I had dreamed of this same white hawk before, many times, only before it had always stayed high in the sky above me, gliding in a circle.

Karl woke me up before sunrise. He had started a fire, and while I got up to make us something to eat, he went outside in the dark, talking to himself in German. I looked out and saw he was swinging the Cortez and doing those little dance steps back and forth. For breakfast we had frijoles and some tortillas, meager for what might be a man's last meal. Karl had already started in on the bucket of beer, and it was more than half empty. I could tell it was boosting his courage, and for that I was happy, but it left me wondering where I was going to find some courage of my own.

We were supposed to meet El Loco at sunrise on a hill between Yerba Buena and the mission. To save his strength Karl rode on Arturo, taking the beer bucket with him to finish on the way. In my waist I'd tucked a few patches of burlap to mark out the "field of honor." Karl had explained that El Loco's second and I had the duty to mark off with handkerchiefs the corners of a square "field" twenty paces wide. Fighting outside the field was cowardice and meant a loss of honor. I didn't understand then, and still don't, why losing honor is a bigger deal than losing life. In most instances, honor is just an ass—braying and every bit as stubborn. I was carrying the Cortez, too, and Karl's frying pan. I'd been too sleepy to ask why he needed the pan, then thought, *It's his last morning, so he can have with him whatever he wants.* But on our way, cat's curiosity made me ask about it. He said, "That pan is not just any pan. It's the one thing of my ancestors that has ever meant anything to me. My grandfather Mordechai carried it from Bohemia to Germany, and it saved his life. He was accosted by a highwayman—a robber on horse—and that pan flattened his face. Family lore has it that if you look hard enough, you can still see the outline of the robber's nose."

I looked but saw no nose.

Right as the sun was coming up, we got to the top of a small sand hill, and on top of the next hill I saw El Loco and another man, both in black clothes, looking all of a piece like two large, hungry ravens. I made a wish that the sun would stop rising and all I had to do was go down to the calm bay and try to catch fish. I touched the shell around my neck and said out loud, "O Lord Jesus, forgive us our sins, save us from the fires of Hell, lead all souls to Heaven, especially those who have most need of your mercy."

"A fine plea for a loser," Karl said. "But let us remember that David slew Goliath."

As we moved up the hill toward the ravens, I saw that I knew the other one; he was a vaquero, a rare bad one, named Fernando. I'd seen him many times at El Loco's, always drinking *aguardiente* and cursing. More than once he'd kicked my backside for not getting, by his measure, his horse ready fast enough. He wore a black leather patch over one eye, and people around the Mission Santa Clara de Asís used to say that if he took it off, you could look into the hole in his head and see all the way to hell. He was a bad man, but I had never seen him with a pistol. This morning, though, he had one tucked under his chaps, near his belly. El Loco already was holding the Wellington sword in one hand and a bottle of *aguardiente* in the other.

I stopped Arturo about forty paces from them, and Karl got down.

El Loco pointed at me, and like a whale blowing its spout, he spit a mouthful of *aguardiente* at us. "Ingrate bastard!" he shouted, still pointing at me. "Thief!"

"We met yesterday but have not been properly introduced," Karl said calmly. "You are Mr. Smith, I believe?"

El Loco laughed and lifted the point of his sword straight toward the sky. "I'm the Duke of bloody Wellington. And this," he said, nodding at Fernando, "is Napoleon Bonaparte."

Karl stepped forward. "Allow me to introduce myself—my name is Karl Marx. I am a native of the Rhineland, but until recently I resided in your native country, sir, in London."

"Enough," El Loco growled. "Let's get on with it."

"I believe," said Karl, "that we should allow our seconds the opportunity to come to a satisfactory resolution. Or in lieu of that, they must mark out the field of honor."

"Sod off, gibface," El Loco said.

Karl turned to me. "Mr. Smith, it seems, does not stand on ceremony. The Cortez, please. And the pan."

I hadn't wanted it to come to this, but I knew now it was up to me to try to stop the whole business. It was painful, but I shouted, "No! You don't have to fight! I am sorry I took Arturo—the burro. Here, you can have him back."

El Loco had never had to take heed of me about anything; whatever he said was what went. So hearing me speak to him like that seemed to throw him for just a moment.

"There's the jackass," he said, "and then there's you, too, half-breed! I gave good money for you!"

Now I was the one to be thrown. What did he mean, he gave good money for me? Did he think he'd given me some money for something?

Karl understood. "Then this is not just for your honor, Sixto," he said. "It is for your freedom."

Then I understood too. A clear memory of something suddenly became something else. I remembered how, while I waited by Mr. Morgan's wagon on the day he handed me over to El Loco, he and El Loco had looked at me and shaken hands before El Loco gave Mr. Morgan some coins. I thought those were for the few things El Loco was buying from the wagon, some jugs and blankets. Now I knew I was one of the things that got sold too.

So in El Loco's view I had stolen not just Arturo but myself as well. I don't believe I'd ever heard the word *slave* before—that word was not used at the mission— but I had some idea of what one was. I knew that at the mission there were *Indios* who were forced to work.

Sometimes they ran away, and soldiers went after them. When they were brought back, they were punished. Whatever they were called, there were people in this world who had to do the bidding of others and had no choice about it. Being at Loco's beck and call was one thing; being *owned* by him was another. That Mr. Morgan had sold me was shock enough that I felt like my feet were sinking into the sand.

But El Loco wasn't going to wait anymore, and he started walking slowly toward us.

"The Cortez, please," Karl said with some urgency, "and pan." I handed them to him, and he turned to face El Loco, the pan held as a shield and the Cortez ready.

It wasn't just my feet sinking then; everything seemed to give way. My head felt heavy, and my heart was galloping like a horse. I was afraid like the men of Israel when they saw Goliath and they ran away, only I knew there was no way I could abandon Karl.

Now El Loco came charging, holding the Wellington up over his head with two hands. At striking range he brought it down like he was chopping wood, but at the moment he began his chop, Karl quickly jumped aside. Had the Wellington landed, he would have been cut in half from head to toe. El Loco went stumbling past him and almost fell. From this swing I saw how heavy the Wellington was, even for a strong man like El Loco. I could move my feet now and so got well out of David and Goliath's way, between Arturo and Fernando, who kept twitching his one eye back and forth from me to El Loco.

El Loco charged again just like before, and again he swung and missed. After this run he was out of breath, and bent over for a moment to catch it. Karl might have attacked then, but he only stood there, waiting. This waiting made El Loco angry. "Bloody bastard!" he shouted, "Fight!" He straightened up and went at Karl again, this time swinging the Wellington wide from one side to the other. When he got close he put his weight into a swing that came sideways right at Karl's neck. I expected Karl to dodge again, but now he stood his ground, and at the last moment put up the ancestral frying pan. The

Cortez would have been sliced in two and Karl's head lopped off, but the pan blocked the Wellington. The pan fell in halves to the ground; ancient, it might have had a deep crack in it.

The blow had knocked Karl sideways and almost off his feet. Not able to follow up on the attack, El Loco was breathless and down on one knee.

"That pan, sir, was a family heirloom," Karl said. "Are you ready to withdraw?"

"Bollocks!" snarled El Loco, too spent to do more than feebly rise.

Karl went on the attack. One hand in the air behind him, the other with the Cortez in front, he twirled it in little circles as he moved forward in the hops and shuffles he had practiced by my adobe. El Loco feinted and weakly swung, Karl ducked away, then Karl lunged and slashed at El Loco's coat and tore it, stepped back, and with another lunge slashed through the string of El Loco's necklace of skulls. The skulls fell to the ground, sending El Loco into even more of a rage. He made a wild but weak swing at Karl's head that Karl ducked, and then Karl struck again with the Cortez, drawing a line of blood from El Loco's ear to his chin. El Loco howled like a coyote, then again swung, this time so hard that, missing, he whirled around and fell on his back. Too tired to get up, he lay there.

In the bullfight there is *el momento de la verdad*, the moment of truth, when the bull is so tired it can barely move, and the matador moves slowly in with his sword to plunge it into the bull at the precise spot, so that the kill is certain. This was such a moment—Karl could have gone in for *la verdad*. I didn't think he would, but I hadn't known him for very long, so I couldn't be sure. And so neither could Fernando, who wasn't going to wait to find out. Just as he had been keeping his evil eye on me, I had kept one on him. When El Loco fell and it was clear he wasn't going to get up, Fernando put his hand on his pistol.

I was ready. Maybe faster than I had ever before thrown a reata, I whipped one around him. Before he knew what had happened, it was around his ankles, and I gave it a good yank. He went down, dropping his pistol, and cursing me as he used to. I tugged at him again, hard, pulling him away from the pistol. When he couldn't reach his pistol he pulled at the reata, trying to get it off his legs. Meanwhile, El Loco had come up on his knees—Karl wasn't going to kill him. I shouted to Karl for help pulling on Fernando, because to keep him off his feet the reata had to stay tight. When I first threw the reata I had no plan, but then one suddenly came to me. "Arturo!" I shouted, pulling on Fernando as hard as I could. Karl, bless him, understood, and we got our end of the reata, even with Fernando tugging at it, to Arturo, who was close by, and I quickly tied it to his saddle. I gave Arturo's lead to Karl, circled my finger in the air and said, "Go!" He and Arturo trotted off, towing Fernando, now so livid that he was wiggling and flopping like a hooked fish on the end of a line.

What I had to do then was to get my other reata around El Loco, which was going to be very hard if he got up and started swinging the Wellington. Just as he stood up, but before he could muster a swing, I roped him. I cinched the reata around his chest and arms so he couldn't lift his sword. But he could use his feet—and came running toward me. I ran hard to one side, and to bring him down I jerked the line hard; he wobbled but stayed on his feet and kept coming. I was just about to turn and run when Karl, leading Arturo and towing Fernando, ran, ducking under my reata, right in front of El Loco, ramming Arturo into him and sending him flying so far that he pulled me with him. El Loco went down, but I kept my feet. From the crash with El Loco, Arturo had slowed a bit, and I ran to tie my reata to his saddle, too, then gave him a hard slap on his hind end. Like a stallion he reared up a little and then charged off in a straight line toward the sea, dragging the two ravens behind him. Coming right by me, I gave Fernando a swift kick in the rear end, to square old accounts.

Like he'd been pulling a plow his whole life—which he had never, as far as I knew—Arturo towed them off through the sand. Everything had happened so fast that it was only then that I realized I might well not see him again. Sooner or later he was going to have to stop, and unless he could somehow run away, El Loco would take him.

With a heavy heart I watched Arturo disappear over a sand hill. Otherwise, you might think I was happy about how the duel had turned out. Karl and I might both be wet with sweat, but he wasn't dead or even hurt, and I wasn't going back to El Loco's rancho, at least for another day. Karl certainly was happy; he was practically glowing with triumph. But I knew that El Loco, and now Fernando, too, weren't going to go away and leave us alone. They saw which way we'd come from, and they would come looking for us.

"Arturo," I said. "He's gone."

"He is a good friend. He will come back."

"Maybe," I said, but didn't believe it. I was sure El Loco would see to him. "El Loco will be back too. He says I belong to him."

"If he comes for you, we will fight him again. It is only by risking life that freedom is obtained."

"But you are going away to the mountains. How can I fight him and maybe Fernando too?"

"Then you must come with me."

"To the mountains?"

"Yes—why not? You are free to go. Freedom is worthless if you don't use it."

Karl, I was beginning to see, was very big on freedom. And that was not something I knew much about. I hadn't run away from El Loco's because I wanted to be free but because I was scared. Even after I ran away, I didn't feel "free" or think of being free in the way Karl did. I was hiding away. I had no real thoughts about the future. I think I expected that sooner or later I would go back to a rancho somewhere because that was where I was meant to be. Yerba Buena was like going on a hunting trip; I had left home but one day would return, and "home" was on a rancho. Now, though, the world had gone more than a little arsy-varsy, me being about the same as one of the cowhides Mr. Morgan used to trade, and Karl inviting me to go to the mountains with him.

For the next few hours I was on edge, expecting Loco and Fernando to appear and hoping Arturo would. I kept a lookout over the top of the sand hill behind the adobe.

Then Karl came to me and said, "You are a young man. You have your life ahead of you. What do you want to do with it? Your life?"

"I want to be a vaquero," I said.

"A vack . . . arrow? What is that?"

"A vaquero is an *hombre de caballos*—a man of horses. He does many things on a rancho. He herds the cows and cares for them. And then he sees them to the *matanza*, the slaughter. He is a hunter too. And he dances with ladies at fandangos."

"I see," said Karl. "You want to be a cowherder."

"A vaquero," I said, "is more than a cowherder. He is brave . . . He can do many things."

"Ah," said Karl, "so he has *Wissenschaft*."

"What is that?"

"It is when a man knows things," Karl said. "How to do things. You, for example, are very good with your rope or whatever you call it. That is something. But more important, a man may know why other men do things."

"I know," I said, "why a vaquero brings the cows to the *matanza*—so they can be killed for their hides. And I know why he dances in the fandango with beautiful ladies. Because they are beautiful!"

I thought Karl was not respecting how worthy a real vaquero is. "And you—what is your . . . shaft?"

"My *Wissenschaft*? I am handy with a pen and paper. But then, many people are. Some of them pen poison and dreck. But to pen the truth of things is not so easy. So I would say that my *Wissenschaft* is to pen the truth of things. And, if I may be so bold to say so, to steer the course of history. Like your vack arrows, I am trying to herd history, if you will . . . or rather, herd the minds of men, and that will then steer history. But the highest *Wissenschaft*—that is to know your own mind! To know if it is free or trying to be free! Knowing why you yourself do things. That may sound like a dog chasing its tail, but it is not."

I knew that I knew a few things—but what did I not know? And how can one know what one does not know? This was the dog chasing its own tail.

"These vack arrows . . ." Karl said. "Would you say they are free men?"

"Yes," I said. "The Don owns the rancho, but he cannot make a vaquero stay there. A vaquero may go to another rancho."

"He may go to another rancho, but are his thoughts free? There are many men with free bodies—they can go wherever they like. But their minds are not free. They don't think free thoughts."

We were quiet for a little while, looking out over the sand hills, and then Karl, as much to the empty hills as to me, said, "The whole history of the world is nothing but the story of the idea of freedom." And then he left me alone to chew on that and think things over.

I can't say that Karl's talk of freedom had much sway with me right then. My fear of El Loco was more persuasive. It wasn't hard to imagine him, after getting hauled for miles through the sand by Arturo, cooking up some special revenge for me—like getting dragged around Yerba Buena behind the fat end of a horse. So El Loco was the "push" for leaving, but there was a pull too—the mountains of the Sierra Nevada. Padre Arturo believed my mother had come from there, that she was a mountain *Indio* who went back home when she left the mission and me. Why she left me behind he didn't know, but he said she must have had a good reason. So those mountains had always had a claim on me, long before I ever made a claim, mining or otherwise, in them. Though I had never been to the Sierras, never even seen them, whenever I imagined them they held a promise of an answer, of something like peace, of belonging maybe, something I had never really known. So, in the end, it was not such a hard decision to make—I told Karl I would go with him.

"Excellent," he said. "*Audaces fortuna juvat*—fortune favors the bold."

He went over to the Wellington and said, "This is yours now."

"I don't want it," I said.

"I'm afraid," he said, "you don't have a choice. You are like King Arthur—the sword has chosen you."

From Karl to Friedrich Engels

May 21, 1849

Dear Friedrich:

Greetings from "splendid California" as you have called it.
And indeed, splendid it can be when the fleas are not dancing in
your underclothes or you're not freezing in a sea fog frostier than
a Prussian baroness's tush on a Berlin park bench in the winter.
Inland from the coast of San Francisco, which I predict will prove
to be permanently uninhabitable, the air gets warmer and there is
an Italian-like sublimity in the landscape of rolling hills until they
flatten out and farther east you enter a hot, broad valley that is less
fit to live in than the hills, though still not without charm. There are
great open expanses that could one day host a prosperous civilization
quite different from the almost feudal-like ranch civilization of the
"Californios" (they do not call themselves Spaniards or Mexicans)
that have occupied it for so long. Their "ranchos" are reported to be
enormous, about equal in extent to many German principalities. It
is a pity that such beautiful and relatively virgin territory is about to
be violated—little do the Californios know that they and their little
kingdoms are about to be steamrolled by the vanguard of capitalistic
force arriving from the American east. I have had little time, so far, for
thinking about much else than my survival, yet I can't help but muse
on what a wondrous picture Socialism could paint on such a canvas.

We are traveling on foot from a settlement called Sacramento.
(Why could the Spaniards not name their villages here other than for
their countless saints or their Popish rituals?) I am with a young man
who aided me immensely when I first arrived in San Francisco. Our
destination is somewhere in the Sierra Nevada mountains, to the gold
mining areas, or the "diggings" as they call it here. My young friend

and I left San Francisco rather in a hurry—it is a long story, but in a sword duel (like my good old student days!) I not only defended his honor but liberated him from slavery! No, he is not an African, but I believe probably a mixture of American Indian and Mexican (a local rancher had bought him from an American merchant). My opponent in the duel and his second were rascals, and the second drew a pistol. But they got their comeuppance from "lassos" expertly thrown by my companion, Sixto, and were dragged away by his donkey. To escape their inevitable revenge, and exercise his new freedom, Sixto has chosen to accompany me to the gold country. We caught a small steam-powered boat out of San Francisco and up the Sacramento River. We had thought we were leaving behind Sixto's beloved and heroic donkey, to whom he is sentimentally attached, but the donkey found us as we were making our way to the boat.

Our steamboat was loaded full with men bound for golden glory. They all believe that they are going to become grandly rich (yes, I suppose even yours truly), that chunks of gold are practically growing out of the ground like cabbages, that under the acorn trees there are pigs running around already cooked with knives and forks sticking in them, and that beer is bubbling out of springs. Ah, the religious and secular superstitions of men! New methods of "divining" gold— note the transfer of religious sentiment to this substance—are being invented right and left. One man means to stick a potato on a twig, another to suspend a can of oysters on a string between two wooden rods. Yet another has devised what he calls a "goldometer," which looks like nothing more than a plumb bob, a ball swinging at the end of some string. He evinces great confidence in this invention, and no king or queen in Europe is looked up to as much!

To while away the time on the boat, some Americans amused themselves by shooting at targets along the riverbanks. Ducks, hogs, coyotes, and anything else that moved were blasted by the fusillade of thirty men firing at the same time. They were, one said, practicing so that up in the mountains they could "take the Pawnees' eyes out without any trouble." I had a grievous toothache that began on the boat, and each fusillade thundered in my head and jaw. I finally remonstrated with them, only to be told to "shut my yap" or they would shut it for me. The only relief came when I could sit and lower my head between my knees; the best relief, if temporary, finally came from standing on my head in a narrow corner of the deck, against the captain's cabin. This brought jeers from some of the fusilladiers unfamiliar with this Hindoo practice. I paid them no mind, although the Americans are loud, rowdy, and aggressive.

On the boat I observed some of the paradoxes of the "land of the free." The Americans dominated the biggest and best area of the boat, consigning us and a few others—foreigners and a black man—first to the back of the boat and then to a cramped area in the bow. We were thus under virtual house arrest, the captain not willing to defy the tyrannical majority. Many of the Americans view the gold as theirs and are not happy to share it with foreigners. Sixto and some Mexicans came into some verbal abuse as "greasers" and had no choice but to tolerate it, given the numbers. The Americans seem to have greater animus toward Mexicans than other Spaniards (such as a couple odd fellows we believed to be Chili-an), no doubt due to the recent war between the two countries. However, not all of the Americans join in, and one hopes they are finer examples of their country's principles. Either that or they believe the newspaper reports that there is enough gold to go around for everyone and turn a blind eye as long as they get their piece of the pie.

Occupying the bow of the boat with us was a black man, the property of his white master who was also on board. Sixto had never seen such a man, nor did he know anything about the American system of Negro enslavement. Despite my toothache, I was able to school Sixto in some of that system's features, and because of his recent discovery of his own former status as property, he was most interested. We learned that the black man had been promised a fraction of his master's findings. If they were lucky, he would earn enough to buy his own freedom—for one thousand American dollars. This got Sixto wondering if he owed his former "master" a debt and if he will ever be able to pay it off. I've told him that he does not owe anyone anything because the whole transaction is morally repugnant and invalid under natural law, but he has a strong sense of obligation and can't seem to "free" himself of the idea that he is in debt. It may not help that he has no idea how much, monetarily, that debt might be.

Rumors of gold strikes are rife. Acting on a tip, we hope to avoid the main "rush" and are heading toward a little-known area called the *Los Infernos*. Before leaving Sacramento—a febrile mudhole prone to calamitous flooding from its river—we bought a few pieces of essential mining equipment: a washbasin, a pick, shovel, pot, knives, and spoons. My trunk was lost in San Francisco, my only surviving possessions the clothing on my back, my favorite frying pan (unfortunately destroyed in my duel), and, yes, a satchel containing the draft of my "work" in progress. As I said, I have had little time for my work, but I'm thinking that in order to have its intended effect, it needs a good, punchy title. Something like "An Indictment of Capitalist Hegemony and Subjugation of Labor and Humanity in the Advanced Economies of Europe and Beyond." What do you think?

In the foothills of the mountains we have passed through a few Indian villages, about which I will perhaps say more later. Only to say now that a ladies' man such as you, Friedrich, would greatly admire the beauties of Nature that the young Indian maidens are. They are as Nature designed them to be, women without stays or padding, and a delight to the eyes.

Please see that you check in on my *Liebchen* Jenny. And, by the way, I assume you received my letter from New York about money—you couldn't send a little cash could you, or does your *Schweinehund* of a father still have you on that strict allowance?

Sincerely yours,
Karl

From Jenny to Karl

February 14, 1849

London, England

Dearest Karl,

We received your letter from New York and were sorry to hear of your rough crossing. Of course the children and I think of your hardship often, and that you are enduring it for our sake, and for the sake of the revolution. I wish I bore good news to lighten your burdens, but we are having our own burdens here. I was not aware of the size of the tab you had run up at the Rose and Crown pub, and the proprietor there, a Mr. Graves, has come by the house twice now to ask how I intend to pay for it. I have had to position our daughter Jennychen as a kind of sentry at the bottom of the stairway for hours at a time, and like a trained parrot she squawks "He ain't here!" in a cockney accent to all of your creditors.

Oh Karl! Our children may have to wash glasses or sweep a pub floor to pay the bill! I know you will say that is nothing compared to the miserable conditions children put up with in the English factories, but that is not the life I and my parents anticipated for von Westphalen children.

I have already pawned everything—there is no jewelry left, nor any other scrap of silver or gold. The next to go is the porcelain and linen. I am so ashamed that I cannot go to the pawnshop myself but instead send Helena. Soon the bailiff will be sending notice he will be coming to seize things. But seize what? It will all be gone! What will we do? Friedrich came for a visit, but he did not offer any money, and I could not ask. He came with his latest girlfriend, that Marshall woman. She is an intriguing, ambitious Lady Macbeth, and I do not trust her. Not only could I not speak my heart with her around, I could not bring myself to sit on the same side of the room as she.

Friedrich was the usual bag of wind—he talks of revolution but lives like a sheik, with his mistresses and his bank accounts. I am not sure how trustworthy he is, either, if you know what I mean. He is some kind of Prussian Priapus, with his pick of all his father's factory girls in Manchester.

Karl, we are nearly desperate—please send some money as soon as you can!

On top of everything else, I may need to find a new nanny. You will be as astonished as I am to hear that Helena is—with child! Yes, our dear Helena, who seems to never go anywhere. How on earth such a thing could have happened is beyond me—it almost makes me wonder if immaculate conception is possible after all.

Your loving Jenny

4
Off to the Diggings

AND SO I BECAME A FORTY-NINER, THOUGH IT'S HARD TO imagine anyone who had less fire in his belly about being a digger than I did. I had no gold fever like all the rest, no dream of becoming rich. The richest men I'd ever seen were a few Dons on their ranchos, and they lived fairly simple lives. I had no real idea what "rich" was and what it all meant. Karl had said the reason I should go was to begin my life as a free man, so I could begin to "form an emancipated consciousness." Well, I had no real idea what that was either. I was going because I was afraid of staying in Yerba Buena, and because I had a kind of superstition, or a wispy hope, that the mountains would somehow "speak" to me, that maybe they could tell me more about myself. Not that I expected to find my mother there. I don't know what I expected, other than to go there and let come what may. That alone, I guess, was a kind of freedom—doing something I was not told to do, something I chose, without knowing exactly why I was doing it. But then, in one of my first positive acts of freedom, I knew exactly what I was doing. Even though he left the Cortez behind, Karl insisted I take the Wellington with us to the mountains. But that damned thing weighed as much as a small anvil, and I refused and stuck it in the sand. I said I didn't know how any Arthur became king or how Wellington did whatever he did lugging around something that burdensome.

I had reasons for not wanting to leave Yerba Buena. One was Arturo. I was mighty torn up about leaving him behind, and didn't know what to do. There was little time to go looking for him, and a lot of danger—El Loco had put a price on my head, and so going to the dock, I wore a sombrero pulled hard down to my nose. When Karl and I left for the dock, it was all I could do not to bust out crying, and then on the way there, lo and behold, Arturo came trotting up behind us, my reatas still tied to his saddle and trailing behind him. He was hot and breathing hard, and even though I was afraid El Loco and Fernando might not be far behind, we stopped to calm him down and let him lap some water from my hands.

At the dock, a steamboat captain said he was leaving for Sacramento the minute he had a full boat and that was going to be soon. But the captain said Domingo could not go with us. There are men who do not like dogs, and that captain was one of that rare and soul-shriveled fraternity. Nothing but trouble, he said. He would take on a donkey—at full human fare. Donkeys and mules were fine, but no dogs, he said, especially coyotes pretending to be dogs.

I didn't like it but had no choice but to leave Domingo behind. I thought maybe I could leave him with Dolores, and then I saw the captain who had paid me to catch rats. Knowing Domingo was a good rat catcher, he promised he would take care of him until he went to sea, and then find someone else who would appreciate his worth. That was a hard thing, leaving Domingo behind, but I told myself it was the best thing for him, staying there on the dock.

The other reason I had for staying in Yerba Buena was Dolores. I'd never forgotten her, and now here she was, and all the feeling that I used to have for her had come back just as it had been. Some men talk about a "girl of my dreams" and don't mean much more by that than wishful thinking, but for me, Dolores veritably was that. After I left the Morgans, I dreamed about her every so often, not the teasing Dolores but the kinder one that I knew she could be, and those dreams were almost like visions of a Virgin to me, leaving me with some hope and believing there might be some good in the world after all. I'm not one for self-pity, but it's God's truth that I'd already had my share of the world's hardness, and dreaming of Dolores always softened it a little. At the time of leaving Yerba Buena, I don't think I knew just what my long-run intentions were toward her. The way I saw it, I was glad she was in a place where God would keep her from harm. That He would also try to keep her from me was a thing I knew I would have to face at some point down the road, but I was content to let that be and deal with it when the time came for it.

I knew I needed to say goodbye to her, to tell her that I was not going to be gone forever. I went to her house and knocked on the door, but no one answered. I went below her window and called her name, and a woman—the one I'd heard squaring off with El Loco, a woman who I think could trade barks and bites with the hound guarding the gate of Hades—popped her head out of the window and told me to skedaddle before she dumped the night bucket on me. That, I thought, was very un-sisterlike, but I heeded the warning. I then asked Karl for a scrap of paper, quill, and ink. I wrote a letter and put it by the door of the house. I did not have the time and the words to tell her about my dreams.

Dear Dolores,

This morning there was something called a duel lala mort with the man who was looking for me, and another man with *mal ojo*. The one looking for me got dragged through the sand by my burro and now might want to kill me. So I must go away for a while. I am going to the mountains with a friend. I came to say goodbye but the sister who is your *jefe* would not let me. This is not goodbye for forever. I will come

back. I did not think I would ever see you again. I am very
happy that I did.

Your friend,
Sixto

I cannot take my dog Domingo on the boat. I had to leave
him at the dock with another captain. Will you please go
tend to him from time to time?
If you want you can send a letter for me to Sacramento.

We boarded the steamboat, a party going full swing up front—a
large pack of piss-and-vinegar yankees tapping brandy casks and
the captain drinking with them. He firmly told us to go "take the
stern"—because of Arturo, I thought, but later I knew otherwise. It
wasn't easy, but I got Arturo to sit back on the deck. Two Mexicans
were already back there and told me they'd been told to go there and
stay there. Two other fellows then came on, an odd-looking pair; one
was tall and goose-necked, the other squat and round. They were
wearing long, brown ponchos not like any *serape* I'd ever seen before, and furry caps stretched around their heads, with little balls on
top. Their hair was so long and falling over their faces that the only
thing you could really see was their noses; the tall one had a prow
like a schooner. Karl said that with their hair all over, they looked like
shaggy llamas, though I had no idea what a llama was. Some men had
brought on full canvas bags or trunks of gear, others nothing. Just before we pushed off, a Negro—I'd never seen one before—came down
the dock, a big trunk hoisted on his shoulder. He had a limp but still
handled the trunk as though it were a snuff box. A man with a cane
walked behind him and ordered him to take his place with us while
he joined the party up front.

Karl was not happy about being "summarily consigned" to the
stern, and even less happy that the captain was fairly swigging brandy
like it was some physic. The wind was rising and bringing in the first

of the sea fog. Waves were capping white out on the bay. I had never been in a boat, and in Monterey I had heard of many a drowning. I could not imagine how that boat could avoid certain doom, loaded to the rails with men and a burro and all but the kitchen sink, and my lungs seemed to tighten up remembering El Loco's drunken sport with me, smothering me to the bottom of the sea.

The captain rang a bell and shouted "Heave ho!" to men who helped push us off the dock. The power of that boat—a steamer, one of the first to run that route—breathed a little hope into my bone-deep dread. On the dock, Domingo barked and jumped, and I waved goodbye. Soon after we pulled away, I saw my adobe down the shore, a brown mound in the fog. I kept an eye on Dolores's house and thought I saw someone in an upper window, and waved, but whoever it was, if anyone, didn't wave back. Farther out on the bay, I took a long look at San Francisco—still Yerba Buena to me—so strange from out on the water. More, it seemed, had happened in my short time there than in all my time at El Loco's.

The boat was slow but steady. The waves bucked it like a wild horse as we went by Yerba Buena island and then the island of Alcatraz. Behind Isla de los Angeles, shielded from the wind, we found some calm. At least, I thought, I was not going to drown in sight of Yerba Buena. Out from behind the island, the wind and waves gradually died down, and we passed by some large rocks, not quite islands, white with guano, hundreds of gulls and pelicans on and above them squawking bloody murder. All of us, except the captain in his little wheelhouse cabin, were wet and cold from the spray, only the yankees were so liquored up they didn't mind. It was then that one of Karl's teeth started to hurt him bad.

By sundown we had left the upper part of the bay and were well up the river channel. I ate a cold tortilla and offered one to the others, only the Mexicans taking one. Karl's toothache seemed to get worse, and the rowdy racket from the yankees' endless shindig wasn't helping. He got some notion then that he thought would help it—to sit on top of a barrel behind the captain's cabin and, holding his head in his hands, bend over and put it between his legs like he was trying to kiss his boots, then come up and do it again. He did this over and over, up and down, groaning the whole time.

The night chill was settling in, and all of us except Karl hunkered low between Arturo and the gunwale, trying to keep warm. Up to that point, no one had said much, all of us keeping to ourselves. I struck up some small talk with the Mexicans. They'd come all the way up from Sonora on horseback, sometimes staying at hospitable ranchos but usually roughing it. Horses, they said, were no good in the mountains, so they had sold theirs. We tried speaking Spanish with the odd fellows in the fur hats but got no answer. Maybe, the Mexicans said, they were *mudos*—mutes—and thought they might be from South America, maybe Chile. Their clothes, the Sonorans said, weren't from anywhere in Mexico that they knew of.

One of the yankees came back and sat near us. He was fairly sober and said he was tired of the ruckus and its makers, mostly "loud Southerners" he said. The Negro—the man with the cane had called him Solomon—then spoke up and said he was from down south, "a place they call Arkansaw," he said, and asked me if I knew it. I confessed I did not. When he'd come on the boat, Solomon was careful not to look anyone in the eye and had stayed that way, and I took him for the quiet type, but once he got going he had a pretty loose jaw. It was hard to tell just how old he might be; he was already graying at the sides and had the limp, but a powerful build. He said he was going up in the "Sarra to dig" with his "master." "And for's myself," he said—out of every one hundred dollars he dug up for his master, he was going to get five. With one thousand dollars, he said, he could buy his freedom.

Now, the whole master and slave business had not really had a chance to sink very far into my head. The duel, coming to the decision to leave, saying goodbye to Dolores and Domingo—all that in one day had been like a big wave crashing on the beach, washing over my learning of it. But Solomon's talk threw me a bit on beam's end—I was the first person I ever knew who was outright owned by another person, and now in the very same day, here was somebody else. And that wasn't the half of it—Solomon said that if he earned more, he might be able to go back and buy his wife and son, and they'd all go to Boston or Philadelphia. I said that if what everyone says is true, he'd be in Boston by the end of the year. But I thought, *One thousand dollars!* Is that what I owed El Loco to buy my own freedom? Karl had said I had no debt because it was immoral, but I thought I was going to want it paid, bad debt or not, so there would be no question at all about my freedom. I told Solomon that I had a master, too—or used to have one—and about the duel.

"So you's runnin away?" he said.

"I guess so," I said.

"Three times I run away," he said. "Last I got up into Missouri and clear across the river to Illinois. Near a place they call Caro. But he come after me, with his brother. I was dog tired. So they take me back and give it to me good. Broke my foot up. No more runnin' for me after that. But I wanna be free."

The yankee had been listening. "You already are free," he said. "Both of you. There's no slavery in California. It's a free territory."

The yankee was well-dressed, with new boots and a clean shave. "I am a lawyer," he said. "Or was one, I guess. In Boston. But I know some of the law here. You might be a slave in a slave state, sir, but once you're here, you are free."

Solomon and I looked at each other. Smiling, he shook his head. "'Ain't that peas and greens!' my mama used to say. 'The Lord answers prayer.'"

This revelation both confused and lifted me. All in the same day, I'd gone from not knowing I wasn't free, to learning I wasn't, then after the duel that I should be by Karl's moral reckoning, but still feeling that I owed El Loco whatever he paid for me—and now, in the eyes of the law, I was free after all.

In the meantime, Karl had been going back and forth between us and the barrel. I went over to the barrel to see how he was and told him what Solomon and the yankee had said, and that's when he told me there were millions of others like Solomon in the southern part of America, people who were owned by men who had farms with enormous fields of cotton and who worked the Negroes to the bone. I could hardly believe it, but then I'd heard other things that day that had stretched belief.

And don't the Catholic priests, Karl said, make slaves out of the Indians here? As I've said, I knew that at the mission there were Indians who did not want to work in the bean and corn fields, who ran away and then were whipped for it. But the padres had said those people belonged to God, that they'd promised their souls to Him, that by taking communion they'd made a vow for life and by running away they were breaking that vow to God, a most serious offense. I'd never questioned any of that, but now I wondered: Was it right for the soldiers to go for them and then punish them—even if it was because they were God's property, not another man's? I'd never heard the padres or anyone else call them slaves. But were they any different from me or Solomon? Did it make a difference who did the owning—God or some man? And what they were called?

Right there on the boat, I couldn't think through all this and come out the other end, but it was beginning to seem all wrong to me—on the other hand, if it was wrong, how could the padres have done it? If you can own a horse or a dog or a reata, isn't it possible you can own a man or woman too? I had a pretty strong notion they weren't the same thing, but I was confused. And then there was Karl with his talk of freedom. I was a little like a horse who's had blinkers on for so long and has no choice, all he can see is what is given to him. You take the blinkers off, the horse might be confused at first by being able to see whatever it wants. That's how I was. But I was a person, not a horse. That's what Karl was trying to get me to understand, that there was more to being a person than just *being*—I was a person who could make choices.

In time we all settled in to sleep, but not much later we had yankees shaking us awake and saying all of us in back now had to go to the front of the boat. We didn't understand why, and Karl—toothache and all—stepped in and wrangled with them, but they weren't hearing it and were ready to toss him overboard, so we all shuffled up there. They let Arturo lay where he was. We soon found out why they put us up there—the wind had changed direction and was cold, and the boat was going straight into it, with spray coming up and over onto the bow. Up there, Karl couldn't sleep and didn't have his barrel anymore, so he took to doing something entirely new to me—standing on his head, up against the wall of the captain's cabin. He'd put his forearms on the deck, tuck his head between them, and then kick his feet up in the air and against the wall and stay there for a few seconds, then come back down and pace around for a while, then repeat the whole thing. This went on all night. I didn't get much sleep, and I'm not sure Karl got any. Later in the night the mosquitos got bad too. The boat would pass through a cloud of them, the quick ones found us, and we'd still be slapping at them by the time we got to the next bunch.

The sun was barely up when the yankees' guns woke us up. Their guns and the mosquitos. At first, I thought they might be hunting coyotes on the riverbank. Then I saw they were shooting at anything that moved—wild pigs, ducks, muskrats. One of them said they were practicing so that up in the mountains they could "put out the Pawnees' eyes without any trouble." The whole boat started to feel then like some kind of floating circus. Arturo started to bawl and wouldn't stop. Karl said it was like cannons booming in his head and begged them to stop shooting, but they kept on firing away, and so he did some more topsy-turvies, and the yankees got to hootin' and hollerin' about that. To tell the truth, I was kind of embarrassed and told the Mexicans it must be a thing people from Germany did.

Pretty soon, Karl said he couldn't take it anymore. He told the captain to stop and let us off, and demanded our money back. At first the captain told us, profanely, to go and saw our timber. But after some more guff from Karl, he angled the boat toward a sandbar just off the middle of the river. The yankees started jeering at us without let up. The captain swung the boat close to the bar and, holding it there in the current, ordered us off. There was no use arguing, as the yankees were about to pick us up and toss us, even Arturo. We were not getting our money back. We got off the boat in chest-deep water and into a sizable current, then made it onto the bar, which was firm sand. As the boat pulled away, the yankees fired their rifles in the air and howled away, a last gift to Karl's head. There was no telling just how deep the water was between the bar and the riverbank about a hundred feet away, and the two of us and Arturo sat there for a bit in a pickle, assessing the situation. As I've said, I'm not the best swimmer. We were maybe going to have to wait until another upstream boat came by and hope it would make a stop. Then a commotion rose up from the steamboat, maybe two hundred feet or so upriver, just as it was about to go around a bend, and we saw something in the water behind it, swimming like an otter toward us—by jiminy, it was Solomon! I have to imagine there was some contention on that boat about if it should turn around or not, but it didn't. And Solomon, helped by the current, made it to us in good time. I wondered how many water courses he'd had to cross in his run aways, because he was a mighty good swimmer. When he got to the bar, we still weren't sure the boat wouldn't be coming back, so he wasted no time testing for us the water between us and the bank. Seeing it seemed no more than chest high, we followed him across the channel.

Now the river "bank" there was not much more than a strip of mud a few feet wide between the river and a thick wall of tule grass almost ten feet high that lined both sides of the river up and downstream as far as the eye could see. We went into the tule, Solomon leading the way and me tugging on Arturo, as he did not want to go through it. The grass swallowed us up good as any jungle. We spooked a flock of ducks and then a pack of wild pigs. After some time fighting that grass, we got into the clear, with dry, flat land ahead of us.

Out in the open, Solomon pointed upstream and said, "If them is a going that a way, I'm a headin' this." He'd find a clearing along the river and see if he could catch a boat back to San Francisco. There, he said, he'd do hauling on the dock to make the money he needed. We wished him well and watched him limp off, his wet clothes on him all he had in the world. He looked happy. He did not need any schooling from Karl in order to prize his freedom.

Karl and I set out northeasterly with slow progress. To relieve his bad tooth, Karl did a kind of topsy-turvy every fifty paces or so, going down onto his hands like an acrobat in the circus. He'd dive toward the ground and kick his legs up into the air, hang there for a second or two and then come back down, gather himself and move on. This gymnastic was even more impressive seeing he was wearing a jacket with gold coins sewn into it, making it heavy. I thought these heels-over-head dives would only make his tooth hurt worse, sending all that blood to his head, but he swore it was "a certain amelioration." I had to hand it to him that he didn't gripe too much to me but was doing what he could for himself.

Between topsy-turvies Karl told me more about the Negro slaves in the South. Without them, he said, there would be no cotton. Without cotton there would be no "industry." Without industry, there would be no trade in the world. And without trade you might as well "erase America from the map." I was seeing more of the world now, he said, so I should learn more about what made it turn—greed.

After a time and many more "ameliorations," we saw smoke in the distance and headed toward it, and soon came to an Indian village—a dozen or so mud-smeared huts with roofs fashioned from tree branches. The village didn't look like any I'd seen before, more like it had just been thrown together the day before. On one roof, a man was sunning himself buck naked. Out of another hut, a man came toward us, wearing striped pants and a straw sombrero, then three more men came out, one with just a shirt on and a pair of boots, another wearing just a vest, and the third one sporting a bandana around his neck and not a lick of clothing more. Some miner, it seemed, had lost or traded away his wardrobe, and they were sharing it. A few women and children came behind them, the children naked, too, but the women more or less covered up. I tried an Ohlone greeting I knew but got no answer. Of a sudden, Karl grunted and went into one of his dives. A woman screamed and ran, and then all the other women and children followed her, back into their huts. The men backed away, sizing us up. Then we heard laughing, and a tall yankee stepped out from a hut.

"Bully!" the yankee said, clapping his hands. "Bully!" He was hairier than a haystack and about half as big as one. Seeing him clap, the Indian men clapped too, and then Karl went down again and they all cheered. When he came up, the yankee said, "Where you fellows from?"

"London, sir," Karl said, holding his jaw. I saw now it was really swelling up.

"Yerba Buena," I said. "San Francisco."

"London!" the yankee said. "Well, welcome to California. You're just a few thousand miles closer to hell."

An Indian came up and offered a bowl of mush to Karl, but he waved it off, pointing to his tooth.

"You got a poison tooth there, friend?" said the yankee. "I believe I can help you with that."

I think Karl would have taken help then from the bad king himself, and he gave the yankee a nod. The yankee whistled, a horse came trotting out, and from a saddle bag the yankee took out a coil of thin string.

"This here," he said, "is what they call catgut. But it ain't from a cat. I pulled it from a mountain goat. Finest string west of the Mississippi. Let me have one of your lassos there, son."

I gave him a reata, and he poked a small hole in the tip of it and threaded the catgut through.

Karl tried to say something but the yankee stopped him. "Just hold on. Open up wide and let's see what we're dealin' with."

Karl obeyed and opened wide.

"Ah," the yankee said, and in no time looped the catgut inside Karl's mouth. "Now, keep your eyes shut."

The yankee tied the other end of the reata to his horse's saddle, then pulled out a pistol, and not far from the poor nag's ear, fired a shot into the air. The horse bolted, the reata and string snapped tight, and Karl's tooth came flying out of his mouth. The Indians cheered. Bad tooth trailing behind it, the yankee's horse went straight off toward the horizon. Karl spit out blood, and the Indians cheered this too. They seemed to think it was an occasion for celebration and wanted us to eat. Karl said he didn't want any, but I was hungry. In a hut, an Indian woman gave me and the yankee bowls of boiled acorn and grasshopper mush. Don't knock it if you haven't tried it—it's much tastier than you think. Arturo got fed, too, a whole basket of one of his favorite grasses.

After a while, the yankee's horse came back with Karl's tooth, but the Indians would not touch it. The yankee gave it to Karl, and I said he should keep it for good luck. Karl said there was no such thing as good or bad luck, just consequences, and he tossed the tooth out the door of the hut. The Indian woman who was feeding us didn't like this at all and told the yankee that it would grow into a big tooth sticking out of the ground, and she and her people did not want a stranger's tooth rising up in the middle of the village. The yankee said there was no sense in not mustering all the luck you could if you were going to dig for gold, so Karl went out and pocketed the tooth.

The yankee never did tell us his name. I know now he was what they called a mountain man, one of the loners who went into the mountains for months at a time to trap and hunt. There may still be some up there, though they're a dying breed. He had done some looking for gold and wanted to tell us about it.

The Mountain Man

"I done some trapping in Colorado and then came west to the Sierra. I wasn't here but two months before I heard of the gold, from a Miwok Indian. Word had got out, and I knew that meant a rush would come. In Colorado, a smart fellow once told me that all the gold in the world had washed down from the north. So while everyone else was heading east of Sacramento, I headed north, way up into country I'd never been before. I didn't know a thing about digging and had nothing to dig with but a tomahawk and a spoon. And sure enough, I was finding nothing. I was fool enough to think the gold would find me. I'd almost given up until one day I saw a lake, a small one, and thought I'd give myself a wash, as I hadn't had a good one in a blue moon. I went down to the lake—and there it was. Gold. All along the shore, out on the ground as thick as pine cones after a storm. I didn't have to dig, just pick up the pieces. I loaded up as many as I could carry and made my way to Sacramento. This was in the early fall, and I had time to go back before the snow came. I have always known my way in and out of places, but damn if I could find that lake again. I looked and looked until the winter got too fierce and I had to hole up until the thaw. In the spring I went looking again, but still no luck. I gave up but I'm going to try once more. Only problem is I got drunk one night in Sacramento and told some fool and he blathered all over. So now every fool and his mother are looking for what they're all calling the 'gold lake.'

"There's diggers in other places making a good out. But they're not telling nobody, and you ain't going to read about it in a newspaper. If'n you see in the papers somebody saying they made a find, more than naught that's somebody just trying to sell you something—picks and shovels."

But a "trusty fellow," he said, had told him of a place that had the kind of wash that had promise, and that is where he would go if he was in our shoes. It was called Los Infernos, and he told us more or less how to get there from Sacramento and what we should buy before heading there. We had at least another day's walk to Sacramento, and from there it was about a two- to three-day trek.

We had a good part of the day ahead of us, so after I ate, we set off. The best route, the yankee said, was to follow a rough trail that pretty much tracked the river. We were both tired from the night on the boat, but with Karl feeling better and not doing his topsies anymore, our progress was much quicker. Karl had said he didn't believe in luck, but I was thinking we'd had some of the good kind by meeting up with the yankee. I'd had little enough of the good kind in my life, so knew that when you did get some you shouldn't ignore it. What if Arturo hadn't been there at the right time and place to kick El Loco? And what was it but luck—or maybe the plan of God—that I'd found Dolores? I wasn't sure if Karl believed in much of anything; however, I didn't see a problem with a man believing in luck and God at the same time. The yankee was right about luck. We were going to need all we could get.

From Dolores to Sixto

May 9, 1849

San Francisco

Dear Sixto,

It was such a surprise to see you, and then I got your letter saying you are going off to the mountains. It is all too much like before—one day you were at our house, and the next day you were gone. I did not know my father was going to take you away, and he would never tell me where he went with you. I really did miss you. I did not have any friends in Monterey before you came, and then none after you left. After my mother and father died, I had no one at all.

I know about your duel. After you left, I heard that that man—I will call him Horribilis—had gone back to the plaza, so I went there too. He was cursing you awfully and said he would give money to anyone who brought you to him. But then a short man with a funny accent said he must take it all back. Horribilis said he would not, and then they said they would duel. Horribilis spied me in the crowd. He came up to me and said, "You know where he is, don't you sweetheart?" He may be Horribilis, but he did not scare me. It was not very polite of me, but I gave him a good kick in the shin. He was ready to swat me, but some gentlemen in the crowd stopped him. I told him I did not know where you were. I was not lying, as I did not know exactly where you were living. Living with such a man as that must have been awful. I am so sorry my father sent you there.

I went to see Domingo. He is not exactly the most handsome dog, but I very much like his spirit. He goes up and down the dock like he owns it, and when he's not sleeping he chases birds off the dock, the captain says. The captain praised you and wished the new boy was as good as you. I will do what I can for Domingo. We sometimes have scraps here that I can give him.

I must say that seeing you brought back many memories and feelings. I don't know how to say this exactly, Sixto, but I will try. When I think of the people who have been in my life—not that many, it is true, but that doesn't matter—when I think of people, I see how you made me feel that life is good, that there can be sweetness in it, that it is not all ashes like I often think it is. Seeing you was like being cold from head to toe, then sitting by a warm fire. We used to do some of my most favorite things. Do you remember when my father had gone to the ranches and my mother was sick in bed and you and I went on the horses all the way out to the Point Pinos? That was a grand day! My mother and father never cared for going to the shore. As you may remember, my mother, may she rest in peace, believed the sea air was unhealthy, but I think it is just the opposite.

You must feel hopeful, going to the mountains. Right now, I must say I do not have much hope for myself. Don't be worried when I say that. That is just the way it is. I can tell you more if I see you—when I see you!

I hope you will understand when I say that you should not come here again. I would like to see you, but if you do come back to San Francisco, please leave me a letter like you did, and tell me where I should meet you. There are some things I need to explain to you.

Please be careful. I have heard there is much sickness up in the mountains. I know you say your prayers—I will say one for you.

Your friend,
Dolores

Karl

May 10, 1849 — I begin here a journal of my observations and experience, perhaps useful in some later work.

All day, despite damnable mosquitos, we kept close to the river, or at least in sight of the tall grass and occasional tree that lined it. Once, from a low rise in a clearing, we saw a maze of ague-and-fever-ridden marshes and smaller channels spreading on the river's far side. On our side there fortunately was not the same web of channels, but several times we had to swing wide around a small bog in order to follow the main channel. The air was still and hot. We saw only one boat going downstream and hoped for the best for our Negro friend.

In the late afternoon, still some time before sunset, the mosquitos began to worsen. We had no tent or any other prospect for lodging, and neither Sixto nor I raised the question of where we were to sleep. The mosquitos—members of the same parasitic civilization that had tormented us on the river boat—made this unthinkable. Airborne nations of them roamed the land and began to swarm us. Sixto and I both swung our arms like mad men, and Arturo's tail twitched furiously. Every ten lengths or so, he jerked his whole head so violently that nearly all four of his feet came off the ground. On the boat we had moved through a horde and had some respite before the next, but on foot we were left to swipe and swat without surcease.

The trail, as it were, had veered a short distance away from the river, and we were hoping to escape the flying devils when ahead, from the direction of the river, we heard a faint noise like the bawling of a calf or the mewling of a spanked child. Closer, it clearly was a human cry for help. With a look of agreement, Sixto and I angled toward the river. As we approached it, we again heard wailing and soon came upon a sight as horrible as any produced by the Spanish Inquisition: a man, naked, strapped to the trunk of a tree, his body serving up a banquet for legions of mosquitos having their bloody fill. He was a thin man, but I could see that almost every inch of his feasted-on flesh, from forehead to *Schwanz* to toes, had puffed up from the horrific insectile tattooing he was getting.

With a blanket Sixto ran and waved at the winged demons while I cut the anguished man's straps. As soon as his hands were free he began to scratch his face so fiercely that it bled. At the same time, he could barely stand, he was so dazed and feeble. Sixto continued to wave off the marauding insects as I helped the man to the river. There he quickly went under, free of his tormentors for precious seconds. As weak as he was, I thought the river might just take him away. But he came up, and we draped the blanket around him and threw him on top of Arturo.

We then did what we should have done for ourselves hours earlier. At a slow run we led Arturo to a spot distant enough from the river that the mosquitos, although not completely left behind, were much fewer and farther between. Flying bloodsuckers or not, it was time and occasion to think about bedding down. It was going to be dark soon, and our poor wretch, draped over Arturo like a sack of grain, had altogether stopped making any sound and seemed to be in a state of shock. Sixto made a fire as I fought mosquitos away with our other blanket. We set the man down, wrapped in the blanket, next to the fire. With a second blanket, Sixto wafted smoke about us, making a cloud of it. That, along with the cooling of the night, seemed to keep at bay most of the flesh-drillers.

It was only then that, despite having seen him naked, I fully assessed the man's physiognomy. He was young, perhaps in his early twenties, and had a flowing but ragged moustache and beard remindful of my comrade Friedrich's. This furry flourish had kept some of his face unmolested. Curiously, half of his right ear was missing, which, together with his facial hair, made him look a little like a cropped-ear schnauzer. He lay for a long time looking at the fire, shivering. Sixto offered him some food, and at first slow to respond, he slowly sat up and then ate with gusto. He soon wanted to talk, and once he started, it more or less poured out of him. It was clear he was indeed a born talker, a talent no doubt inspired by finding himself among the living after looking at a death from sanguinary draining by volant parasites.

"Sir," he said, "I done fought with Sam Houston and gone face to face with the Mexicans"—he gave Sixto a glance—"and I was damn near caught up in the Alamo. I have tangled with gilas and rattlers and Apaches. All of 'em have tried for a piece of me, but none of 'em was as bloodthirsty as those skeeters."

"How," I asked, "did you come to get tied up to that tree?" He was still wrapped in the blanket, only his miserably bitten face visible.

"Well, sir," he said, "I can see that you—both of you—are kind people, and so I can tell you all that happened. And it looks to me that you're off to the diggins to find some gold, so I can tell you things about that too. Even where you can find it. That'd be the least I can do for you boys."

The Gila Argonaut

"I told you I was in the war with the Mexicans. I was with them Texans that went all the way down to the Mexico City. When we come back, at the border they told us all to go home. Just like that. I set out for the New Mexico territory and worked on Kit Carson's ranch there. And then last year, word started comin' in about gold in California. There were ten of us boys on the ranch, and we all left together, hit the Gila Trail through the desert. One of the boys called us the 'Gila Argonauts.' I liked that, even if I didn't know exactly what an argonaut is. Of the bunch of us, he was the only one that died in the desert, just plumb fell off his horse one day like lightnin' had a hit him. The rest of us spent the winter down south on a ranch in California. We had some differences then, and we split up. I went off on my own, first to Sutter's, where they said was the first gold spotted, but already there was too many diggin' all around there. Mexicans and Mormons and even some Frenchies. I didn't want to be diggin' next to no Mexicans. I had enough of their kind in the war. So I headed out on my own. I didn't have no map nor no one tellin' me where to go. I just knew the more I got away from Sutter's, the better. And I was right. There are all kinds of canyons up there waitin' for you. You just have to be willin' to go a little farther than most, and you can find one of your own. But I don't recommend either of you be all by yerself. It's good to have a little company to help protect against the Injuns and the grizzlies.

"So, one can say I was lucky, but I was smart too, wanderin' off. There are some who been up there for a year or more, ever since the first whisper of gold. They scratch out a little dust every day. They're like ants, puttin' a little bit on their pile each day, and in time they come to think that's their due, that's all they're ever gonna get, and they're happy with that. Well, I ain't got the patience for that. I'm like most of the rest—we all want a big strike and want it yesterday. And I must a been livin' right, because that's just what I did. I always have had the luck when I need it. Just like you comin' along.

"Lickety split, I found me a pretty good vein, and I took it out as fast as I could. I figure I had close to six thousand dollars of nuggets and dust. After that vein cleaned out, I went at it in a couple other diggins for longer than I oughta and only came up with a bit of dust. I was losin' money then, payin' more for food than I was findin', so I thought to quit while I was ahead. So I set off for San Francisco. I didn't have no horse, so I was walkin'. Had a horse once but sold it after I got up in the diggins. Had no use for it. A horse is fussier about its feed than mules and eats more. A mule will chew on rocks and survive. So keep that jackass of yours and don't let him go. I was walkin' back through the hills and couldn't find me a soul who'd sell me anythin' with four legs.

"Even before I set out, I was already tyin' my boots to my feet, and after three days of walkin', my feet were tore up somethin' fierce. Not even marchin' in Mexico tore 'em up that way. I'd a

walked to San Francisco in bare feet if I had to, but I was gettin'
keener by the hour on findin' a horse or a mule. And then yesterday,
I got another piece of luck. Or so I thought.

"I was comin' up on a little hill, and on top of it was a drove of
horses. Right off, I thought they must be wild and I had no chance
on foot of gettin' one. But when I got close to them, they didn't run.
I saw then they were used-up packhorses with sore backs, every bit
as sore as my feet. About a dozen of 'em. They must a been turned
out to pasture because they weren't no use to no one no more.
They couldn't run with the wild ones, but they had each other,
like a family. And I had one more piece of luck: Right nearby were
some dead trees that'd come down so they made a nice little corral.
It didn't take much to drive most of 'em in there. Once in there,
though, they showed more fight than I expected. I woulda liked
one of the more spirited ones, but I took what I could get. I finally
handled a gray mustang. She was so worn down I felt sorry for her.
Bein' a pack horse, she wasn't used to riders, but I went easy on
her, and she must have come to see I was lighter than the packs she
used to carry. I rode her out of the corral, and we were on our way.
I put a piece of rope through her mouth for a bridle, Indian style,
and it worked just fine. I thought it would be two, maybe three, days
before I was in San Francisco. My feet were happier than a gold
digger in a whorehouse. And when your feet are happy, the whole
world is right.

"Even though she weren't too fast, I believe I had only a couple
hours to Sacramento. I got maybe half that far when I met up with
three men. They were on foot. I seen some rough customers in
my life, and these fellas looked to be as rough as any. There was
somethin' about 'em—they looked to be on a warpath of some kind.
Each of 'em had a rifle, a big pistol, and a bowie knife. We traded
howdies, and then they asked me if I'da seen any horses on the trail.
I said there was a pack of horses back on a hill and kept movin'. But
I didn't get very far when one of 'em said, 'Joe, that there looks like
your mare! I know her by her crooked tail!'

"Over my shoulder, I saw Joe givin' my mustang a hard look. 'By God,' he said, 'that is my mare!'

"Now, around here, stealin' a horse, even a worn-down pack, is worse than killin' a man. In my time here, I seen more than one horse thief strung up on a tree. If I'd the time to think straight about it, I woulda explained everythin' and handed over the mare. But I was a little put out, and truth is I was mighty eager to get to San Francisco. What's more, I had to wonder how much use the mare was gonna be to Joe and his sidekicks. If they tried to load her down at all, she'd die. All this was spinnin' round in my head. So to be honest with you, I told 'em a little white lie and said I hired the mare back at Woods Creek.

"'Who did you hire it of?' the one named Joe said. 'What's his name?'

"'Peters,' I said, as I knew a Peters from the Mexican war.

"'And what kind of lookin' man is he?' Joe wanted to know.

"Now—if you're in for a penny, you're in for a pound, right? So I said, 'Tall, slim. About thirty years old. Sandy hair, beard. From Alabama.'

"One of Joe's sidekicks said, 'Is he comin' after it?'

"'No,' I said, 'he told me to just turn it loose tonight and it will find its way home.'

"Well, they got together out of my earshot and talked it over. I know now the fear that a guilty man feels when his jury is meetin'. I guess I was about as ready to die as I've ever been—and then wasn't sure I was hearin' right when they said I could keep the mare but I had to leave it at a corral in Sacramento run by a man named Curtis—and give it a good feed of barley! I said I certainly would, and they said they were goin' to go find Peters and teach him a lesson.

"Now, I know you're gonna think I'm a horse thief when I tell you what I did pretty soon after, but I had no choice. My little white lie had put me in a fix. I thought that if I went to Sacramento, and given there ain't boats there every day going down to San Francisco and I had to wait, they might well find me there after not finding Peters. So

I figured I had no choice but to skip Sacramento and push on toward San Francisco on the mare. So I went as far as the mare could take me, until her legs were bucklin'. That was a place not terribly far from here, up the river. There's a trader there with a camp, he'll sell you a plate of beef and beans. And he pours whiskey from a barrel. He keeps a big campfire, and you can bed down by it for nothin'.

"I had a few whiskeys, maybe a couple more than was wise. I paid for them straight from my dust bag—I had one bag for dust, and one for nuggets. And I maybe said some things about my luck that I oughta not said. But I was feelin' pretty good. I was pretty damn near home free. But whiskey or not, I still had some wits about me. I got to thinkin' that sayin' what I did wasn't too smart. So I said I had to piss, and I went off, and right close to the camp there was a tree with a hollow I could just shimmy up a little and reach up into, and I put my bags up in there. I stuffed some chunks of dirt into my pockets to look like I was still carryin' the bags, and I went to bed down.

"Well, just as I was settlin' in, who comes into camp? Joe and his pardners. There was nothin' I could do. They saw me right off. I thought for sure I was a dead man right there and then, and I almost had to laugh on how fast a man's luck can sour. They were on horses now, good ones, and after they set them for the night, they had some whiskeys themselves. It's easier hangin' a man, I suppose, with a whiskey or two in you. Once in a while, one of 'em gave me a look and a snicker, but otherwise they didn't say a word to me. All that time, I'm in my blankets, waitin'. When they were done drinkin,' I thought, *This is it*. But instead of haulin' me up, Joe bedded down right next to me! One of them went out to sleep by their horses, and the other one sat on a rock and stared at me. After a while, Joe and the one on the rock switched watch, and later, they switched again. I guess they all thought the hangin' could wait for daylight.

"I don't have to tell you I did not sleep. I laid there listenin' to Joe breathin' next to me, and every once in a while took a peek at the guy on the rock. There were other fellas sleepin' around the fire, too, but it was only Joe and his sidekick that I minded. In the meanwhile, I laid there tryin' to think what to do, but in the end, there was only one thing to do. I waited until the deepest hour of the night. There was no moon anymore, and the fire had died down to almost nothin'. The hombre on the rock had nodded off to sleep. I got up and stepped over Joe like he was a water moccasin. I went for the tree where my bags were—and there was the other fella! They'd tied their horses to the same tree with my bags, and they had the mare tied up too. The fella was leaning against the tree, so that there was no way for me to reach up and get my bags!

"I wasn't about to try shimmyin' up the tree. It was two bags of gold or my life—an easy choice. I set off runnin'. I wanted to cross the river, but I don't swim too good. It was too early for boats, so I kept on movin'. Then just before sunrise, I saw them comin'. I had a hope they weren't goin' to be. They had the mare, why'd they have to have my neck? I hid in the weeds by the river, but they were good trackers and they found me. Swim or no swim, I oughta have took my chances with the river. We can't ask the dead, but I'd say drownin' is a better way to go. I was sure they were goin' to hang me. But now it weren't the mare they were after, it was gold. Somebody'd told 'em about my bags. But hang me and they don't get 'em. I told 'em bad luck dropped the bags in the river when I was runnin' away, but they weren't goin' for that.

"It was Joe said to take my clothes off and tie me to the tree. That's just what they did—stripped me clean and doused me with river water to bring on the skeeters. They said if I told 'em where the gold was, they'd let me go. I figured if they didn't want to hang me no more, and they believed I didn't have the gold, they'd let me go. And then the skeeters started comin' on somethin' fierce. It was like there was more of 'em than there's stars in a Texas sky. And each one is diggin' for the red gold in my veins. My mama raised me stubborn. But each one of those skeeters was a powerful persuader. Gettin' that many skeeter bites at once is worse than fallin' in a cactus patch. They crawl up your nose so thick you can't breathe, and they fly into your mouth. But that ain't the worst of it. The worst is the itchin' you can't scratch. I howled like an Apache. Finally, I couldn't take it no longer. I told 'em where the gold was. I damn near wanted 'em to hang me then, but they said hangin' was too good for me and rode off. They were pretty sure the skeeters were goin' to do their work for 'em, and they were right. They woulda if you hadn't a come along."

"What will you do now?" Sixto asked.

"I reckon it's time to go home," the young man said. "I ain't no cat with nine lives."

After telling us his story in what seemed like one long breath, the "argonaut"—was he lucky or luckless?—lay by the fire and suddenly dropped off to sleep, and Sixto generously tucked our other blanket around him. As Sixto and I had had a restless night before and our own trying day, we, too, readied for bed. Sixto cut some soft grass for me to bed down on, and, nestling by the fire, I used my coat as a blanket. Sixto put down some grass a little away from the fire and cozied up against Arturo for warmth and to ward off coyotes. It was a good thing Sixto did so, as I listened to those American hyenas endlessly bay at the moon or each other until I, too, came under the spell of Morpheus.

My next moment of consciousness came with Sixto shaking me awake.

"Don Karl! Don Karl!"

"You must not call me that, Sixto," I said.

"He is gone!"

That news did not immediately register—who was "he"?

Most alarming was Sixto's next news: "And your poncho is gone!"

It took me a moment to realize that Sixto was referring to my blue coat, and only another moment, in my morning fogginess, to register the gravity of the news. My beloved blue coat that held all but a stray coin or two of my "seed money" had been pinched. I sat up and spat the Lord's name in vain—in German to spare Sixto's ears.

"He tried to take Arturo too," Sixto said.

Some distance from us, Arturo stood gnawing at a bush crookedly crowned by his saddle, the thief apparently having tossed it there. I was puzzled by how Sixto could have slept through the attempted theft of Arturo but later came to learn that Sixto might have slept through the French Revolution.

My satchel had been rifled through, but the coat was the only thing taken. The young man had, after all, admitted he was a thief, and now proved it. One had to assume he was a liar as well. I wondered how far, and in which direction, a naked man wearing or carrying only a coat could get, although he would fit right in at the Indian village we had been to the day before.

There was no telling just how long he'd been gone. The question was whether the two of us and a donkey should try to pursue him, or one of us on a donkey, or none of us. We decided we must try to find him together. Sixto rode ahead on Arturo while I did my best to keep up in the rear. It was doubtful, we thought, that he would head up the river, so we started back toward the way we had come.

Sixto soon went far ahead. There, walking alone halfway around the world from London and nearly possessionless, I had an odd feeling of liberation, which though I knew to be temporary and would later turn to hardship, was exhilarating. The river was flowing; birds were singing. The life of the earth carried on, regardless of my troubles. I felt an optimism that, come what may, the earth's life force was my life force and it would sustain me. But this fugue-like reverie was not long lived, broken by seeing Sixto in the distance, coming my way. He said he had made it almost as far as the Indian village, then met a party of gold seekers who reported seeing the thief get onto a downstream boat. It went without saying that we were not going to pursue him to San Francisco. It also went without saying that the road ahead had just gotten harder and longer than we had bargained for when leaving San Francisco.

From Lt. Junger and Lt. Fischel to King Frederick William IV

May 14, 1849

To: His Excellency King of Prussia Frederick William IV
Re: Herr Karl Marx

To our most high King, the greatest sovereign in all of Europe—
Ja in all the world! Your servants have cleverly followed, if we do
humbly say so ourselves, Herr Marx and his *Junge* companion to
this settlement called Sacramento, in the hinterland of California.
It is a place even more remote and *Scheiß*-ridden than San
Francisco. A flood came and turned the entire settlement into one
great cesspool of *Scheiß*, mud, offal, garbage, and dead beasts.
There are no wonderful water closets here like those your Majesty
has at Sanssouci—in fact, there are no water closets at all. Always
the whole settlement smells like the hind end of a peasant horse.

Expertly disguised as miners from Chili, we left San Francisco
on the same steamboat as did Marx, the *Junge*, and their donkey.
Because of our Chilian dress, we met on the boat the hostility
of some drunken Americans, who insisted we must keep first
to the aft, then to the forward part of the boat. This conformed
perfectly with our plan, as we could then stay close to Marx and his
accomplice.

In the morning, we witnessed Herr Marx engage in argument
with some of the passengers and then, as seems to be his habit, with
the boat captain. Marx cannot tolerate anyone other than himself
being the "captain." As is also his habit of late, he came out on the
losing end. He then ordered the boat captain to deliver him and the
Junge to the bank of the river. The captain resisted but finally gave

in, no doubt thinking it best just to be rid of Marx, and abruptly deposited them on a spit of sand in the river channel.

Soon after, we asked the captain to bank the boat and we disembarked. After fighting our way through the bulrushes, we came out at a point from which we saw Marx and the *Junge* setting off overland. On the boat, Marx had been engaging in some very odd gymnastics, and he continued these as they set off toward the east. They, and we, did not know that they were headed in the direction of a native village, which they eventually entered.

From a distance we waited as the subversives conducted in the village what we believe to be benign business with an American woodsman. After seeing them leave, we entered the village. Through the woodsman there, we learned that the natives had been entertained by Marx, and that they expected us to perform for them too. Wanting to please, your servants proudly represented the Prussian nation by performing a very creditable *Lauschaer Galopp*, for which we received a standing ovation. The woodsman also revealed to us Marx's probable ultimate destination in the mountains beyond Sacramento. As much as we then wanted to continue with our surveillance, our native hosts said we must, before leaving, eat a local dish of mashed boiled acorns garnished with bits of tuberous material. We acceded, unfortunately, as almost immediately we were both befallen with, we are sorry to offend your Excellency, *explosiver Durchfall*, which disabled us for the rest of the day and that night.

However, the next day, we were able to muster the strength to set off for this sorry settlement that makes a Latvian hamlet seem like Baden-Baden. Here ensued some temporary trouble from which we will soon extricate ourselves and again be hot on the trail of Herr Marx, to wit: We eventually located Marx and the *Junge* in one of the several houses of drink and gambling—an establishment charmingly referred to locally as a "*café chantant*." This house also featured music provided by a French woman and an American piano player who had to be, we are sure, working together for the first time. The music was not to our taste, nor was the very bad beer—how we greatly miss the beloved brews of home! The French woman was an apparent lady of the night posing as a mumbling *chanteuse*. The American played in the style of a Lutheran church organist, and the mismatch resulted in loud catcalls from the surly patrons.

We followed Marx and companion to a gambling table with the intent that we might be able to bankrupt him, but quickly discovered that the table, run by a Mexican card dealer, was exclusively for speakers of Spanish. The confusion caused by this language obstacle was compounded by the unfamiliar game being played, and further so by having to endure the awful music. Oh how we miss the strain of accordions playing the *Hohenfriedberger Marsch* in a *Biergarten*! In short, we have been unusually frugal with your Excellency's money, but we risked an imprudently large bet in the game and lost. Conversely, Marx, aided by the Spanish-speaking *Junge*, bet against long odds with what we believe was one of his last coins—and won.

Apparently feeling flush, Herr Marx proceeded to drink several glasses of the lousy beer. Then, in a break in the *chanteuse's* "music," and presumably inspired by her nationality, Marx stood upon a table and began singing the revolutionary Marseillaise anthem. We were alert that this might be a signal or coded message to other revolutionaries in and around the "*chantant*," but the catcalls grew very loud and Herr Marx was struck by bottles thrown by a table of Australians. One of the Australians then turned his attention to us. He wanted to know "what the hell you're gawkin' at" and wrongly accused us of Sodomitic desires. His compatriots soon joined in abusing us. We could not speak openly without giving away our identities to Marx. And we are not French puffs "*de crème*." One thing led to another, and we found ourselves outside in a fistfight with the Australians. We fought bravely but were outnumbered and were pitched into a mudhole caused by the recent flooding. To add insult to injury, the Australians exposed us to several lewd gestures which were of a nature unlike any we have ever seen, even in a Prussian enlisted men's barracks. However, the Australians received a comeuppance of sorts as they—and we, too, unfortunately—were arrested by constables and arraigned by the local justice of the peace, who apparently makes his living by taxing foreigners with outrageous fines, nonpayment of which results in confinement. We had only a small sum left after the gambling table and thus are enduring an unpleasant stay in the "hoosegow" with the Australians but expect to be released shortly.

Your Excellency may be assured that despite losing Herr Marx's trail for a short time, we are confident we will be able to find him, as we know of his intended destination. However, we regret to report that we are very short of funds. Our accidental gambling loss has drained our "treasury," so to speak—please send money, your Highness! You may send it to Sacramento, in care of our cover names, "Hozay and Horhay the Chilians."

We thank you profusely and remain deeply dedicated to your service.

Your servants,
Lt. Ernst Junger
Lt. Franz Fischel

From Karl to Jenny

May 21, 1849

Dear Jenny,

After some ordeal, my young comrade Sixto and I arrived in
the settlement of Sacramento. "Settlement" is not quite right, as
very few are settling here. Everyone is either going to or coming
from the gold "diggings," so that collectively the place feels like a
dusty, ramshackle *Bahnhof.* Due to a thief's knavery, Sixto and I
were nearly broke when we arrived, but with some good fortune at
a gaming table we managed to parlay our last coin into a pile large
enough to underwrite the supplies we need for mining.

As we were preparing to leave Sacramento, Sixto was struck
down by a mysterious pain in his chest. He felt it so acutely and
deeply that he could not stand. He is, I believe, not yet eighteen
years old, and is otherwise robust, so there was no answer for this.

I intended to find a real doctor (quacks abound here) to exam
him, but he would not have it. He insisted that he knew what the
malady was and how to cure it. It may be the "new world" here, but
there is still very much of the old blight of witchery and magic that
only a real New Order can eradicate. He was suffering, he said, from
the "*mal ojo*"—the so-called evil eye. He was certain that the eye in
question was cast by the scoundrelly second (who had only one eye)
in a duel that in San Francisco I was obligated to fight for his honor
and, as it happened, his freedom (I know: gaming tables, thieves,
duels—the "new world" is not so wholesome either). He'd known
others to suffer the "*ojo*," he said, and what he was feeling exactly fit
what they had felt.

The remedy involved first obtaining an egg from a black
chicken. No other color would suffice. I thus had to venture out and

about the lampless settlement, in search of a melanoid fowl—on a moonless night. Taking my own lamp wasn't possible, as I didn't own one, and besides, the light would have given me away.

Hence, I was to be guided first by my sense of smell—the nostalgia of the acrid dung of my father's chicken coop. This smell so often wafted through the open windows of my childhood breakfast room that I grew to find it no less agreeable than that of *Schneckennudeln* or fried bacon. As it happened, I could locate only one coop in the entire settlement, behind what appeared to be a mound of brush and bramble. The coop was an impressive residence, a long, rectangular wooden box on stilts—a palace for poultry. I neither saw nor heard any chickens about in the "yard" around it, and curiously, there was no rooster to sound an alarm, but there was no chance of mistake about the odor. Even without moonlight, any white chicken would be visible, so I thought that if something moved and I could scarcely see it, it would be either red or black. I opened one of the doors, and a low squawking and clucking began. I was careful not to let out any of the creatures, and just as I stuck my head into the coop—boom!—a terrific peal of thunder cracked not fifty paces away. Every chicken in that box instantly shrieked bloody murder and, flapping their wings, produced such a cloud of dust, dried dung, and feathers that I was almost completely blinded. Another peal, and I realized it was not thunder but gunshot—the nearby seeming mound of brush was a habitation, and in it a vigilant protector of poultry who, to miss me, had to be nearly as blind as I was at the moment. While before I had been inconvenienced by the dark night, now I was grateful for it. A voice in an unknown language shrieked at me from the bramble pile. I frantically searched in the dung and feathers and with each hand clutched an egg, wiped the smut from my eyes, then managed to run away from the coop without breaking my neck.

With a piece of canvas we'd bought, Sixto and I had rigged up a tent next to the stable where Sixto's donkey, Arturo, could get a full feed before venturing into the mountains. When I returned with the eggs, Sixto was lying in the tent in a feverish daze. Fortunately, he had told me earlier what I was supposed to do. Lighting a candle, I saw no black feathers in either of the handfuls I'd taken. However, I told Sixto I'd had rare luck and found a *poulet noir* and we could proceed with his remedy—called "*la limpia*" in Spanish, meaning "the cleaning." Both eggs were white, but as you know, there are dark chickens that lay white eggs; besides, Sixto was in no condition to examine eggs. The first step of the *limpia* was the most difficult for me. Sitting Sixto up, I was obligated to recite the "Lord's Prayer" while passing an egg over and around his body. On "thy kingdom come," I nearly choked. I then broke the egg into a small metal mug, along with some water. By Sixto's prescription, the egg and water had to be placed under, not next to, him for the night. As Sixto would be sleeping on the ground, I had to first gently move him, then dig a small hole where he would lay on his back. The hole dug, I placed the mug in it and assured Sixto that he would be cured—an incantation as smooth as any shaman's! If the *limpia* were to work, in the morning there was to be a tiny dark spot in the egg's yolk— the concentrated spirit of the evil eye! Both Sixto and I slept fitfully. I confess that, despite myself, I sometimes when awake kept one curious ear alert for the magical moment—an otherworldly grunt or groan marking the transportation of the "eye"—but heard nothing out of the ordinary. However, in the morning—*mirabile visu!*— there was indeed a speck in the yolk! At first, I believed it was only a crumb of dirt on top, but no, it was indeed embedded in the yolk. Sixto was heartened by this news, and for his sake I did not express doubt or experimentally poke the speck and release it into the world. The *Geist* of placebo is as powerful a spirit as most.

For Sixto's sake, the final step of the *limpia* had to be seen through. I found a clear patch of earth, and with my back directly toward the sun, I threw egg and water over my shoulder without looking, then walked away. Lo and behold, Sixto almost immediately began recovering, sitting up to eat. He continued to progress over several days, each day walking with me down to the river. I believe, as you know, that there is a salubrious effect from watching flowing water. He is now fully himself again. I am convinced his "cure" to be coincidence, but there was no reason to say so to Sixto. Vodou or no vodou, I was happy for his recovery.

Today we are leaving for the quaintly named "Los Infernos," a believed-to-be hot spot, so to speak, in the mountains. I have put in a "forward" at the post office in Sacramento for your letters to be sent to a trading post near the Infernos.

Ah Jenny!—do not let lack of money best you. It is the ruin of society, the bond of all bonds, the universal confusion of all things.

Your truly beloved,
Karl

5

From Paradise to Los Infernos

IN HIGH SPIRITS WE SET OUT FROM SACRAMENTO AT SUN-rise. With some winnings from gambling Karl's last gold coin—he again reminded me that fortune favors the bold—we had bought corn-meal, jerky, beans, a boiling pot and mugs, canvas for rigging a tent, a pick and shovels, and two "pans" for panning gold. Karl also had to have a small barrel of whiskey. Much of this we were able to load onto Arturo, but not wanting to overload him, Karl and I carried packs, too, saddle-bags rigged with ropes that cut into our shoulders. A burro, even one as agreeable as Arturo, can turn stubborn if you overload it. It will sit down and not move an inch until you have eased its load, and because it is in a superior bargaining position, it will insist on more easing than needed. It is best, then, to avoid getting into that spot in the first place.

From the mountain man we had the general directions to Los Infernos: Head east to northeast out of Sacramento following the big river, then take the trail that goes due east and we will come to Frenchie's, a trading post run by a Frenchman. Just past that, we were to turn northeasterly up a valley, then over the hills and down into another smaller valley. At the very end of that was a small river in a narrow canyon. He'd said we would know we were in the right place when we couldn't go any farther and were wondering why the hell we were where we were.

Our first day out from Sacramento was hot and clear, and I thought Karl might complain, but he was in a good mood. From time to time we soaked our hats in the cold river, which was wide and flowing fast, and drank from it.

"Isn't this marvelous, Sixto? This landscape?" he said. "So fecund you can hear it groaning. I don't know if there are any other spots on earth quite like it that are still so virgin."

I knew what a virgin was but had never thought of the countryside as one. All I felt was the heat, and was thinking that the cold fog of Yerba Buena was not such a bad thing after all.

"There is water and sun and soil," he said. "That's all you need to grow whatever you want."

"What can you grow here?" I asked. I saw only thirsty-looking bushes and trees, and here and there sprouts of wild grass.

"People," he said. "They could grow here, into something better than they are now."

"From the people we have met so far, I am not so sure."

"But they grew up elsewhere, not here," he said. "If they had had everything material they needed, they would not have come here. So, in a way, they were deprived, or stunted. But if they'd started here, they'd be rich already—like you—and wouldn't need more."

I wanted to ask him why, if I was rich already, I was baking in the sun on my way to some distant canyon to break my back digging for something that likely wasn't even there. But that would have been ungrateful and quarrelsome. Despite some doubt about what we were setting out to do, I felt indebted to Karl for "freeing" me.

"Once the revolution does its work," Karl said, "people will have the time to develop their capabilities. If you wanted, you could, for example, learn to paint beautiful paintings."

"In the church at the mission there was a beautiful painting. It was of San Pablo on the road to Damascus. I most liked his beautiful horse—the padres would not have liked that. There were many fine horses in the picture, but San Pablo's was the finest of all."

"Ah yes, Saint . . . San Pablo again. But paintings don't need to be of saints or of Jesus. You can paint other people. Or no people at all—just hills and trees and flowers. You would be free to choose whatever you wanted. That's the point—you would be free. You could paint only the horses."

"What if I did not want to paint? I could ride horses all day, like the vaqueros do?"

"Well, I guess that would be fine too," Karl said. "There is an art to that, I suppose. You have to know what you're doing. But some things are more . . . elevating than others. Do you understand? It would be good to have a mix of things. You could ride horses in the morning and in the afternoon do your painting or write poetry. Some things are good for the body. Others are good for your mind. You seem to have a good mind, Sixto. You want to use it, don't you?"

"Yes," I said, wondering when I was ever not using my mind. "But you must always use your mind when you are riding a horse."

Along the trail we met up with a fellow who looked like he had not walked down from the mountains but rolled down them. His clothes were torn and hanging on him. He seemed to want something from us, but after being thieved by the "Gila argonaut" rascal, we were wary. It turned out all he wanted was a shot of whiskey from Karl's barrel and an ear to gripe to. He was so forlorn that we obliged. He'd come from New England, he said, and was sorry he'd ever heard of California. Or, as he called it, "Humbugnia." For his trouble, he said, all he'd been paid was scurvy and the sharp points of Indian arrowheads. He'd given up his search and wanted to go home but had no money for the passage. His best and only hope was the same as Solomon's—hire himself out as a laborer in San Francisco and earn the fare home.

At midday we stopped under an oak by the river to rest and eat. Meeting up with the Humbugnia fellow had seemed to put a damper on Karl's cheerfulness. While we were eating he said, "The world is at a turning point, Sixto. It is on the verge of immense change, but it doesn't know it yet. This land is like a virgin, yes. But a sleepy one on the day before her father will marry her off to a lusty rake. She may guess at what's coming but won't know what until she experiences it fully. Your world here—the ranchers, the Mexicans. You can see the change already. The Americans are coming, and others."

When we set out again, I went ahead of Karl, leading Arturo. We'd gone maybe only a mile or so when, out of nowhere, just upstream from us and across the river, a white horse came running with a full head of speed, straight at the river. Right before it hit the river, I saw it wasn't a horse at all but a mule—one with fine lines, but mule ears. Without a break in stride, it flew off the riverbank and plunged into the water. At that spot, the river was eight or nine rods wide. It looked to be deep, too, and the current was swift from the melting snow still running down from the high mountains. The mule's head popped up out of the water, and it was fighting hard to keep it up. A mule can swim, but I'd heard vaqueros say that if its ears filled with water it would drown.

On the far bank, a fellow came running up, cursing a blue streak. He was fit to be tied, shaking his fist at that poor thing in the river. For three or so rods the mule fought the current, not getting pulled downstream by it as much as I thought it would, until ears and all it sank out of sight. I felt sorry for it, more so because the fellow on the far bank clearly didn't. He kept up his cursing even when the mule went under. Turned out he knew something about that mule we didn't, because before long, like a muskrat it rose up out of the river and lunged onto the riverbank just ahead of us. To this day I believe that mule didn't swim but walked across the bottom of that river. Karl and I were flabbergasted, but the fellow across the river didn't seem surprised at all. The mule—a she, I saw—gave a shake like a wet dog and then stood there calmly, eyeing us and Arturo. She was the color of white corn flour and had finer bones than many horses. My first thought was how were we going to get her back to the fellow across the river, but he threw his hands up and walked away, seeming to say that we could have her if we wanted her. And we did. She was still wearing a *cabezon* of rope and, without the least bit of fuss, she let Karl take her and lead her off the bank. She went along with him as though we'd had her for years. Karl walked her about, and in that sun she started to dry off pretty fast. But before loading her with our packs and having her run off with them, I thought one of us should try to ride her, and Karl said he would give her a try.

"Do you know how?" I asked.

"I have been on a few horses," he said. "I am familiar with the rules of English riding. And German as well."

"But you had saddles then, yes?" I said. "It is much different without one."

Karl took the *cabezon* reins and said, "Help me up, please."

With my hands together to make a stirrup, I lifted him up on the mule.

"A first principle is to sit up straight," he said. "In Germany they say only a rider who sits correctly can ride correctly."

I sensed that, for a mule, this animal was high-strung. I half expected her to bolt back into the river and take Karl with her, but after a gentle kick he trotted her around in a big circle like she was a show horse. Karl was as pleased as a new father.

"I do not need to tell you, a Master of the Stalls, that riding is the art of keeping the horse between you and the ground," Karl said. "To do so, you must communicate with the nature of the horse. In the English fashion, I am rising and sitting in rhythm with it."

I wanted to tell him, but didn't, that was all well and good but he wasn't on a horse. He was on a mule. And a mule is, so to speak, a horse of a different color.

"I will call her Alborak," he said, "after the horse that the Musselman prophet rode off into paradise. Because to me today, California feels like a paradise."

I asked him who that prophet was, and he said he'd tell me about him later. "How," I asked, "can it be paradise when it has men in it like the ones we have met? Bad men. Or sad ones."

"Just look around you," he said. "At the wildflowers. And these magnificent oak trees. Someday, when you have seen more of the world, you will know what I am talking about."

Two yellowjacket hornets then came circling round Arturo's nose. One landed on it and must have stung him good, because in one big spasm he shuddered from head to tail, making the pots and pans and mugs hanging on him clank together like cowbells. Faster than a dropped hat, Alborak went from show horse to bucking bronco. Her first kick pitched Karl straight forward over her head. She kept on bucking and almost trampled him, and then, just like that, she stopped like nothing had happened at all. We were lucky Karl didn't get hurt. As much as we could use a mule, I wanted to send Alborak off, but Karl said he had known a horse in Germany that did much the same thing. Whenever it heard two beer mugs clink together, however softly, it went berserk and caused all kinds of trouble. All we had to do, he said, was pack Arturo and the mule such that no piece of metal could touch another. This was easier said than done, but after some time repacking and padding, we were fairly satisfied that it would be all right. We hadn't said so, but carrying packs had been tiring us out, and we were ready to take a chance on this free mule.

A burro and a mule are different creatures, but Arturo and Alborak seemed to hit it off just right. When we stopped later to rest, they didn't mind sharing the same bush of pin grass. I asked Karl then about Alborak's name and the Musselman prophet he'd mentioned. He said the prophet's name was Mohammed and that he'd started a new religion some hundreds of years after Jesus. This was news to me. I'd never heard of this prophet or the religion. I wanted to know how many people went to that church, and Karl said he wasn't sure but he thought two or three hundred million or more. I was thunder-struck—how many people were there in the whole world? He told me there were other religions, too, besides that one.

"There are people," he said, "many people—in India—they are called Indians, by the way. That's another story, complicated . . . there are people there called Hindoos who believe that cows are very holy. That you must not kill one."

"You must not kill a cow?"

"That's right. Because they believe there are people inside them.

Not people exactly. Rather, there is a life inside them that once was human and died but now has come back to live inside the cow. And once the cow dies, that life will go on to another life somewhere—I forget where. Into greener pastures, so to speak."

"If this is true, then our sin is very great. We have killed many, many cows."

"It's not just cows. It goes for horses or any living thing."

"For burros?"

"Yes, I believe so," Karl said. "But cows are special. It is like a ladder. There are steps, different lives, that the inside life—I guess you can compare it to a soul—must pass up through before it gets to the top. So these people, the Hindoos, respect the life that is in all living things."

"That is like the Indians here," I said. "They believe there is a spirit inside many things. Not just animals but also a tree or a river. I have wondered about Arturo—the way he looks at me sometimes."

"Hindooism is very old. But you have a new religion here in America. I have heard of it. They are called Mormons. They believe you can have more than one wife. How about that? You could have five wives!"

"I think," I said, "you are telling me a story. You are having your fun with me."

"I would not do such a thing," he said. "I am telling you the truth. Someday you may see for yourself."

"Then I can only say the devil is very busy these days. He is always busy."

"Ah yes, the devil. He takes the blame for a lot, no?"

"He has much—how do you say—*vissen shaft*? He is very clever."

"Maybe," Karl said, "we could make a deal with him, as they say. Teach us a few things about how to find gold, and we would give him some of it. What do you think?"

"You would do such a thing?"

"Ah—now I *am* having fun with you. Still, I might listen to an offer."

"I do not think that is funny, Karl. I have heard of a person who met the devil, and said the wrong thing, and was turned into a goat."

"I know what I would say to him if I met him: Who do you think you are? Really?"

I already knew that Karl was not afraid to speak his mind, but I thought that talk of the devil took the cake. We set off again, and with our packs now on Alborak we made quicker progress. We soon left the river behind us and headed due east. By sundown we were into the lower hills, and pressed on in the twilight into the night until we reached the Frenchman's trading post. We spent the night there with Jean the Frenchman, he and Karl parlaying away in Jean's lingo like old friends.

The next day, we took from the post the first trail that headed north-easterly, into a narrow valley. But then, deep into it, we came to a fork, one branch going more north over hills, the other heading east across hills. We couldn't remember the mountain man telling us about this fork, and were stumped as to which way to go. I then saw a white hawk up in a tree. It looked to me to be the same hawk I'd seen in my dreams, the same that had swooped down on the bear on the dock. After surveying me it took off and flew over the path on the right, the one going east. Karl didn't see it at all, but that was enough for me. I told him I did remember, after all, the mountain man saying something about another fork, and that we were to keep to the right, and so we did.

That night, we made our camp away from the trail, behind some rocks in what wasn't more than a gully with a trickle of water in it. When I woke up in the morning, Karl's blanket was right on the spot where he'd slept, but there was no Karl. And then what did I see drinking at the trickle—a goat! Not a mountain goat but a skinny, flop-eared ranch goat that looked at me cock-headed and every bit as much as if someone was inside it and wanted to say something but knew it couldn't, and so went back to drinking. I had the strongest conviction that that goat was Karl—that he'd made a deal with the devil that had gone wrong. I ran at it, and it bolted. I fell into the trickle, got up, and chased it down the gully. Then what did I see—Karl behind a rock, taking care of some personal business, as it were. And he saw me, chasing the goat. We were both embarrassed, but I had to feel more the fool. He never did ask why I was chasing that goat, and I wasn't about to tell him.

Karl

June 10, 1849 — Ah Lucre! that lures men from every corner of the planet to these mountains and then toys with them. It is a jealous god before whom no other may stand. And I now a pilgrim, and its plaything, as much as any other. There is great hope, but already there are plenty who are disillusioned. On the trail we met a pathetic creature who is sorry he ever came to "Humbugnia." The poor fellow looked more forlorn than any London beggar. We met other defeated ones who had little to say other than a shoulder shrug and a shake of the head when we asked for directions. Fortuna favors the bold, as it did us at the gambling table in Sacramento, but it also flattens men under its wheel.

We are encamped in an area called by the Spanish "Los Infernos," but which its new citizens call "Chucklehead Diggings," so called because, according to one of the American miners here, only "chuckleheads" would choose to come and stay here. A chucklehead, I gather, is a person of questionable judgment. Sixto and I have been here for more than a fortnight with little more than a few pinches of sparkly gold dust to show for our work. After the fortnight passed, I suggested we move on, but Sixto resisted this, saying he had reason to believe we should stay here. He did not want to tell me what "reason" that was, but I pressed him on it, and although he knows how I view such things, he said that on the way here, at a point when we were unsure of the trail, he saw a "special" white bird in a tree. That bird then flew off and supposedly led us here—little did I know! And Sixto says he has seen the bird once more since then, as further omen of this being the right place for us. To Sixto, this all adds up. I am willing to indulge him in his little superstition and stay a while longer but have to say I feel the "chucklehead" for it.

In the local geographical vernacular, our "diggings" are in the bottom of a "canyon"—essentially a narrow ravine. The canyon sides are steep but not such that a man can't, with some difficulty, climb one of the less severe inclines all the way to the top. A creek called Los Infernos runs down through the canyon. Sixto gathered from a Spanish speaker we met on the way here that the canyon is so named because of hot springs that are said to be located higher up the ravine, but it could just as well be because the California sun mercilessly radiates the rocky sides of the canyon, making the whole a furnace as hot as Hell. Despite any hot springs there may be, the water in the creek is bracing cold and good for drink but breathtaking for bathing. There must be another watercourse, likely with melted snow from the mountains, that somewhere joins the creek.

For the denizens of Chucklehead, the only tolerably habitable portion of the canyon is along a short length of the creek where the land on both sides is flat and broad enough to camp, and there are a few oak trees for shade. Above and below this section is mostly narrow, rocky gorge. Intersecting the canyon at angles are smaller defiles called, wonderfully, "gulches." The largest of these may be called a valley, though still narrow; it has some brush and a few trees but no water, and serves as the only feasible entry to our canyon. Through this gulch and over a few steep hills at its far end is a passage that connects with the trail that leads back to Sacramento.

The peopling of this place is curious. Before the gold mania it could not have seen more than a passing native, and now it nearly has the start of a small village. An odd village, however, as it is all men. One habitable side of the creek is fully claimed by Americans, the other by "furriners" (not people who skin animals; rather, in a provincial American accent, anyone not an American). Oddly, this latter category includes Sixto, the only native Californian here. The creek serves as a kind of international border. All but one of the Americans are a band of twenty or so roughnecks from a place called Kentucky, which, judging by their fierce behavior and mien, I imagine in its culture to be similar to the steppe of Attila the Hun. Many of them have shaggy, uncombed beards, and all wear a uniform of sorts consisting of identical long boots and red shirts. Even when digging they carry revolvers in their belts. They love their guns and will fire them off any time of the day or night, for any reason or none. At times they glare at us as though we are their next meal. On one hand they are as dirty as Welsh coal miners, and on the other as fussy as Hindoo Brahmins. They've made it clear that only they can bathe—if they ever do—upstream, lest any foreigner-tainted water sully the stream. They can be prickly about identity—their leader especially, a brusque-tongued roisterer named Burns. He overheard Sixto refer to them as "yankees," and he forcefully corrected him—they are "proud Kentuckians" (though Sixto continues to refer to all Americans as "yankees"). The one American on the other side of the creek who is not a member of the Kentucky band dresses too well for a miner, is older than the roughnecks, and mostly keeps his distance from them. He is alone and has set up his camp apart from theirs. I have heard him called "Doc," though a doctor of what I don't know.

On our "foreigner" side of the creek, the right-hand side as you face upstream, are myself, Sixto, and four Mexicans. The Mexicans, who arrived just after we did, camped fifty or so paces downstream from us. At night they play a guitar quietly and sing. Their guitar player and apparent leader, Pablo, has befriended Sixto, who sometimes joins their campfire. The saddles of their mules are edged with gold and silver, and around their camp they fly red and yellow silk flags tied to bushes and tree branches. In the evening for warmth they wear a marvelous one-piece, blanket-like article called a *serape*. They go to sleep very early and are the first in the morning to start working, not "panning" for gold in the creek as we and the Americans do but in a method called "dry digging." They dig deep holes, piling up a mound of chunky rock, and then employ a kind of primitive grist mill to crush the rock. In a large, stone-lined circle, they sink in the middle a sturdy vertical post and atop it attach a long horizontal cross post that revolves like the hands of a clock. One end of a rope is tied to this cross post, the other end to a large stone. A mule pulls the cross post around in the circle, the large stone crushing or "gristing" the smaller rock. Once the rock is pulverized, the Mexicans then use a pan, though not with water. They put the pulverized rock into the pan and shake it to settle the heavy gold, then skillfully blow off the finer, lighter dirt and dust on top. They repeat this shaking and blowing until most of what is left is gold.

Despite being Sixto's partner, the Mexicans seem wary of me, perhaps lumping me together with the Americans who are ready to abuse them as "greasers." The Americans have aimed more than a few taunts at them, using this epithet and others, but the Mexicans ignore them and go on with their business. They have their own guns but are not trigger happy like the Americans.

I've tried engaging some of the Kentucky band in conversation across the "border," but one might as well try talking to wild beasts. They are fond of their drink, and at night around their campfire they swear like demons. During the day, a fight will break out, and rather than settle it they will form a human boxing ring and let the combatants go at it, punching or wrestling or both. When they've had enough, they simply pick up where they left off and go back to work. Before retiring for the night, they love to bang their pots and pans on the rocks and make them echo in the canyon. The first time they did this, the banging so agitated Alborak that she uprooted the entire bush she was tied to and dragged it with her down the canyon, as far away as she could get. I asked them not to bang, but this only made them bang louder. After that night I no longer tie Alborak, leaving her to roam the hillsides. Each morning I wonder at her survival and that she's willing to come back for more.

With four-legged beasts Sixto and I have had trouble too. Wild pigs come in the night to scratch themselves against our tent and rut about. I whack them with a shovel, and Sixto has thrown boiling water at them, but they are not deterred. They so vigorously poke their snouts and rub their behinds on the canvas that they bump up against us in our sleep and threaten to smother us. One night, the dogs owned by the Mexicans attacked the pigs. The pigs formed a defensive phalanx, their rear ends bulging against our tent until it collapsed on us. The Kentuckians have two or three dogs as well. When the moon is up, the dogs bark, which starts a chorus of mule and donkey and horse (the Americans have foolishly brought a couple of horses up here) braying and neighing like beer-bloated Oktoberfesters until a multilingual hue and cry rises for them all to shut up.

We likewise are assaulted by the animal kingdom from other directions—all variety of mountain mice and other rodents, chipmunks, squirrels, raccoons, et cetera. There are mercifully few mosquitos, but plenty of arthropodic creepers and crawlers, including some finger-length scorpions that lie in ambush in your boots or bedding. Daily we must take our bedding out for a shake and drape it over a bush in the sun.

As noted, the Mexicans do not use the creek's water for their mining, but Sixto and I, and the Americans, use it for "panning." Panning is tedious work. In short, it involves much digging and stooping and bending over a "pan"—a shallow circular basin— loaded with water and gravel. You must take this heavy pan and move it in a steady circular motion. The water and gravel (lighter than gold) are "swirled," then the water and gravel poured, the pan then swirled and poured again and again until the gold, the heaviest material, eventually settles to the bottom. At the end of the process there is—*voila!*—the mineral for which the Spanish pillaged entire civilizations. The pan's utility is wondrous—when not digging with it, you can soak blistered feet in it or fry bacon.

A miner can stake a "claim" anywhere he likes, marking it out by leaving his tools in sight. A claim is all of a square, ten by ten feet, that must be worked at least one day in a week. Moving a man's tools and encroaching on his claim is perilous. He can either take the matter into his own hands and kill you with impunity or resort to the simple system of miner justice. There is no real law or lawmen here but rather a brutally efficient do-it-yourself system. You can have a killing over a disputed claim, a trial by jury, and a man go free or hang all in one morning. Here in our little canyon, so far everyone knows his place and there has been no trouble. That is not to say there won't be, what with the Kentuckians' hostility.

My diet has been as dreary, though not as disgusting, as it was out at sea. At first we had a daily monotony of beans, cornmeal, and jerky, but the jerky soon ran out. Recently, Sixto made a trip over the hills to the trader who has set up shop on the trail to Sacramento, which also serves as a post office. Like all merchants in California, that trader is likely making much more money selling goods than he would breaking his back digging for gold dust. From this trader, Sixto bought some potatoes and onions and a bit of bacon that have somewhat broken the gustatory monotony. I also have had my complement of whiskey, which helps with my digestion. I confess I sometimes overindulge in this treat, but it's necessary in order to sleep well and keep up spirits. The trader stocks small kegs of it, and Sixto cooperated in getting me another.

I have always maintained that men are coincidental with their production: They become one with what they produce and how they produce it. As such, I am now equal to a rodent or beetle burrowing into the ground, looking for a "grubstake" of essentially useless (other than to fill teeth or make shiny jewelry) metal. Its only real use lies in its exchange value—for money, that ruin of society and bond of all bonds. However, as of now, Sixto and I could use a little exchange value. Our expenses (whiskey, yes) are outrunning our revenue, and we can sustain that for only a few more weeks. If our luck doesn't improve, we may have to join the Humbugnia crowd and hire ourselves out as labor in a town. No money has been received from Engels or other quarters. I may have to write to my mother, which I certainly do not want to do. We spent much in Sacramento buying our supplies at exorbitant, gouging prices. It's unclear how much the little gold we've found is worth, but I'm certain not as much as we need.

I note with interest the political state of man here in California, including Chucklehead and its peculiarities. Yes, nationalities are divided, reflecting the limited vision of men. But in other respects, the whole presents, in theory, the possibility of a genuine democracy. There is no class system—all men are equally debased by their greed. There is no state that stands against and opposed to men. They are their own law. Apart from their slavishness to gold, men here are essentially emancipated (sadly, women may be another story altogether), only they do not fully know it. Or rather, they may know it but do not care to use that emancipation for anything other than the pursuit of gain. Gold, the search for it, now controls their destinies. Still, they may be one or more steps closer to real emancipation than most other men on the planet. The situation is a fine example of how the social and political structure is determined by the means of production. The hand mill created the feudal lord, the steam mill the industrial capitalist. Here, we all employ essentially the same means, the pan. It is thus our democratic equalizer.

CHUCKLEHEADS

From Thomas Stilwell to his mother

June 14, 1849

Dear Mother,

I hope this will ease you, as I know it has been a long time with no word from me. I am now in California. I hope too you will understand why I lit out like I did without a goodbye. That woulda been very hard, as I knew you would make a fuss and we woulda argued and I didn't want any of that. Someday I will come back and be able to help you out a heap more than if I stayed home. Maybe I will be rich enough so you can have your very own cook just for you, like I heard some people in Cincinnati do. A cook and other help too, who do not do much besides scratch your back or put on your boots. Or maybe even you can come out to California. You always said miracles happen all the time. I already have found a little gold here. Just a few pinches of dust, but where there is smoke there is fire, right?

By now I am sure you know I went with those men who were at the lodge. After the war we all felt pretty much the same itch that nothing could scratch. I am cooking for them, and they treat me all right, even if they do sometimes call me a belly robber. They mostly are good Kentucky men. They can be ornery but then the patience of Job himself would be tried by crossing the country. They can be sour in the morning after they drink. I am making a promise to you that I will not touch whisky or any other moonshine.

Across the prairie we burned rosin weed in my stove, and then in buffalo country we burned dried buffalo chips and anything else that would light up. Trying to stretch our bacon we tried eating some rare things like raccoon and even a badger. I had to boil the raccoon for a hour to get the smell off, and after that he wasn't all that bad. There were other things too I learned about, wild onions and potatoes, and a thing I never heard of called an artchoke thistle, though eating a raccoon or badger is easier than it. Here in California we slaughtered our oxes. They were mostly skin and bones, and their livers looked like honeycomb from all the bad water in the desert. We did not eat them but threw them into a river.

Before coming up here we got supply in a town called Sacramento. We can resupply with a trader over the way that gets meat and beans and coffee from town. And there are some wild plants in this valley that one can eat. The trader gets mail sent up to him from town, so you can send me a letter. It will take a while but send it to the Emporium de Paris, as the trader is a Frenchy from France. I will find it there.

Our camp is in a steep valley in the hills below the mountains here. It is very hot, but at night it cools down so much you can get the chills even in summer. There is a creek we use for panning gold. On the other side of it there are some Mexicans. Some of the men are a little tender about that, but I think the hash was settled back in Mexico, so I have no beef with them.

I brought some paper and pencil and am drawing a bit. A man in Nevada named a ox team you woulda had a kick out of—Empty Bucket, Bucksnort, Possum Trot, Lickskillet, Doughplate, and Buzzard Roost. He was from Texas and said those were all one-horse places there. I drew them and gave it to him. At times I get away from camp to draw. There is a boy from the other side of the creek who came around with his donkey. We have met up a couple times down the valley by the creek. He is not with the Mexicans but has a partner that is German, I think. He is a friendly sort and speaks good English, even though I think he might be Mexican too. I drew him a quick one he was pleased with. He is taller than I am and skinny but strong looking. He can stare at you for a long time like a cat and not give away a thing.

You should know I think of you often, and you must not worry. I promise to write again soon.

Your son,
Thomas

From Lucas (Doc) to his sister Amelia

June 15, 1849

Mrs. Amelia Carpenter
947 Carondolet Street
New Orleans, Louisiana

Dear Sissy,

I have made it to California. (I have, by the way, been taught
the meaning of "California"—it is a Spanish word from "cali"
meaning "Get rich" and "fornia," meaning "or die trying.") In San
Francisco I had a little luck at the gambling table (please, no
chastisement) and bought passage up the river to Sacramento. I
took some time there to bottle up some of my lithintropic potion,
good for whatever ails you, and sold many to miners back from the
mountains who were suffering from everything from rheumatism
to bunion to Sacramento fever. Most of them were in a pretty state
of hardupitiveness. I know you don't approve of my potion, but I
believe in the power of belief. If those miners think they are going
to get better, many of them will, just for believing it. And who's
to say my potion isn't medicinal after all? As for my own health,
I've learned to stomach food that would destroy the digestion of a
coyote. What I wouldn't give for a plate of Eggs Sardou at Antoine's!

All in all, out here I am just one soldier in what has to be one
of the queerest army of invaders ever. There are all stripes here,
from Chinese to Swedes to Pacific Islanders to New York lawyers.
It doesn't seem to matter where they come from, they all have their
queer beliefs. Some have dreams of eggs or snakes and think that
will determine their luck. Others carry horseshoes from home or sit
looking at the moon to find signs in it of where the Mother Lode is.

Me, I discount nothing and am treating every man I meet as though he's a sage or a seer who might end up being my King Midas. The world is in fact queerer than any of us knows, and we may as well learn from it.

I am now in a canyon aptly called Chucklehead Diggings. My camp is on the side of a creek that runs through the canyon. The rest of this creek side is taken up by a company of men from Kentucky. They were all soldiers together in the Mexican war and are as tough as pine knots. I would not want trouble with them. They like their drink, and when they are not panning for gold, their camp is pretty much one constant carnival of whiskey. For former soldiers they have, to a man, a surprising lack of discipline and disregard for personal hygiene and appearance. You might imagine how they feel about a few Mexicans who have set up camp across the creek. Only short years ago they were fighting a war against them. The leader of the Kentuckians explained to me that it wasn't just about the war. He says that Mexicans came from the Spanish, that the Spanish came from Arabs, and the Arabs came from Africans, so that makes the Mexicans no better than a bunch of African bushmen. I tried but could not change this view of genealogy. They are like almost all other Americans I have met, believing they are the Israelites taking the promised land by force of arms. Anyone in their way is a motley race of Hittites. That whole business might be well and good if they could show the divine warrant of the Hebrews.

The Mexicans appear to be finding gold that the Kentuckians feel should have been theirs, as the Kentuckians first camped over there and then moved. Burns, their leader, told me, "We beat the bush and now another is catching the bird." That is not quite accurate, as the Mexicans have a different way of digging, going deeper into the ground, than the Kentuckians do. The Mexicans are beating a different bush altogether. The Kentuckians, as I am, are panning for gold, washing gravel in pans in the creek but not digging very deep.

As I said, there are many here disillusioned and disappointed to find that gold nuggets are not as common as cowpies on the prairie. I believe the truth is that mining here will be no different from spinning a roulette wheel. Your village idiot (and more than a few of them have come west) will be just as likely to strike it big as your professor. On the way to the diggings I witnessed a powerful lesson in just how lucky any man can get—and of course, we all believe we will be lucky. I wandered off my trail one day to find water I'd been told about. I went into a box canyon with a creek and came upon a solitary soul down at luck, sitting on a small rock. It seems other miners had once been there, too, but all but him had left after panning out nothing but gravel. For him the game was all up—high, low, and jack—and he was about to leave but I guess needed to melancholically meditate on it all before doing so. He had a beard that a family of sparrows could nest in, and his clothes, even though the creek was right there for washing, could have walked down Canal Street on their own. He told me he'd been digging there for almost twenty days and had one pinch of gold dust to show for it. I said, "Sounds like you've left no stone unturned." He said that was right. Then I said, as much to humor him as anything else, "What about that rock you're sitting on? Why don't you turn it over?" In a Tennessee accent, he said, "Mister, I'll do it to please you, but I might as well look for a weasel in a watchman's rattle." He got up and rolled the rock, barely glancing into the mossy hole he made, then peered into it more intently, and with bare hand reached down and pulled up a piece of gold as big as my thumb. We both had a good laugh, at his fortune and Fortune generally. He made no offer to share it and I no claim to it—the claim was his, and the twenty days' sweat.

Worry not about me. Worry is, as our dear father used to say so elegantly, about as useful as teats on a boar. But I welcome whatever well wishes you send my way—they won't put lines in your pretty face like worry will. I don't want to be the author of any of those.

I think of you and Earl and your children daily, and vision the day I see you again.

Your loving brother,
Lucas

From Jeremiah Burns to his brother Jim

June 15, 1849

Dear Jim,

You know I aint a letter writer so do not expect too much. But you should know I am in Californnia and well enough as is Billy and the other boys from home. We did have a little accident here the other day. Caleb Putney filled up on whisky to the gills and instead of gettin up on a rock and callin all the bears in the woods to a wrestle like he sometimes does he went off to do some more diggin in the gravel here. Usually whisky comes after workin but you know Caleb a little he has a mind of his own. He went to work with his boots off and came down with a pick on his big toe and sliced it right off. He howled like a wolf in heat while we tended to his foot. There is a fellow here who says he is a doctor though I believe he aint a real one but a quack. He has tried to sell us some magic potion he brews up that he calls his vegtable tropical mixter or some such thing but none of us was born yesterday and have seen one or two of his kind before. I told the quack that maybe if Caleb drank a bottle of the mixter he would just grow a big toe back as good as new. Besides stoppin the bleedin there werent much else we could do, but we did let the quack mix up a poltiss and put a patch of it around Calebs toe and then put his boot on and he told Caleb to leave the boot on for the next 20 days. If that dont rot his whole foot and his toes all fall off I dont know what wont.

Me and some of the other boys had some rumatism and spots of lung fever but we all shook it off. Most days we are standin in the creek here in cold water up above our ankles but above them the sun feels like a blacksmith fire burnin up the rest of your body. So far no one has come down with nothin worse like Sacramento fever that can kill a man. That gets in your head and most times stays there until it does you in. The fleas here cant kill a man but they can dam sure make you wish they could. They pretty much own the whole dam territory and every nook and cranny in it and will go at you any time of day or night even when you are standin out in the creek. If the quack Doc was smart he would come up with a flea poison and make more money than any gold digger.

We are in the hills short of the mountains here. Theres a creek here runs through a gulch that widens out. Our camp is on one side of the creek and on the other side are some Mexicans and a German with a boy who looks Mexican too. None of us is too pleased about the Mexicans comin in here. We did not go down into Mexico and fight them and many Kentucky boys die there so they can come up here just as they please. We fought them so as to put them back into their own country. For the time being there is no trouble as long as they stay on their side of the creek, but I dont even want to have to look at them. At night I can smell their cookin, they got some kind of boil that stinks up the whole gulch. And they carved a cross into an oak tree and I seen one or two of them down on their knees in front of it doin those hand things they do in their church.

We have our own preacher with us now too, a part time one anyway. He joined up with us in Nevada. We did not know he was a preacher at the time but he made that known by and by and now he holds a service on Sunday mornings. Only a few of the boys go to it because they feel guilty for this or that. Out here in the gulch there is little sinnin to be done, some cuss words and maybe a little friendly gamblin. Nothin like what you see in the towns. We do got plenty of whisky but that is a necessity of life. It aint good Kentucky whisky but it still is whisky. The preacher lets us have it about intemprence but we pay him no mind. There aint many pleasures here and plenty of hardship and the whisky is the closest thing to the balm of Gilead that we have. The preacher says we will reap what we sow, but aint no man sowin gold and there is word that plenty are reapin it.

Some of the boys think we ought to leave here and head far north, as there is word of whole lakes of gold that way. That may be true, but even so there is plenty to be found around here, you just have to be payshent and maybe a little lucky. We just crossed dam near the whole country. I am not about to pick up and cross it again in another direction and go to Canada where it is cold as hell.

You would think it a dam sight funny how I wear my trousers always tucked inside my boots. I do that as my pockets are full of holes. I am always forgettin that and puttin things in there, so instead of mendin the holes all I have to do is dump out my boots. Much easier!

I hope the tobacco crop is lookin good. Sure wouldnt mind a fresh pipe. I hope mother and father are well and you are mindin them.

Your brother,
Jeremiah

From Karl to Jenny

June 12, 1849

Dearest Liebchen Jenny,

I am sorry to hear that the swinish "Mister" Graves from the Rose and Crown has been to our door. I promised him satisfaction and had his promise not to bother you. As for the tab at his pub, what can I say? Being one of the few men (or the only!) articulating the direction of history is hard work! The wheels of my mental locomotion must be greased or they will lock up, and then where will I and the future of the world be? I will write to Graves and threaten to thrash him if he dares to come by again. In the meantime, you must be brave and find a way to continue. Is there not another piece of porcelain or two that you could pawn—and send some part of it my way? In the life process of individuals seeking emancipation there will always be a great deal of hardship, and you and our daughters are not, unfortunately, exempt.

Speaking of pigs, we witnessed a priceless porcine scene at a camp we passed on our way here. A man was touting a pig that he had supposedly trained to sniff out gold. A pack of newly arrived miners, their own mouths and nostrils extended, followed the beast around, and when it stopped to poke its nose at the root of a weed, fifty axes struck the spot at once, threatening the life of the "goose" that they believed had lain the golden egg. They dug until they finally gave up in a storm of profanity. The pig's owner made the excuse that the wind had changed direction and confused the pig, and then the whole drama began again, the pig finding some worm or other larvae in the ground, pushing at it with his snout, and then had to leap aside for his life before the miners stabbed him to death with their tools. Again no gold, and this time the excuse that something must be blocking the pig's nose. The owner used the kerchief round his neck to wipe the pig's nose, and all were expectant that this would be the lucky third try. Indeed, the miners did that time find a minute scattering of dust. Suddenly, no monarch in Europe has ever been as revered as was that hog. All attributed the "success" to the pig rather than pure chance, and the owner proceeded to auction off the pig for what had to be a sum many times what he paid for it. There is no limit to the fantastic devices that greed is dreaming up: potatoes skewered on twigs; a can of oysters suspended on a line strung between handheld tree branches; a "goldometer," which is nothing more than a plumb bob swaying in the wind but to which is attributed the divinatory power of a saint.

I and my comrade Sixto are optimistic that we will find gold soon. Our chances must be as good as a pig's! Our manual labor is hard but ennobling, and any day now I may have the good fortune that will free us from poverty and enable me to support the revolution. But until then, please send money if you can. Mr. Engels's *Schweinehund* of a father has cut him off, at least temporarily, so I am not getting any support from that quarter. I note your displeasure regarding Mr. Engels's latest companion. He is a great friend of the female proletarians, no? Our Prussian lad may not have the mind needed to lead to the revolution, but he must have other gifts that English factory girls admire. Maybe just maybe he is responsible for *enceinte* Helena?

Your dearest,
Karl

6
Chucklehead Diggings

I CAN'T SAY I WAS UNHAPPY EVERY DAY OF MY LIFE AT EL Loco's. At times he would drink more than usual and sleep the whole next day, and Arturo and Domingo and I would go off into the hills and be back before he woke. But I was always very lonely. At the mission I had the padres, and in Monterey the Morgans, but at El Loco's I had no one except Arturo and Domingo. I knew why someone like El Loco was alone. He wanted to be. But I wondered why God had made it that way for me and if it would always be so. For a long time, I thought it wouldn't be right to ask God to change this plan for me. That would be the same as telling Him the plan wasn't a good one—and who was I to tell Him that? But I also knew that, if they have been good and patient and feel perhaps deserving, people ask for things. They may even not feel deserving but nevertheless ask because God, being merciful, may all the same grant their requests.

So the time came when, though for a long time I had not confessed my sins, I began praying for a family. A real family of my own, not how it was with the Morgans. How this could be I didn't know; I guess I thought that was His problem to figure out. It might take a small *milagro*, but would that be so hard for Him? I felt shame thinking that, yes, even for Him this may not be possible. So even while asking, I doubted I would ever receive.

They were not exactly the family I once prayed for, but up there in the diggings I felt as though I had brothers. Life was hard there, and we shared it. Karl had become more than an amigo. Dueling for my freedom had made him my brother for life, even if he did not see it that way. And near our camp were four Mexicans, Sonorans, who treated me not as a boy but as a *compadre*. At the mission and the Morgans and El Loco's, I was always a boy among men—the padres or vaqueros, Mr. Morgan and the boatmen, or El Loco. But there in the mountains, I began to feel like a man just as much as others.

During the day the Sonorans worked hard and kept to themselves, but at night I often went to their campfire and listened to them play the guitar and sing *corridos*. These were songs from Mexico about vaqueros, the trials of lovers, and heroes in the revolution against Spain. In my favorite, a peasant farmer, Valentin, joins other *campesinos* to fight against the soldiers. He is captured but refuses to tell *el colonel* where his compadres are. The colonel kills him, but he is a hero and lives on in the song. Pablo played the guitar and knew many *corridos*. He had a silver front tooth that shined in the campfire light, and he was fatter than the others. They sometimes called him *Gordo*—fat—but he didn't mind. Timoteo was his brother. They called him *Dedos*, or "fingers," as he had only three fingers on his right hand, the other two bitten off by a puma in Mexico. Jose and Ramiro were their *primos*, their cousins, and were brothers too. Every morning on waking, I heard their shovels scraping away before anyone else was at it. They didn't drink too much *aguardiente*, and went to sleep early. They worked without talking, because they knew that's how work gets done, and they were finding much more gold than us and the yankees. They bagged up their gold dust not caring if the yankees watched them like hungry coyotes fixing to pounce on a limp steer.

Around their fire they told me stories from Mexico about poor *campesinos* standing up to the rich, or about the war for independence from Spain. They never spoke of the war with the yankees, and I didn't ask. Pablo especially liked to tell "tall" tales, the ones I liked most. He told of *el jinete sin cabeza del camino del diablo*—the headless horseman of the devil's highroad—a Spanish soldier who appeared on stormy nights to help vaqueros stop stampeding cattle. Ahead of his horse went a flame as tall as an oak tree that turned the cattle around like they were sheep. He told of Juan Oso, who could move whole mountains and pull up pine trees, who bit the ears off his enemies, making them his henchmen. He told of men finding gold and silver treasure buried in Mexico and California, others losing their lives looking for it. If it was a man's destiny to find treasure, he would see an orb of light glowing above it—but if not, the glow would lead him off a cliff.

One night, Pablo told the story of Joaquin Murrieta:

"Joaquin Murrieta was born a Californio. He was the third son in his family. He did not get along with his oldest brother, who was very cruel, and who was going to receive the rancho from their father. So when he was young, he left his home and became a vaquero on a rancho not far from the Sierra Nevada, the rancho of Don Raimundo, who was a good man and was generous to all his vaqueros. Don Raimundo had a beautiful daughter named Rosa. Like other rancheros, Don Raimundo wanted his daughter to marry a man who would have his own rancho someday. But Rosa and Joaquin fell in love, and though Joaquin was not going to have his own rancho, Don Raimundo gave his blessing, because he knew Joaquin was a good man and came from a fine family. Joaquin and Rosa were married, with a big fandango. Joaquin would still be a vaquero, because he loved the life of one, but he and Rosa would live together in the Don's house.

"Every year after the *matanza*, the vaqueros from Don Raimundo's rancho would go into the Sierra to hunt. That year, after they were married, Joaquin and Rosa chose to go alone to a cabin high in the mountains. Rosa could ride a horse as well as most men and knew how to hunt too. One day, soon before returning to their rancho, Joaquin went out hunting on his own. When he came back to the cabin, he saw a terrible thing—evil men, *yanquis*, attacking Rosa.

Joaquin fought bravely and killed one of the *yanquis*, but there were too many of them. They tied him up and whipped him until they thought he was dead. Rosa was dead, her throat slit. They put Joaquin in the cabin and set it on fire. In God's eye, he awoke and escaped the fire. With no horse, after many days he made his way on foot back to Don Raimundo's rancho. There, Joaquin swore to Rosa's father and to himself that he would have revenge. He vowed to become a hawk preying on *yanqui* chickens and to find the men who killed Rosa. Over time, vaqueros from other ranchos joined him. He and his men now ride in California, in the desert in the winter, in the mountains in the summer. He steals only from *yanquis* and will kill a man only to defend himself and his men or to have his vengeance.

"He carries around his waist two silver-plated pistols in calfskin holsters and wears a sombrero lined with a ring of silver skulls that smile like those on the Day of the Dead. They say he has killed two of the men who killed Rosa and still searches for the others. To the *yanquis* he is a *bandito*, a criminal. Their soldiers in Yerba Buena will pay one thousand *yanqui* dollars in gold for the head of Joaquin Murrieta."

I felt at home at the Sonorans' fire, and Pablo told me that I could come whenever I wanted. He joked that I might want to get away from my "*tio*"—uncle—Karl once in a while. The Sonorans weren't sure what to make of him. They were amused by the way he sometimes bantered with the yankees across the creek. They also thought it was dangerous, as for them it would have been. On most days when we were done working, Karl would pour a mug of whiskey and take it with him to the creek when he went for a wash or to soak his feet, and I'd often go with him, without the whiskey. If the yankees were there too, just up the stream, Karl sometimes tried to start a conversation. He'd say something he'd been thinking about, something I guess he'd been writing in his letter to the world. Their head man, Burns, at times answered him, other times just stared and laughed. Burns called him "the Philosopher" and said that back in Kentucky, he knew more than a few "bottle philosophers." One day, Burns was not in a good humor. I could see this, and hoped Karl would too, but he asked Burns if he ever thought about what his "essence" was.

"What are you gettin' at?" Burns said—he was standing naked in the creek, washing.

Karl thought that Burns seemed to be serious about the question. "What I'm getting at," he said, "is what makes a man what he really is—inside. Some, although I don't, call it their 'soul.' Or you might say it's the *prima materia* of your life, your existence. But I prefer to call it your essence."

"And what do you know about that?" Burns said, looking at us the way you might at a noisy rattlesnake. "About my 'essence'?"

"Well, it is about you and every man. Your essence is not what you are or *what* you make in this world. It is as much, or more so, *how* you make it."

Burns looked around the canyon, thinking hard. "So you're sayin', then, that I—we—are all just a pile of dirt? Because that's about all we've been makin' here."

"Dirt, yes," Karl said, "but not just dirt. You could say that you are also moles blindly digging through it."

With that, Burns shook his head and went on washing, but I think being called dirt and moles didn't go down very well with him and his company. That night, Karl shook me awake, thinking a wild pig had got inside our tent. I sat up straight and saw something small, not a pig, and tried to kick it out of the tent, which was a mistake. Skunk stink burned my eyes, a smell that up close is like an arrow through your skull. I heard yankees laughing as they splashed across the creek. Karl and I dived out of the tent. Our eyes were burned so bad we were blinded, and we crawled to the creek to wash them out. Cold water is about the only thing you can do for skunk spray. We cleared it out enough to see, but the tent smelled too bad to get back in it, and we spent the rest of the night in the open in stinky blankets. In the morning, the yankees all had wide grins while we tried to wash the skunk out of everything. Try as we might, we couldn't get the smell out of the tent, even after washing it twice. It smelled as much like dead coyote as it did skunk. For some reason, our blankets and clothes washed out better.

By our fire the next night, I told Karl that these yankees seemed a little high strung and even more tetchy than other ones I had met.

Karl said, "They are desperate men. And they are just the first wind of the storm. These Americans are even worse than the English. They are energetic, without the drag of centuries, the drag of history."

I offered that maybe it would be better from now on if we and they just minded our own business.

Karl didn't answer that but said, "If thousands of desperate men do not find what they are looking for, what then? There will have to be an unimaginable amount of gold for them all to be satisfied."

I said, "They say there may be many mountains of gold."

"If that is true, then there will be a different kind of storm," he said. "The havoc that thousands of newly rich would wreak on the land. In England we've already seen that—the rich buying their machines and putting the rest of humanity in their factories.

"You don't know," Karl said, "what a factory is, do you? Here you have your Don or your padron, or whatever it is you call him. He is a 'big man,' powerful, because he owns a lot of land and cattle. But in England, and now in America too, if you have a factory you can be powerful without owning a single cow or any other animal. A factory is a building ten times larger than most churches, and inside it, they make one thing. Three hundred men and women and children— mostly women and children—will stand all day at machines and make that one thing—shoes or shirts or hats. It is like working in a cave. It is dark and the air is full of dust. The workers can go an entire day without seeing a tree or the sky. The smoke from the factory covers the sky. And these workers may not even notice. One day is like any other in a string of unending days of senseless work."

"Why do the workers stay there?"

"They have little or no choice. They have no land or too little to live on. But I will tell you a secret. Almost no one knows this."

"A secret?"

"Yes. The secret of our time right now, and the future, is the freeing of these people—of the common man. People like you, Sixto, are the secret."

"I know the secret?"

"You *are* the secret."

I felt pretty special being *the* secret, even if I didn't entirely understand why I was. But that wasn't going to help us with angry yankees or with shelter. From time to time there were some hard storms up there, and while our tent hadn't been perfect, it had kept us mostly dry.

I decided to make a lean-to for us—a more or less three-sided one, with a high rock as the fourth. It would be bigger than the tent and strong enough to fend off the pigs. Some thick pine branch walls would be warmer than the tent, and the skunked canvas could go over the top, to keep the rain out, with a smoke hole cut in it. We wouldn't smell it much, and in a short time it would get smoked like jerky. To get the pine branches I needed, I went with Arturo up the hill right behind our camp. I thought there might be some pine or fir at the top, and more grass for Arturo, as he and Alborak had thinned out the grasses lower on the hill. Arturo and I were nearing the top when a fellow popped up from behind a bush. He looked a little caught out by me barging in on what was probably his daily squat, and at first glared at me like an angry cow, then turned and went off toward the top of the hill. On his bottom he had on blue long johns; on top he was naked except for a *serape* slung around his neck. I recognized the *serape*—it was just like one of those that the odd fellows on the river boat wore, the ones we'd thought were maybe from South America. Other than his considerable snout, this fellow didn't look at all like either of those fellows. He was about the same size as one of them, but they were very hairy, and brown, and this fellow had short blond hair. Later, I told Pablo about this, and he said he had been up there once and saw two men. It was curious they were up there, he said, and he thought they were a little strange looking too. Maybe, he said, it's because they're from Texas, where all the men are large and none of them are quite right in the head.

At that time we had only a small handful of gold dust for all our trouble. Most nights I prayed that we would find more. I asked this more for Karl than for myself. He very much wanted it, but for myself I didn't care that much. What would I do with a lot of gold? Would I go to El Loco and pay him off, even if the law said I didn't have to? But how much gold would that take? Was I the same price as Solomon? And after paying him, then what? Buy a horse, maybe. But if I was going to be a vaquero, I didn't need to buy one. A little extra gold might be nice, but a Don provides for his vaqueros. On the other hand, I knew that my wanting to be a vaquero was not so simple anymore because of finding Dolores. What if she did not want that life? Would it not then be good for me to have some gold for us? So I was confused—for the moment being in Chucklehead was enough, but I knew that there were questions that were going to have to be answered.

Every night after sunset, I prayed behind a small juniper by our camp. Karl knew I went there, and one night when I came back to our fire, he said, "You do that every night, yes? Pray?"

"Yes," I said.

"I'm curious—what do you say when you pray?"

"Many things. I ask Him to keep us safe."

"How do you know that He hears you?"

"Because He can hear everything. And you have seen that He does. When you were sick, I asked Him if He would make you better, and He did."

"That is what made me better? I thought you did."

"But with God's help. You got well very quickly. You were like the mother of a boy at the mission. He saw a virgin who told him she would heal his mother's sickness. And she was healed the next day."

"Does He give you everything you ask for?"

"No, but that is because He is wiser than I am. He knows what is best."

"I see. Were you asking for something tonight?"

"Yes—I was asking for gold. For you and me to find more of

it—for you."

"That would be a nice irony—your God giving gold to me."

"Do you never pray to God?"

"When I was a boy, I did, yes. But now, no. If there is a God, I don't think he'd listen to me."

This talk of "if" there is a God burned my ears. El Loco was the only other person I'd known who might have thought there is no God, and even he seemed to talk to Him sometimes—after much drink. He'd talk straight to the sky, and then he would curse at it too. As for Karl, I kept praying. I asked God to have mercy on both of us, and, if He thought it fit and meet, to show Himself to us at the right time.

The next day, Karl said to me, "What do you think God looks like?" He wasn't one to let things be. He himself once gave me the word for what he was: a "*Kochlöffel*," a spoon used to stir soup or stew in a pot; and that's what he liked to do, stir things up.

"I don't know," I said. "But I have seen a painting of Jesus. And the son will look like the father, yes?"

Karl laughed—not unkindly—and said, "I wonder about those paintings of Jesus. I don't recall a description of him in the scripture. Do you? Other than that odd one of white hair—for a supposedly young man."

I did not, I said. I was still feeling pretty sharp about Karl's blasphemy the day before. "Why do you say 'if' there is God? How can you say that?"

"Well," he said, "I just think that God is . . . an idea. He is real but only in your head. Not real in the world or in the sky or anyplace else. Or you might say that I believe that you, Sixto, are God."

My ears had never heard the like of this. It was enough to make me think the "bad king" was maybe not so bad after all, and Karl had gotten what was coming to him when the king booted him out of Germany.

Karl could tell I was scandalized. "What I mean," he said, "is that you and I, and other people—that whatever is the best of us—we've taken that and put it into one thing, one container, and called it God. We all have an idea what these things are, and we want them to be true, we want them to be the things that are strongest in the world—that is, we want to believe in them. Things like loving your fellow man, justice, kindness, forgiveness. We bundle them all together and call them God. But they really belong to us—to humans—not to the sky."

Padre Arturo could have told Karl a thing or two about God that I didn't know how to then. I was sure Karl was a blasphemer, and that could have made me shun him, except I'd been taught that the sinner and his sin were not the same thing, that all of us were God's children, and that like children, some behave better than others. You don't write off a child because of what he might say; there's always hope he will see the error of his ways and come around. Padre Arturo used to say that all of us are born in the light, but not all of us see it until we're led to it.

I had another amigo of a kind there in Chucklehead. His name was Thomas. He was one of the yankees but he was a different sort, he had an easier temperament than the others. Only a little older than I was, he had already fought in a war and come all the way across the country. I first met up with him down the canyon one day when I went there with Arturo. Thomas was there, and it looked to me like he was pulling weeds. Turned out he was picking something called miner's lettuce, a plant with long stems and round leaves that you could eat like a salad. He did most of the cooking for the yankees and said his grandma had taught him to eat wild things like that lettuce and nettles and even dandelions. At first the yankees weren't too keen on eating the lettuce, but the fellow on their side who said he was a doctor told them it fought off scurvy, so they ate it as medicine. Karl and I started eating it, too, and found it not at all bad. Only problem was too much of it gave a man the runs.

Thomas was a talker and didn't shun me at all like any of the other yankees would have. We saw each other by chance a few times down the canyon, and it got so that I'd go to find him there, for a change of company. I would watch to see when he would go, then wait, and go down after him. He told me he wanted to get rich enough to buy his mother a big house somewhere where she could sit on the porch all day in a rocking chair and watch the world go by and have her very own cook. She had shed a bucket of tears, he said, when he went off to the war. He wanted to know about my family, and I'm ashamed to say I lied and told him about a mother and father I wished I'd had. I said they were back in the pueblo where I was born, that they had a *milpa*, a little cornfield, of their own, and that my father was a fine hunter and kept them fed.

I was impressed that Thomas had been in the war. Being at El Loco's, I knew little about it—had only heard it meant that California would become yankee territory. In the war he'd been a cook for the same kind of men as the yankees, but he wanted me to know he'd been a fighter as well. "I didn't even know which way Mexico was," he said, "only that the Mexicans had moved into Texas and everyone said it couldn't stand. It was pure hell down there. As many died from their guts rotting out as from anything else. It weren't the cooks' fault, it was the water. It was almost seven months before we got to fighting, at a place they called Buena Vista. You know what that means?"

Yes, I said, it means good or beautiful view.

"The view we had was the Mexicans coming up the valley. That day decided the war. They say more Kentuckians died that day than from anywhere else. Jake Burns died there, Jeremiah's brother. I suppose that's why he's hard on Mexicans."

Thomas drew pictures with pencil and paper. That was why he went down the canyon—so he could do it without being bothered about it. He made a picture of me and gave it to me, but I lost it in the events that came to pass.

There was one other person much on my mind in those days who I thought of as family—Dolores. I got one letter from her, and Karl gave me what I needed to write several to her. I did not have any idea what to write about. Even if I had known how, I would not have professed love. I was afraid I might spook her with what might seem like wild dreams about the future, so I mostly wrote to her about our past, things I remembered from living with her family, and a little about El Loco's. I went easy on the El Loco years, not wanting her to think badly of her dead father. I never did tell her that he sold me like a side of beef. With the letters I just wanted her to know I was alive, to keep me alive in her head. The closest I came to proclaiming love was telling her she should not leave San Francisco and should expect to see me there one day soon and I would take her on a long ride to the seashore.

From Friedrich Engels to Karl

March 20, 1849

London, England

Dear Comrade Karl,

It is all well and good that you are on your "mission" in splendid California. Whatever troubles you're having, just be glad your arse isn't target practice for Prussian sharpshooters. I was fighting the King's soldiers in the Palatinate but we were routed and I had to run to Switzerland, and from there back here to England. It's a good thing one of us is willing to put his arse on the line, otherwise the whole band of democratic bums would claim we are yellow and can only talk the talk. I have had to deal not only with Prussian bullets and bayonets but my father bombarding me with letters telling me that you and all the other godless Communist rabble have thrown me under a buggy.

From New York you ask for money but know that my old man has essentially cut me off, putting me on a monthly allowance that barely covers my living costs. I'm left to pen as many bad IOUs as you—the master author of them. Maybe there's room in California for one more seeker of fortune?

I visited your wife the other day, and she had the brass to suggest that I *shtupped* her nanny Helena! Apparently the woman is swelling up. You should be grateful that I didn't give anything away. You and I know who the *Shtupper* is—*Ja*? As much as I'd like to take a California vacation, I am tied here to my father's factories, so don't look for me soon.

Yours in the furtherance of the revolution,
Friedrich

From Thomas Stilwell to his mother

June 21, 1849

Dear Mother,

I am well, though I have had a little fever of late. I am lucky as
there is a doctor here by our camp. He gave me some medicine for
my fever, a few swallows of whisky with some peppermint and then
some sugar in something he called absinth. I know I promised not
to drink whisky but this was for medicine only, not for unmoral
reasons. The doctor has his own vegetable potion that he says is best
to take when you are still healthy and it will keep you that way. But
for fever he said the other is better. He is a colorful sight and one
day he let me draw him even with no color. Most miners don't give
a rip what they wear, but he dresses up like he's going to a dance.
Even when he is panning for gold he wears red trousers under a
blue jacket with silver buttons. When he is in the creek he wears
a pair of deerskin shoes with fancy stitching on them. He keeps a
little box around his neck on a gold chain and has a dirk knife that
he uses for practically everything.

I have gabbed a couple times more with the boy here I told
you about. Turns out he's not Mexican but Indian, so he's the first
real Indian I have ever talked to. He knows some things about the
Indians out here and said they believe that deer give themselves up
to hunters because of a deal the Indians made with the animals a
long time ago. So when an Indian kills a deer, he thanks the animal
for holding up its end of the deal and thinks the deer can hear him.
I don't quite believe any of that, but I didn't say so. The boy said
his partner has told him how important it is to learn as many ways
of knowhow as you can in order to make your way in this world.
And that means not just how folks might do things but how they

might look at things, like the Indians and the deer. Even if you don't believe it others might, and so you can understand why they do what they do.

I hope you are well and work is not too hard for you. I am sorry I cannot be there to help.

Love,
Thomas

From Lucas (Doc) to his sister Amelia

June 24,1849

Mrs. Amelia Carpenter
947 Carondolet Street
New Orleans, Louisiana

Dear Sissy,

I have been meaning to tell you more about what a miner's life is like, but my heart is rather heavy today. A young man here in the camp died. He couldn't have been more than twenty years old, as he was still smooth faced. I'd taken a liking to him and did what I could for him.

Sickness and death are all part of the roulette here. There is plenty of fever, and you die or recover as heaven might please—Joe neglects his sick partner Jim; Jim recovers and then Joe gets sick and dies. There is some kind of preacher here with us, and we had what passed for a funeral. He said "our treasures we must resign at the dark portal of the grave." The funeral done, most here went right back to digging, dark portal notwithstanding.

All in all, I am ready to throw up the sponge and head back to San Francisco, and will do so, maybe even today. I mean to try my luck at the gambling tables there, where I can at least have a pillow and a half decent meal while I fritter away my money. With any luck I'll be able to buy my way on a boat at least as far as Panama. I'll figure out the rest from there. Don't be surprised to see me at your door before Christmas.

Your loving brother,
Lucas

From Jenny to Karl

April 1, 1849

To Karl the Adulterer,

"*Mein Liebling Jenny*"—what a bunch of Prussian prattle! My
family always warned me about you, and they were right! Helena
has admitted everything! I've thrown her out into the street where
she belongs with other tramps! I don't know or care where she has
gone. Maybe she and your lovechild will follow you to California
someday. I learned about it all after Mr. Engels came here again
and very generously gave us a little money so we can scrape by.
Before he left he said he needed to use the WC, but I heard him in
the kitchen where I found him giving money to Helena. I accused
him of being a scoundrel and said he should do the right thing by
Helena, not sneak around and keep her quiet with hush money. He
lost his temper and said that if I wanted to know who the father is,
I need not do more than ask you. Helena then broke down and told
all—the two of you having it on while I was away visiting my uncle
in Holland! How could you? She has the sex appeal of a hunchback!
Mr. Engels comforted me, and I'm beginning to see him in a new
light. Maybe I should look a little closer at the "qualities" that
so many of his factory girls admire! Don't bother to defend the
indefensible. Our marriage is, as you might put it, a dialectical
wreck—we had the thesis, you *shtupped* the antithesis, and now you
will have to live with the synthesis!

At any rate, I've had enough of your Communist (im)morality.
The children and I are staying here for the meantime—thanks
to Mr. Engels—but we may go back to Germany where there are
people who still observe the Ten Commandments.

Just to spite you, I might even raise the children to be good Christians!

Your long suffering and newly former wife,
Jenny

From Lt. Junger and Lt. Fischel
to King Frederick William IV

July 1, 1849

Chucklehead Diggings, California

To: His Excellency King of Prussia Frederick William IV
Re: Herr Karl Marx—An Alarming New Development

To our most high King, the greatest sovereign in all of Europe—
Ja in all the world! Your servants have been closely watching all
the goings on in another California hellhole called Los Infurnace,
looking for signs of sinister Communist plotting by Herr Marx and
his *Junge* accomplice. Almost daily, Herr Marx has had dialogue
with potentially dangerous American allies. Meanwhile, the *Junge*
may be forging an alliance with some Mexicans here. They may
have chosen this remote mining camp for security. We cannot hear
what is being said, but from our vantage point above the camp, it
appears Marx and the Americans may be planning something. The
Americans sometimes appear to dissent vigorously, but this is to
be expected from what we know of the Communists in Europe—
they are a disagreeable bunch. Still, we believe an international
conspiracy may be brewing, and now things have taken a dangerous
turn and it is time for us to act swiftly.

To wit: We have seen nearly every day how Marx drinks the
local rotgut whiskey to the point of extreme gesloshment. Today,
after much whiskey, he read what appeared to be a letter, and after
doing so he staggered about his camp, wailing and pulling at his
hair, waving the thing in the air. The *Junge* tried to calm him down,
but Marx wouldn't hear it and proceeded to tank up more whiskey.

Thoroughly soused, he took off running up the hill on which we are camped, as if he were making a charge at us, but then fell and rolled down the hill. He went at it again, but this time sharply stubbed his toe on a rock at the base of the hill. He then threw a characteristic temper tantrum, repeatedly kicking the guilty rock until he dislodged it. Then at once, he stopped kicking the rock and examined it—and a different wail began, of delight. In short, Marx had found a chunk of gold larger even than a loaf of pumpernickel.

We believe that Marx, with an untold amount of gold at his disposal, has now become much more dangerous. We believe that he may be ready to unleash on the world—targeting specifically your Excellency and your Kingdom—his new Communistic screed. He may also be readying violent co-conspirators, here and at home, to act with him imminently, and now has the means to arm and supply them. Specific instructions from your Excellency may take too long to arrive. Therefore, we will proceed under the discretion allowed by our general instructions: We will soon take steps to "liquidate" Herr Marx (he is already doing plenty of self "liquidation") in order to prevent the publication of his scurrilous propaganda and to forestall his Communist plot.

Your faithful servants,
Lt. Ernst Junger ("Hozay")
Lt. Franz Fischel ("Horhay")

July 5, 1849

SACRAMENTO SPECULATOR

**"There are more things in heaven and earth, Horatio,
than are dreamt of in your philosophy."**

Word has it there's been a big strike in what might be some very rich diggings. Reports are that a German known as "The Philosopher" hit upon a nugget that would be the biggest find yet in the Sierra foothills. "Crazy as a coot and lucky as a leprechaun," one miner says about The Philosopher. They say this could be the Mother Lode, an entire mountain of gold, with nuggets as common as cowpies on the prairie. The exact location is still unknown, but it is believed to be somewhere in the general vicinity between the Delirium Tremens and Pinchemtight diggings. Wherever it is, we always knew German philosophy would be good for something someday. Interested parties ought to hightail it to the aforementioned diggings and inquire while the getting is still good.

Before you go, get your gear at the Stanford store! Mr. Josiah Stanford will outfit you with all you need to get to the diggings and mine your claim once you're there!

7

A Black Beetle
and a Blue Bear

THE MORNING AFTER KARL GOT THE HEAVE-HO LETTER from his wife, I woke up with something crawling in my ear—a black beetle, an ill omen of that day, to be sure. I flicked it out of our lean-to and looked around. It was just before dawn, a bright glow over the east end of the canyon. The Sonorans were up but not working yet. Karl was on the ground near the dead campfire, no blanket, sleeping off his sorrow-driven whiskey binge. Ill omen aside, it was the time of day I liked most in Chucklehead, before the heat and the work of digging, before the air of hostility.

His wife's letter had sent Karl into one of the biggest conniption fits I'd ever seen, a whiskey-fueled one. He stomped around groaning and howling and pulling his hair, until he went off running up the hill like there was a nest of hornets after him. I got the gist of the letter—that he'd wronged her and she didn't want him anymore. Between hair pulling and whiskey drinking, he said lots of things in English and German. I gathered their marrying had been a bit scandalous, that her parents didn't approve of him because he had no "prospects" and she had no dowry, but she and Karl defied them and married anyway. And he said more—that he'd been a fool and an "exploiter," and that men lust after women even more than they lust after money. That sex was the ruination of the world and the one thing the Christians got right was the story of Adam and Eve, even if it was a fairy tale. He said he'd been cast out of the garden and into Los Infernos, and then started in laughing crazy as a loon. Then, just like that, he stopped it all and went running straight up the hill behind our camp. He didn't get far before he fell and rolled down, got up and went at it again, tripped on a rock and fell again, then got up and started kicking at that rock and cursing it. He kicked it so long and hard it came loose. And that is how he found what everyone, it seems, came to call the "Chucklehead Nugget."

He was yowling like a madman when he was kicking, but when he saw it was gold, he started a yawping altogether different. I think his whiskey-soaked brain thought that nugget was going to be the answer to all his problems, his money ones and his wife ones too. He brought the nugget over and laid it at my feet and told me to lift it. It was a piece of quartz bigger than a cow's head and heavy, with wide veins of gold running through it. We took it to the creek and washed it like a baby, the yankees gawking at us with no less adoration than the wise men did at the baby Jesus and the Virgin Mary in the manger. Only the yankees had envy, too, and could only take so much. I heard Burns say, "I guess I'll go and get drunk too, and see if my luck changes," and he told his men to get on with their business. It was all the worse for them because they had once dug on our side of the creek, and that nugget had been theirs for the finding. Karl and I washed it until the veins practically shined like the gold flakes in the altar at the Mission San Juan Bautista church, and then Karl sat it in his lap stroking it and drinking more whiskey until he passed out on the spot, hugging the blasted thing.

Now, in the morning, he was on his back, his beard looking like a clump of dirty tumbleweed, sticking straight up. The nugget was off to the side of his head. I went to wash my face in the creek when, all of a sudden, I heard a low rumbling like wild horses stampeding. Then I looked up the hill behind us and saw it coming—a giant boulder crashing down, headed straight for us. At the very same time, I saw something else move at the top of the hill. A bear? But—a blue bear? I had only two, maybe three seconds. There was nothing I could do about Karl. I froze, not sure how to move. I knew rocks don't always roll straight, but I had a deep conviction nothing was going to change this one's mind. Right about when it hit the bottom of the hill, I leaped to my left. I don't know what possessed me, but I kept an eye on Karl even while I did. I didn't want to see, but I couldn't not look either. It all happened in the blink of an eye, a *milagro*—the boulder skimmed just over Karl's head so close it might have brushed a twig out of his beard, then it rolled across the creek and rammed into a small oak and took it down. Only then did I realize how big that rock was—as high and wide as a full horse and a half, maybe even two. The yankees sprang out of their tents loaded for bear. The boulder just missed Burns's tent, and he came out looking daggers at me like I was the one who'd rolled it there.

Karl slept through the whole thing. Near his head where the nugget had been was a pancake of crushed quartz and gold dust. That nugget was or wasn't going to be the answer to all of Karl's problems, but it had answered that boulder. Somehow it had held together enough to skip a few thousand pounds of stone just over his skull.

I then saw again, at the top of the hill, the "blue bear"—a man— looking down on us. He saw that I saw him, and he ran back out of sight. I grabbed my reatas and woke Karl up. He wanted to sleep, and said something about cats yammering in his head. I told him what had happened, that someone up on the hill was up to no good, and that he had to come with me to see who was up there. And so he did go with me, all the way up the hill griping about the *schmerz* in his head, and I told him better having a bad head than no head at all, and to keep quiet. We climbed fast and pretty soon heard what sounded like arguing coming from the top.

Staying behind bushes, we saw two men. "Prussians!" Karl said. They were arguing nose to nose, wearing only boots and blue long johns. One—the one I'd seen before—was tall and burly, big at the hips, and long necked. The other seemed about half as tall as his partner and fleshy, round about the middle. As they faced off, they looked a bit like a bowling pin and a ball. They were doing a kind of dance step—the Pin bending over into the face of the Ball and shaking his fist, and then the Ball stamping his feet; and then the Ball taking a turn shaking his fist and the Pin stamping, and so on. Seeing both at the same time, and remembering the *serape* around the Pin, I realized they were the odd fellows on the river boat.

"The bad king's men," Karl said. "Though there is no good king."

I asked Karl what they were saying. "They are calling each other *Dummkopfs* and idiots. They blame each other for missing me with the rock."

I had no idea what we could do, but then the Pin spit into the face of the Ball, and the Ball straight away clamped the Pin in a bear hug around the waist. The Pin yowled like a bobcat and drummed his fists on the Ball's head, but the Ball kept squeezing. I saw our chance—I moved in and looped a reata around them both, cinching it tight. Already clasped together in the bear hug, they didn't even feel the reata. I handed that one to Karl and then fast roped them with my other one. The Pin then saw us and must have said something, as the Ball let go his bear hug, but we had them—kind of. If you rope a grizzly, you should have a plan. We had no plan, and this was a grizzly with four hands, four feet, and two heads.

I told Karl to pull hard. We yanked together, and the Prussians went down, the Pin on top of the Ball. They and Karl were screaming at each other in their awful tongue. But then each of them got hold of a reata and was pulling on it. The Ball was pulling on mine. He got up on one knee, and I managed to get him back down; he got up, and I yanked him down again. The Pin was doing the same with Karl but getting tangled up with his partner too. I knew I was wrong about "having them"—sooner or later they were going to get on their feet, and because they were heavier and stronger, they could reel us in like fish. We were going to have to drop the reatas and run—but then a notion came to me.

The top of that hill was almost flat, like a small mesa or table. The "edges" weren't sharp, but the slope angled off pretty steeply, and the

Prussians were close to that slope. I wrapped the end of my reata tight around my wrist and told Karl to do the same and to follow me. I ran hard, first right at the Prussians, then broke hard away. The Prussians had got on their feet but were confused—where were we going? In a dead run, I flew straight off the hill and out into the air for a few feet and then—*wham!*—came to a sudden stop, my whole body jerked so hard I got spun around and came face down on the side of the hill. Karl came down right near me. Above us, the Prussians, now on the start of the slope, were down too. They tried to get up, but the slope made the footing tricky, what I had hoped, and a good jerk on a reata took them back down. One of the Pin's boots came off, and papers flew out. Karl let out a whoop, and then they were all squawking away in their German lingo again so bad my ears ached. The Prussians got wise and sat back and dug in their heels so we couldn't pull them down the hill. We might have been at that all day, a kind of Mexican standoff, if the real Mexicans, Pablo and Dedos, hadn't shown up with pistols and rope. The Prussians gave up, and Karl went chasing after his papers. I might have helped him, I suppose, but I was bushed. He could pick up his own letter to humanity. How they'd got hold of it was a head-scratcher, but they must have come down into our lean-to during the night while Karl was passed out and I slept hard.

Down in the canyon we tied the Prussians to an oak tree and took their boots for good measure. The yankees had watched most of our little rodeo up on the hill and showed keen interest in two white men in blue long johns being led along by me, Pablo, and Dedos. Burns wanted to know who they were, and I told him they were Prussians from Karl's country out to get him—and that they were the ones who rolled the boulder down. He showed even keener interest then, as they'd almost flattened his tent, and said that after morning chow we would all deal with the "Persians."

After eating, the yankees came across the creek for the first time since skunking our tent. They intended to hold what was known as a miners' court. More precisely, this was a yankee miners' court, as Burns was going to be the judge and only yankees would be the jurors. Karl kicked up a fuss about Burns taking charge and not bringing in any of us from our side of the creek, but Burns told him to clam up and asked him what foreigners knew about how to do an American court. Six of his men sat on a log like turtles in the sun, lined in a row, mostly sober because it wasn't noon yet. I have to say they appeared impressively ready to take their duty seriously. The Prussians stayed tied to the oak.

Burns started off by asking me to say what had happened with the "Persians." Karl corrected him: "They are Prussians, not Persians. Persians are an ancient Asian people. Prussians are Teutons from northern Europe."

"Two tons?" Burns said. "I swear you must have knocked your head up there on the hill, Philosopher. Go ahead, boy," he told me.

I told "the court" how the Prussians had been on our river boat, dressed like South Americans, and how I'd seen one of them up there before, and how I spotted one of them at the same time I saw the boulder coming down, and then I started in on how I'd roped them, but Burns stopped me and said he'd heard enough. He then said Karl could have his say and to keep it short. Karl told the court what he'd heard when they were arguing—that they'd dug out beneath the rock and pushed it off, meaning to kill him, and that somehow they'd got hold of his papers. He then went off on a tongue-lashing of the bad king, but Burns stopped him too.

"You have anything to say for yourselves?" he asked the Prussians.

"What is the wrong you are accusing?" the Pin said. "What is the law?"

"The law here," Burns said, "is the law of common sense. We ain't blessed with law books confusin' as a Chinese bible. Or with double-talkin' lawyers. What's fair is fair. So say your piece, and we'll all get this job done. What do you say?"

"We have done nothing," said the Ball.

Burns scratched his head. "Then why were you goin' round dressed like greasers when you're Persians? And why did this one here," he said, pointing at me, "see you up there just when that big old rock came down? You sayin' that was just happenstance?"

"We make morning exercise," the Pin said.

"Maybe so," Burn said, "maybe so—but how is it you had the Philosopher's scribblins on you? What business is that of yours?"

The Prussians looked at each other. The Ball smiled and said, "We are students of the great 'philosopher.'"

This really set Karl off—he called them Christian German jackasses and then some worse things, I'm sure, in German.

"All right," Burns said, "all right. That's enough. It's clear they're lyin' through their teeth. Gentlemen of the jury, what do you say? Guilty or not guilty?"

The yankees didn't even talk about it. They looked around at each other, a couple of them nodded, and then one of them stood and said, "Guilty!"

"All right, then," said Burns. "I say that a whippin's too little. That might be enough for thievin', but you damn near put not just the Philosopher here out of business but some of us too. By rights you oughta hang for that. But you're in luck as I don't feel like a hangin' today. So you're gonna get a whippin'—forty each, less one—and a head shavin'. And while we're at the shavin' we'll take a piece of ear too."

"That is barbaric!" said Karl.

Burns scratched his cheek and ran his tongue over his teeth. "Philosopher, I'd be careful what you say here. You done called us dirt once. Now you're sayin' we're barbers too?"

"There is no need for blood. We can take them to a sheriff."

"Sheriff?" Burns said. "No need for a sheriff we don't have. We can teach them a lesson or two on our own."

"It is useless bloodletting."

"Ain't much more than a nosebleed. And you don't have to do the shavin'. But you can keep a piece of ear if you want. The judge and jury have spoken, Philosopher. So let us take care of this."

"And what happens after you 'shave' them?" Karl asked.

"Well," said Burns, "we'll take them over to the trail. And if they want to stay Angus instead of Angie, they won't show their faces around here no more."

I'd had my beatings in life, on the business end of El Loco's cat tails, but only once, in Monterey as a boy, had I seen a full, barebacked whipping. It was the *alcalde* himself—the mayor—who did it, with a horsewhip. The whipped man was big and strong but cried like a baby, the *alcalde* laying the marks down on his back like wagon tracks crossing in sand. Whipping is cruel, but a man can put his shirt on his back and carry on. Cut off a piece of his ear and it will never grow back, and the only way to hide it is to grow your hair over it or pull your hat down. I'd learn later that men all over the mountains had their ears clipped, so much so I'm surprised that a whole generation of California babies weren't born with half an ear.

Karl and I did not want to stick around for the punishment. We collected the dust, quartz and all, from the crushed nugget, then took Arturo and Alborak over into the dry *arroyo* that connected with the canyon. I had some questions, but they could wait: Why did the bad king want to kill Karl so much that he sent men so far to do it? Would more men be coming? What did Karl's letter have to do with it all? With all the goings on, I hadn't really had the chance to tell Karl I was sorry about his wife, and I did so then.

"Ach!" he said. "Men and women are like puppy dogs."

"What do you mean?"

"I mean they get infatuated and think that infatuation is real."

"They become fat?" I said.

"No, no," he said, "infatuation means short-lived foolishness. A passing state of endocrinology."

"A passing state of—but you have been married for many years, yes?"

"Yes," he said. "All right, then, infatuation may not always be short-lived. Even if it is long, romantic love is not real."

"Love is not real? How can you say that? Jesus said we should love our neighbor as our self."

"Ah, yes. One of your commandments. There are different kinds of love. Your love for your neighbor, if it exists at all, is not the romantic love I'm referring to. It is more like what you may feel for Arturo. That love may be more stable than romantic love, but neither kind of love is real. Neither one is a material reality. You can't see it or touch it. It is just a feeling that comes and that may go just as easily. You are more likely to kill your neighbor than you are a complete stranger."

"But I love Dolores," I said. "That has never gone away. To me, it is real."

"Of course," he said. "We all want to believe in the illusion, the dream. Not unlike all the men—including us—boring into these mountains. Our hearts dream and our heads stop working."

"But it is real for you!" I said. "You have found gold! It is not a dream! And I think you still love your wife, yes? You are sad, and that is real."

"I'm saying that I should have known better," Karl said. "A man and a woman should never think that they own each other. That another person is your property and only yours. It is more natural for someone to share his or herself with more than one person. In your Old Testament, some men had more than one wife."

If that was in the Old Testament, it was not something the padres or Mrs. Morgan had ever brought to my attention. "I do not believe that—you must be wrong. The Bible says that you should not covet your neighbor's wife."

"Yes, but—if a woman is not just one man's wife, or if a man is not just one woman's husband, then no one can covet anyone. Do you see?"

"But I would not want to share Dolores with anyone. Did you ever share your wife—Jenny?"

"No. I did not."

"Why not?"

"Men and women are not ready for that yet."

"But you—are you ready for it? She does not want to share you."

"I'm describing a more perfect, a better world than the one we are in now."

"This sharing—is this part of your letter to the world?"

"Maybe. Or it's at least related to it. It's one of many things related to it."

"I hope you understand—I don't mean that the bad king is right to want to kill you. But I am maybe starting to see why he may be vexed with you."

"Kings don't like to be told that things should be any way other than the way they think they should be."

For what seemed like many hours, we stayed in the arroyo, trying to keep to the shade, looking for the yankees to come through with the Prussians. Arturo and Alborak feasted. Karl and I kept to ourselves. We needed to talk about the nugget, but that could wait. In the middle of the afternoon we saw them, the blue-long-johned men being led on horses, each man with a rag wrapped around his ear and head. I thought of Padre Arturo, how he often said there was no virtue higher than mercy. On one hand, Burns had shown some mercy, and on the other, none. I said this to Karl and remembered Jesus saying, "Blessed are the merciful, for they shall obtain mercy."

Karl seemed somber. "Yes," he said, "but in your Good Book it also says 'If any have an ear'—and those two still have one and a half—'let him hear. He that leadeth into captivity shall go into captivity. He that killeth with the sword must be killed with the sword.'"

I thought this was harsh, given how Karl had not wanted any bloodletting for the Prussians. But over time I would come to see that it wasn't just Karl but maybe all men—maybe even padres—who, in their heart of hearts, lacked the blessings of mercy toward others.

8
The Carrera del Gallo

AFTER KARL'S FINDING OF THE "CHUCKLEHEAD NUGGET"—now dust in a canvas bag I cut from our old tent—I was of the mind to leave Los Infernos and go back to San Francisco. Karl was of another mind, one struck with gold fever. After a find like ours, he said, there had to be more where it came from. His was like most minds with gold fever, not knowing the meaning of "enough." At the same time, and perversely, he believed the yankees would soon pull up stakes, which made no sense to me. They were just as fevered as he was and had to be thinking that if fortune chose that spot to favor a scruffy "kraut," how could it not, there and soon, smile upon them too.

I knew the yankees were not finding much at all, and I feared what they might do when they were liquored up. So the morning after the Prussians' trial, even before the Sonorans were up and about, I buried our bag of dust in a shallow hole a few paces from the lean-to. I thought it best that Karl not know where I'd put it, in the event he would have too much to drink and would somehow give away the spot or even dig up the bag just to fondle it. He surprised me in agreeing to this.

A day or two later, it was one of those days when the heat shimmered back and forth in waves from one side of the canyon to the other, when even in the shade of an oak tree it felt like an oven. After a morning of panning, I wanted to do nothing but sleep in our lean-to. Arturo, needing a good feed, had something else in mind for me. His and Alborak's greedy bellies were thinning out the grass in the canyon, and he was giving me long hungry looks I couldn't ignore. So even though I was tuckered out, I took Arturo over into the arroyo. I would have taken Alborak, too, but she was too ornery that day to follow.

The arroyo was much wider than our canyon, and longer, and was curved like a new moon or a slice of melon. Arturo and I had not gone very far into it when I heard voices coming from farther back in it, around the bend. Staying up on the side of the arroyo, we went to have a look. There, in the bottom of the arroyo in a wide, flat wash, were about twenty men with horses. Even at a distance I saw what they were doing—the *carrera del gallo*—and went closer to watch, staying a little above them on the slope.

In the *carrera*, a chicken is buried in the ground with only its head and neck sticking out. From many paces away, a rider breaks into full gallop, and then, holding his saddle with one hand and dropping low to one side, he must reach down and grab the chicken by its neck. Sometimes the chicken will come with the neck—usually not. Sometimes the rider makes a mistake and falls from his saddle, and so he is the one who suffers. These men in the arroyo did not have a chicken. A man, who seemed to me the *jefe*, the boss, went out and stuck a knife into the ground all the way to the handle. I watched a few riders try for the knife; only two snatched it, and the others cheered when they pulled it out. I was puzzled by these men. They rode like vaqueros and wore vaquero hats with a leather string under the chin, but they did not wear buckskin breeches or spurs or carry reatas. They did not look like hunters, either, and it was too early in the year for vaqueros to hunt.

Arturo and I went closer. Many of the men saw us but paid us no mind. The *jefe* again went out and stuck the knife into the earth. As he walked back, I saw a band of silver around his black sombrero, and two shining, silver-handled pistols holstered at his waist. A new rider trotted out to about fifty paces from the knife, turned, and whip-started his horse into a dead run. At the right moment, he leaned down and out of his saddle as far as he could, touching the knife, but he couldn't snatch it, and it tumbled.

Again the *jefe* went out and stabbed the knife. Then, in Spanish, he called to me: "*¡Muchacho!* Do you want to try this on your burro?"

His men laughed, and I said, "I can do it. On a horse."

"*Bueno*," he said. "You can have mine."

I knew that for him this was a *chiste*, a joke. But I have always hated people making fun of me like the children at the mission did, or even when Dolores did it. I am always quick, sometimes too quick, to answer it. So I was not going to let even Joaquin Murrieta—if it really was him—get away with teasing me. I was going to show him, even though I had never tried the *carrera*, had only watched it.

I left Arturo and made my way down to the *jefe* and his horse, through his men. They were amused, as he was, but he seemed curious too. He was a little shorter than me, though not a small man. I saw he was strong, with a round chest and thick legs. Though he had a scar from his forehead to his chin, there was something simpatico about his face—a face that maybe smiled and laughed easily.

His horse was a tall copper stallion. It was all I could do to swing myself up onto it, and I knew right away that reaching the knife from the saddle was going to be all but impossible without a trick of some kind.

"You are ready, *muchacho*?" the *jefe* said.

I nodded and walked the stallion out to the start. On the way, I wound my reata a few times around the horn of the saddle and knotted it, then gave myself three feet of it and made some wraps around my left wrist. The rider who'd been ready to go when the *jefe* called me out was waiting for me. Seeing what I'd done with the reata, he grinned and spit, and said, "*Buena suerte, amigo*."

In my left hand I had the reata and the reins. With my right I gave the stallion's haunch a good slap. It bolted forward and I hung on, gripping with my legs. The stallion was faster than I expected. Before I knew it, I was coming to the knife. I dropped to my right, my left foot coming out of the stirrup. But I had guessed wrong about the reata on the saddle. It was too long, and my shoulder and arm hit the ground, again and again, bumping along like a stone skipping on water. Somehow, I kept my right foot in the stirrup, or I would have come out of the saddle and been dragged by the stallion or trampled by its rear legs. There had been no way to get the knife. With one hand I pulled myself up into the saddle and brought the stallion to a stop. I heard the *jefe's* men laughing and whistling—for me, not at me. My shoulder felt broken, and I was bleeding from my elbow to my knuckles, but I was ready to try again, and started back.

But the *jefe* waved for me to bring him the horse and said, "*Está bien, muchacho.* That was a good try." He offered me a hand to get out of the saddle, but I got down on my own. I'd been a piece of fun for them, but I'd won respect. I let the *jefe* take my arm and clean it with a wet bandana, then he tore strips and tied another bandana to cover the wound. I did not expect such a man to care about my arm. As he tied it, he said, "*Muchacho.* What is your name?"

I told him, and smiling, he said, "Sixto. I will call you *Sixto de Sangre*, yes? How old are you?"

"Seventeen years," I said.

"You are brave. It doesn't matter if you don't get the knife. Being brave is the thing. And it's good you are not afraid to bleed a little."

"I will give you the bandana tomorrow," I said.

He laughed and said, "No, it is yours. We will not be here tomorrow."

Some of his men had started to eat. He told one of them to bring him a piece of jerky, and he cut off a piece for me. "What are you doing here in the mountains, Sixto de Sangre?"

"I am looking for gold," I said.

"Ah, of course," he said. "By yourself?"

"I have an amigo," I said. "But there are others."

He pointed toward the end of the arroyo where the trail led to Sacramento and said, "You did not come that way." Then he pointed toward the canyon. "But that. By chance, is that the place they call Los Infernos?"

I think I was in some shock, so at first this seemed an innocent question, but it quickly came to me why he would want to know that. I wanted to lie and say no, but it stuck in my throat.

"They," I said, "the yankees, they call it Chucklehead."

"A funny name, yes?" he said. "The yankees have such a talent for naming things."

For a while we ate the jerky and said nothing. He offered me more, but I didn't want it. I thought how there were still a couple of hours before the sun went behind the hill. In the canyon they would start cooking soon. My shoulder and arm were throbbing, and I would not have minded resting longer, but I said, "*Muchas gracias, señor*, for the bandana. But I must go to feed my burro more before the sun goes down." I got up to leave, and the *jefe* got up and put a hand on my good shoulder.

"It is best, Sixto de Sangre," he said, "if you stay here for a while. You can go with us."

I sat with Arturo until the *jefe* called for his men to saddle up. Believing I knew what was about to happen, I rode some distance behind them, as I did not want anyone at Chucklehead to think that I had led them there. The men rode slowly, and soon the *jefe* came back to me. He had questions: How many men were in the camp? How many were yankees? Were they all in the canyon, or were some in side canyons? How many had guns and what kind? I answered all these, with a heavy heart.

"Gracias, Sixto de Sangre," he said. "You are brave—and intelligent."

I said, "Señor, if you are who I believe you are, please tell me—is it true you take gold only from the yankees?"

He cocked his head and smiled. "I am sorry to disappoint you, Sixto, but that is not true. It is true that yankees get special consideration, you might say. But we take what we need. And sometimes more."

"Do you need much today?" I asked.

"We will see," he said and then rode up to the front.

Murrieta surely would have made it to Chucklehead no matter what I did or said, but right then and there I felt I had opened the door and let him in. If someone got killed, blood was going to be on my hands. I could have stayed away, stayed in the arroyo, but I'd have been a coward. And, I have to say, I was curious to see just how Murrieta and his men did what the stories said they did. Also, if I am to be honest, I will admit that a little part of me wanted to see the yankees get some "special consideration," while our bag of dust was safe in its hole in the ground.

Close to the canyon, the banditos charged ahead, their guns out. They surely knew that that time of day, an hour or two before sunset, was a slow one for miners—the time for washing, drying boots, writing letters, cooking supper. A cavalry charge out of the blue might literally catch them with their pants down.

I heard shots fired, but I believe the yankees didn't get off a single shot, surprised as they were. It was a small miracle that only one of them was wounded, in the leg. When I came into camp, it was in full commotion—a whole lot of loud and blunt back and forth, you might say, the yankees with their hands in the air, the banditos collecting their guns and gold, here and there firing a few warning shots to keep the yankees in line. I knew the yankees hated losing their guns more than their gold. Even in all the commotion, Burns saw me come in and gave me the worst *mal ojo* of my life, before or since.

A bandito was holding Karl's arms behind his back while another was tugging on his beard but good. Murrieta, on his horse, was near them, his pistols at the ready. He was keeping an eye and ear on everything. One of his men, across the creek, was shouting, wondering how much longer they had to keep the yankees at bay. The Sonorans were standing around their grist mill, quietly watching the whole thing.

I ran up to the men working Karl over and demanded they stop. Murrieta gave a sign and they let him go, but then Karl tried kicking at the one that had been yanking his beard. The bandito behind him grabbed him again and twisted his arm hard, and the one in front was readying to slug him, but Murrieta said, "*¡Basta!* Enough.

Señor—please tell us where your gold nugget is. Then we will leave you alone."

"I tell you I don't know!" said Karl.

Murrieta nodded, and the beard yanker grabbed a fistful and jerked hard enough to come away with a few hairs in his hand. Karl let fly in German with what must have been some pretty rich curses.

Afraid that one of the banditos might lose his temper and shoot Karl, I said, "I have it. Let him go."

Murrieta had to be wondering why I was defending Karl in the first place, and when I said I had the gold, I saw that really did put him to wondering. I went for the buried bag, and with a couple strikes of a shovel I got it out and gave it to Murrieta. Looking inside the bag, he stirred the dust with his finger. A man who'd seen plenty of gold, even he was impressed by what he saw. He bounced the bag up and down in both hands like it was a fat melon. All the while, more of Murrieta's men were coming across the creek, leaving just a few to hold off the yankees. Some of the yankees had started to throw rocks, and I was afraid there was going to be bloodshed.

"Señor Murrieta," I said. "I have heard how the yankees were wicked to you. But we are honest men and have never done you any wrong."

Murrieta looked up and away, toward a hilltop, and I was afraid I had made a very bad mistake, speaking of his past and its grief. Then he looked square at me and said, "Yes. Gold is not the most important thing. I can take it. I can leave it. Usually I take it. Your gold here is very valuable. But there is other gold for us." He dropped the bag to the ground. "I will let you find out if your dust is a good thing or not," he said. "It is just dust. So you keep it, Sixto de Sangre. *Vaya con Dios.*" He then fired a pistol in the air and galloped off toward the arroyo, his men following him.

I knew of course that stealing is wrong, and there was no denying that, strictly speaking, Murrieta and his gang were thieves. But at that moment there was a big piece of me that wanted to ride off with them. If freedom, as Karl said, was pretty much the most important thing, those men seemed to me the freest I'd ever seen. Free enough to leave behind a fat bag of gold. And since I was not riding off with them, there was another part of me that wished Murrieta had taken that dust, as having it then was like bringing on a curse as bad as any *mal ojo*. Being the only ones to lose their gold and guns made the yankees mighty sore, and indeed, they went from mere surly to downright wrathful. To them, I was a kind of Judas who had betrayed them, and if looks could kill, I'd have been dead as a steer in the *matanza*. They gave the Sonorans even more heat too.

Still, seeing Murrieta had been a secret joy to me, as much because I saw he was real as because of what he did. I'd never really been sure he wasn't another one of Pablo's tall tales, like Juan Oso or the headless horseman. I took to heart his words that there were things more important than gold, such as pride. He and his men had shown me that we did not all have to bow down to the yankees. At the same time, I wondered if Karl was right, that there were never going to be enough Murrietas to save California from the stampede that was already rushing it.

From Karl to Friedrich Engels

July 3, 1849

Dear Friedrich,

I know you know about the whole business with Jenny. I absolve you from blame for telling her about me and Helena, even if it wouldn't have hurt you to take the rap for me and the Greater Cause. But I will not forgive you for trying to charm Jenny while she is angry with me. You can have all the factory girls you like, but hands off my wife! She may go back to Germany, but I will follow her there—the king be damned—as a new man. And a rich one! Maybe richer than your old man!

Yes, I have made a find of gold here, a large find perhaps big enough to serve my personal needs and our political ones. At the moment, however, I do not know exactly where it is, as my colleague Sixto has hidden it somewhere—for my own good and safety he says, and he may be right.

I am writing this by the light of our campfire, and a hungry coyote, a kind of American jackal, is eyeing me as though I'm a *Knackwurst*. I have to wave a fire stick at him every few sentences. We had an incident here with two of Frederick's finest. They'd followed me and tried to do me in but, not surprisingly, bungled it. No doubt they, like their Christian German jackass brethren, hold their Lord in Berlin and their Lord in heaven in equal veneration. The Americans gave them some barbaric justice and then deposited them at a distance from here with the threat that if they return, they will have a future as *castrati* in the Vienna Boys' Choir. Maybe what we need is to enlist some Americans in our fight there. Their one virtue may be their truculence.

There is something going on in our little canyon here for which we could use a good lad who is battle-tried and true. More about that soon.

Please do what you can for poor Helena.

Yours truly,
Karl

From Karl to Friedrich Engels

July 13, 1849

The Emancipated Socialist Republic of Chucklehead

Dear Friedrich,

It is an irony not lost on me that, from a place without history, I am writing to you about events of possible profound historical importance. I am also writing in the fever of revolutionary fervor in the middle of a quickened pace of events here. First, as backdrop: The social mood in our little "canyon" here has been more charged than usual lately, as some Mexican bandits came through and took our American neighbors' gold and guns but took neither from Sixto and me (who have gold but no guns) nor our Mexican miner friends (who have both). Without their guns the Americans have been pouting like toddlers deprived of their Christmas candy. Some days later, a new band of Americans came into the canyon and camped upstream. Three days later, we heard two tremendous explosions in that direction, and almost immediately the water in our creek here was reduced to little more than a dribble. Inquiry discovered the newcomers had purposely blown up the sides of the gulch so that debris would tumble down and create a dam to block the creek. The inquirers, some of our headstrong American neighbors, got into a scrape with the newcomers and came back the worse for it. After allowing tempers to cool, I wanted to see things for myself and went to talk to the head man there. He is a big, red-haired ruffian called Rusty, and a more unpleasant man couldn't be found in the Prussian officer corps. He had some sport, firing his pistol near my feet when I approached him, and then made fun of my English accent. He wouldn't tell me what they were up to but said that if we had a "beef" we could take it up with his boss, a Mr. Stanford in Sacramento, and suggested that the best thing to do would be to "hightail it" out of the gulch "pronto" before someone got hurt. I told him I did not care to be threatened, whereupon he fired another shot at my feet and said the next one would give me a new hole to whistle out of. I stood my ground and told him I did not know how to whistle out of the old one!

A further outrage was that among his crew I saw the man who was the scoundrelly second in our duel in San Francisco, the one-eyed Fernando. He was with others of the same ilk—thugs hired by this Mr. Stanford to forcibly evict us from our claims here. Somehow, Stanford must have gotten word of the find I made, and where.

Having lost their guns to the Mexican bandits, our American neighbors across the creek wasted no time in sending men to Sacramento to buy new ones. In the meantime, hanging on to their prejudices, they've kept those of us on this side of the creek in the dark about whatever they intend to do about the new situation, even though we are all in the same straits. We have barely enough water for daily essentials, and it is all but impossible to keep panning for gold (our Mexican friends here have continued what is called "dry digging," but Sixto and I and the Americans are not keen on this method).

Matters then went from bad to worse, as we and the Americans had another encounter with Rusty, and a sobering vision of the future. Two mornings after the explosions, a new and terrible noise came down the canyon from the newcomers' direction. None of us had ever heard anything quite like it—even you in your factories may not have heard such a din. It was a continuous low scream, echoing down the gulch, as though the earth was in pain and cracking apart. Risking Rusty's six-shooter, Sixto and I, ahead of a few of the Americans, went to see what this could be. What we saw: a machine, assembled from pieces the newcomers had brought in, that was one part large steam boiler and other part hydraulic cannon, all of it together almost one-half the size of a locomotive engine. From it ran a long hose, and from the end of that, two men were directing a bolt of streaming water into the rock and soil forty paces distant, boring into the earth and sending it flying. The water's force was so great the men struggled to keep the hose end in place. A wooden flume running from the new dam fed water into the hose. As startling as the sound was, and the sight, I was not surprised. The reach of machines, even to this remote gulch, was inevitable. These men, and other men like them elsewhere, are not going to be satisfied to sift soil patiently by hand and collect small bags of gold dust. They are going to mechanically strip away whole mountains in order to find it, hoping for pieces of ore that will make my nugget seem an acorn.

A hundred or so paces from the juggernaut, Rusty spotted us and ordered the men to turn the hose on us. Even at that distance, the force was immense. I was hit as though by the end of a battering ram. Struck in the chest, I was lifted from my feet and hurled backwards against Sixto, and both of us fell hard on the rocks. I have bruises from my neck to my ankles. Some of the Americans took lumps, too, and all of us beat a retreat. I think the machine bruised the Americans' minds even more than their bodies. Nursing insult more than injury, they were strangely subdued the rest of that day while the machine roared away.

Their men who were sent for guns returned this afternoon. For this there was a big hooray, even though their guns were not rifles but pistols. They also brought back more whiskey, and earlier this evening they had what Sixto calls a "fandango," a revel with whiskey, fiddle music, and dancing. These Americans, from a place called Kentucky, have had some kind of revel two out of every three nights, but tonight they were in especially high spirits. Like you, they put much faith in the ability of guns to solve problems. And yes, I know that in Europe we've seen that guns have been and will again be needed, but they are only tools, one means to an end. It is always the mind of the tool user that is our first interest. It was with

that thought that, as I listened to the Americans whooping it up—
and, I confess, was enjoying some of the last few cups of my own
whiskey—I had a kind of, dare I say, "vision," a most secular one
that moved me to action.

I told Sixto what I intended to do, and he tried to talk me out
of it, but I would not be. I marched across the bed of our all but
dried-up riverlet and into the fandango, Sixto reluctantly following
me. I climbed onto a large rock and expected abuse, but the fiddler
ended his song, and whether because of the humbling they'd had
by the machine or from the opening of the mind that whiskey can
sometimes make possible, or because the time had arrived when
the cumulative truth of what little I'd told them, combined with
the course of events, had penetrated their skulls, they listened
to me. I do not remember verbatim what I said; I myself was in
a heightened state. But I told them that unless men such as they
unite and resist, other men will use not just this machine but other
kinds as well to dominate them. More so, men will not stop with
machines until they stop living only to dominate one another. They
did not cross, I said, a continent just to stay under the oppressive
thumb of an overlord such as Rusty or Stanford, who uses power
and machinery to dispossess them. Men of all nationalities and
colors should unite and work together against such oppression.
What did one of your country's founders, Jefferson, mean but just
what he said when he wrote that all men are created equal? And
when all men regard each other as such and are united, you will
not be alone. As individuals or riven factions, a cruel randomness
determines your fate. It is mainly by chance that you have survived
the heat, the coyotes, the rattlesnakes, the fevers. How much better
could you live and prosper if you worked together! No matter how
hard you work now, you may not find gold, while others literally
stumble upon it!

They reminded me that I have quite a bit of gold while they
have little or none. In our unity, I said, we shall all share and share
alike—I pledge to share my nugget with all of you, as you will share

with me! We shall be a true republic—the Emancipated Socialist Republic of Chucklehead!

I swear their cheering was heard in Berlin! One even shouted that I should be the president of the Republic, but I explained that our republic would have no head of state, no political hierarchy. They had no conceptual difficulty with this—they seemed to instantly grasp its truth and power.

Friedrich, you know I did not come to America to found a communist colony. There are some in Europe who want to, and who wanted me to. I admit I came for selfish reasons. But history, as you and I learned from Hegel, has a way of going forward that pays no attention to individual wishes. Hence, I am coming to the realization that here in California may be the most fertile ground for our ideas. There is no state here to oppose, no kings with their secret police. Besides its unsettledness, there is much else here in California that commends it to such a future—if watered, the soil should be immensely productive, and the climate is Edenic. Between the cold fog of the coast and the heat of the mountains, there is a large territory conducive to a collective paradise. But most important, there are Americans here by the thousands who have come to escape the already turgid capitalism and class strictures of their eastern states, or the feudalistic torpor of their Southern plantations. There are Frenchmen exiled here by their police, Mexicans fleeing class-based neocolonialism, and Pacific Islanders escaping tribal kingdoms. They are all deluded by the fantasy of gold, when what they are really seeking is self-respect and dignity. Many of them already are, or will be, disillusioned, and if they can be made to see that the absurdly random lottery of gold mining will not be their escape, they can be made to see the sense in uniting and working together. The California Manifesto that I am now writing will only make clear what their miserable experiences here have already taught them. Yes, the Chucklehead Republic is small, but even the French Revolution had its beginning somewhere!

The potential for true democracy only needed an external shock to become real. Word will spread to other camps here in the mountains, and I can imagine an entire federation of canton-like republics forming and functioning on the principles you and I have so far elaborated, and they will then, someday, combine into one large socialist republic!

But first, the Chucklehead Republic must deal with the immediate threat from this gang of bullies and their machine. If we allow them to scatter us, this moment of historic creation could all be for nothing.

Your comrade,
Karl

9

The Emancipated Socialist Republic of Chucklehead

IT WASN'T EXACTLY ON ACCOUNT OF HIM, BUT AFTER Murrieta came to Chucklehead, a wave of trouble came on us as thick as Old Testament plagues, until the morning I found myself up on a hill watching Karl getting led away to Sacramento—for a hanging.

Real trouble started with some new yankees coming into the canyon a couple days after Murrieta came through. They set up camp a few long stone throws upstream, and other than wonder why they would want to be up there, in the rocky part of the canyon, no one much heeded them. But they soon dynamited the sides of the canyon to make a dam, and the water flow in the creek went so low that Arturo and Alborak could barely lap it up. All that water behind their dam fed a hydraulic machine that they used to blast the earth, and us as well when we faced off with them.

Burns and company got into high dudgeon about the water, but they weren't about to do any dry digging like the "greasers" did. Karl and I weren't too keen on dry digging, either, and we talked again about leaving the canyon but decided to stay. Greed, I suppose, was at the bottom of it. Our dust was worth a lot, but just how much we didn't know. Murrieta had said gold was not the most important thing, but it had started to figure more and more in my thinking about my and Dolores's future. So I can't blame our staying all on Karl. He said the new yankees couldn't keep the creek stopped up forever, and it might just be the thing to get Burns and his men to move out of the canyon. But they stayed because they were like ornery goats; if you want them to go somewhere, they won't, for no other reason than you want them to. And they'd been seeing the Sonorans making a decent haul, so there was no sense going to beat the bush in some other crowded diggings when they knew there were birds right there. The Sonorans stayed, too, of the mind that none of it was their business.

We should have seen it that Burns and his men would set on having it out with the new yankees. Even before the creek got dammed, they'd sent men to Sacramento for some new guns. Those men got back after the creek was dammed and some of us had been hammered by the hydraulic monster the new yankees had built. Pistols were the best they could get—all the rifles in Sacramento claimed for—and that night, they had their biggest fandango. They built a bonfire and soaked up whiskey, danced, and shot their new pistols into the air. These were men who had fought in a war. I knew nothing about that, but I had to wonder how wise it was to go firing off those pistols, letting the other yankees know they now had guns.

Karl drank plenty of whiskey that night too. We had our own fire, and he was drinking and writing by it. The fire had gone low when he stopped writing and stared into it for a long time. He did that often, look off into the distance for a spell like a bored or daydreaming heifer, his mind ruminating on some cud or other. Then all at once, he snapped out of it and said he was going over to the fandango. I said that was loco and he shouldn't go, but he was intent. And I sure didn't want to, but I followed him over there. He walked straight into the fandango, like Daniel into the den of lions, and climbed up on a big rock. He right looked like a prophet, too, standing straight and fearless, believing he had something mighty to say. I expected the worst, the yankees hauling him down and stomping a jig on him, but they didn't. Maybe not a prophet, but they may have seen him as some kind of lucky charm. Miners were even more superstitious than sailors—laying a hand on the finder of the Chucklehead Nugget might jinx their own luck. Whatever the reason, they quieted down, eerie-like. Then Karl raised his hand and told them he'd had a "vision."

"Comrades! I ask you: Why did you make the journey across this continent? Why did you brave the desolate desert, the wracking fevers, the wild storms, the foul food? You believe it was your hearts' cry for gold, but I tell you it was to answer a different cry: The cry for freedom! Freedom: That, comrades, is your hearts' deepest yearning. But you will not be free as long as you are a slave to random chance. An inch from where you lay your head tonight may be a lump of gold, but you will never know it. Then another man by chance may find it. Can that cruel chance be called freedom? And now you see that even if you accept the cruelty of chance, there are other men who will take even that from you. Men with machines. At home, you were oppressed by the gentry; here, you are exploited by merchants, lied to by newspapers—and now men with machines will oppress you too. You crossed this land to be free, but you will not be free as long as there are others who have the power to take everything and leave you the scraps, like dogs. This is your future: There will be more, other machines, and men not afraid to use them against you. They will be the bosses unless we resist them. And so we must unite—all of us. Not just blood brothers or boon companions. Your Thomas Jefferson said that all men are created equal. To defeat the bosses we must unite as equals, men of all colors and nations. We will share the work of the fight and will share the rewards. Together we shall be a free republic! Free in every sense, standing on an equal plain, a nobility whose title is manhood! We shall be the Emancipated Socialist Republic of Chucklehead!"

The yankees did not quite know what to make of all that and kept eerie quiet. Then Burns said, "That's all very fine, Philosopher. You've got yours. Are you going to share *that* 'reward'?"

"Man's misery," Karl said, "began not with the bite of an apple but with the first person who said, 'This is mine.' In your Kentucky, one man has his, and the others have nothing. Those fine gentry have never not had theirs! I did not make my nugget. It belongs to the earth. As you belong to the earth, so it belongs to you too. In our republic, I will share mine with you!"

With that—the gift of free gold—the yankees put up a rousing cheer and took Karl down from his rock and circled him around the bonfire on their shoulders. They poured more whiskey, and Karl drank with them; I wouldn't have drunk it anyway, but they did not offer me any—so much for being equals.

I didn't set any store at all in Karl's republic and the yankees joining in on it. All of it was just whiskey talk, as far as I was concerned. I let them carry on with their fandango, and then I slipped away to dig up our bag of dust and put it in a saddlebag, to sleep with it. Before handing anything over to the yankees, he and I needed to talk.

I went to sleep, then woke up to gunshots. At first, I thought it was still the fandango, but then I knew something was wrong. There were too many gunshots, and fierce hollering. I went out of the lean-to, and someone grabbed my arm—Pablo. He said "*los nuevos*," the new ones, had come and that I should go with him. There was some moonlight, but even without it I could see he was afraid, something I hadn't seen before. The "new ones" wouldn't know, especially at night, that he and the others wanted no part of the fight. I trusted that he had a plan of some kind or he would not have come for me. I went back into the lean-to, to wake Karl and get our dust bag, and he was awake, stuffing his papers into his satchel. Pablo said to hurry, and I told Karl we were going with him. Across the creek, gunshots were going off like firecrackers on the Fourth of July, and there was more crying in pain than I'd ever heard before and hope never to hear again. I got Arturo, but Alborak bolted down the canyon. We followed Pablo, and

I thought Karl was behind me, but when I looked, he was running across the creek, into the fight. What he thought he was doing without a gun was beyond me, but there was no stopping him.

Pablo led us down the creek bed, and then Dedos and the *primos* came up behind us with their mule and burro. We went a short way down the creek bed, then up the hill behind the yankee camp. As we climbed we saw and heard men running down the creek and shooting, but soon the shots were fewer and more scattered. Clouds had covered the moon—a half one—and then it cleared, and as we got near the top of the hill we saw below us, coming up the way we had, someone leading a horse with a body thrown across it like a sack of feed.

At the top of the hill, the Sonorans went apart from me to talk, and I wondered what they had in mind from there. I had a feeling they weren't wanting me to go with them, but even if so, I wasn't going. I had no idea how, but I was going to find Karl, dead or alive.

The moon was going in and out of clouds. It was just two or three minutes or so, the Sonorans still talking things through, when a man, alone, came up onto the hill from the direction of the yankee camp. It was Karl in one piece. All he knew was that Rusty and gang had come and given the ultimatum—leave now and take nothing with you—and that had been more than enough to combust the lot. Karl's satchel was still strung around his chest, and he had a pistol, taken from a dead man, and had used it till he'd run out of bullets and had to run.

Before we had much of a chance to talk about what to do next, the man we'd seen below us came up, leading the horse. It was Burns, and he said it was Billy slung on the horse and he was bleeding bad. We helped him take Billy down, but we saw it was too late, he was dead. Burns didn't want to believe it; he talked to him and tried to get him to come to, but then he knew it, too, and covered Billy's face with a kerchief. I felt sorry for Burns. That shouldn't have surprised me, but it did.

I can't remember if the Sonorans were still there when Burns came, but at some point they slipped away without a word of *adios*. Most likely they bushwhacked down the far side of that hill. For a while, Burns kneeled by Billy, not a sound of grief from him. Down below, men were still shouting up and down the canyon, finding each other, someone barking orders. There were voices on hillsides too-- Burns's men scattered in retreat.

Still quiet, Burns went over to the horse and took off a keg that was strapped on its back. I'd thought it peculiar but not wholly surprising that the one thing he'd want to save besides Billy was a keg of whiskey. He brought the keg over to us and set it down.

"How about it, Philosopher? All for one and one for all, right?"

"Whiskey?" Karl said.

"Not whiskey," Burns said. "I'm going to blow a hole in that goddamn dam. Are you coming with me?"

The keg had rope handles on each end. I knew then what it was— powder. I'd seen ones like it before, in Monterey, by the cannons at the fort. It was smaller than most whiskey kegs, but it looked heavy when Burns carried it.

Burns said, "For the 'republic,' right? Sharing and all that?"

"Yes," Karl said, standing up. If he thought about it much, I didn't see it.

"All right, then," said Burns. "I got the lucifers. We're going to need that jackass. This horse is too jittery."

"Jackass" meant Arturo.

Burns was evidently set on this, but I didn't understand the why or how. I didn't want Arturo going anywhere, but if he was going, I was going too. And not just me but Billy too. Burns said he would not leave him there. Burns was possessed and Karl willing, and I had no standing to say otherwise.

We put the keg and Billy on Arturo and set off bushwhacking along the backside of the ridge that sided the canyon, Burns first, then Karl, me, and Arturo carrying Billy and the keg. The bush wasn't thick, but the going was slow, especially when the moon went under the clouds. When the moon came out, the pale silver light made the whole canyon look like we were all in a dream, the kind where one thing is following another toward an unknown but surely bad end. The dam wasn't far, not even three hundred feet as the crow flies, but we had to go down into a shallow saddle between hills and then up again. We had to make sure of our footing, and I guided Arturo carefully. In that canyon, sound traveled easier uphill than down, but tripping and falling might give us away.

Still out of sight from the canyon, we stopped on the hill above the dam. Burns said we would wait until there was a long patch of cloud cover, then he and Karl would take the powder from there.

Sitting there waiting for the moon to go under, I felt small and scared and sick. I was a boy. I did not have the stomach needed to take in all that had passed that night, and what I imagined was about to. I had seen dead men, probably killed, floating in the water at Yerba Buena, but I had never been around the killing itself. Now Billy was lying dead on my burro and there were sure to be others below. I knew, too, that what Burns was going to do could lead to more, not just for him and Karl but others too. I wanted no more dying but felt helpless sick to stop it.

The cloud cover came, and Burns and Karl each took a handle of the keg and went off down the hill. Burns had said for me to wait there, and I did for a bit. But after a while I couldn't do it; I had to see what they were up to. I tied Arturo, and, the moon still under, I went out on a knob of the hill to look down into the canyon. I couldn't see Karl and Burns or the dam, but then the moon came out, and I saw the backed-up water, a small lake, long and narrow, looking like a silvery fish in the moonshine. Below the dam the machine was shining, too, like a new toy.

The next cloud cover was a ways off. Below the dam, I heard men and could make out two or three of them moving. Karl and Burns had to be on a part of the slope that wasn't in my line of sight, but then I saw them moving out on the dam, out to the middle of it, and then I lost sight of them again for a moment. They must have squatted around the keg, because then they were running off the dam, back toward the hill, and on the dam there were sparks flickering. I held my breath, and then—nothing, no sparks, no voices. I heard the creek running above the dam, and a whisper of wind. Someone ran back out onto the dam—I couldn't tell who, he was nearly just a shadow. A shot went off, and another, and on the dam the shadow went down. Not a moment later, the blast went off—a flash and sound so powerful my arms went up over my head and I flew backwards. There was too much dust and smoke to see anything, but I heard rushing water and a queer sound—metal scraping on rock, and I knew it had to be the machine tumbling down the canyon. Then the dust and smoke cleared some, and I saw the water pouring fast through the dam. I waited, looking for Karl and Burns to come up the hill, knowing in my gut that if anyone was coming, there'd only be one of them.

Then a loud ruckus rose up at the bottom of the hill, and in it all, I heard that unmistakable German, fiercer even than I'd ever heard it before. The whole cluster of the ruckus, maybe a half dozen men, came into sight and was moving downstream, the sound of German moving with it. I could hear Karl in there, even if I couldn't see him. Burns, I was now sure, had to be dead, joining Billy and an untold number of their crew. Karl was alive—but for how long? He had once told me that to be free, you may have to risk your life. He had, and where had it gotten him? They were likely going to shoot or hang him on the spot, and there was nothing I could do about it.

That night was the second most miserable night of my life. It was only dead Billy who reminded me things could be worse. I had heard men dying; I had all but seen one shot down. I had no food and no blanket. The one good compadre I had in the world was most certainly a dead man walking. What to do weighed on me, not least how to give Billy his Christian due. That saddlebag of gold dust felt exactly like what Murrieta said it was, nothing more than powdered rock. I slept very little and got up before sunrise and waited for it.

With the sun up, I saw the creek running through the hole in the dam and the wrecked machine on its side down the canyon. With my bare hands and a stick, I dug a poor shallow grave for Billy and said a prayer. Down the canyon, campfire smoke came up, and I saw men moving about, but no sign of Karl. And then around midmorning, three men on horses headed toward the arroyo—Karl, Rusty, and another. My guess was they were going to Sacramento, and I had a sound idea why. I took Arturo, and we began going down the ridge line we'd come up in the night. He and I were going to Sacramento too.

July 16, 1849

SACRAMENTO SPECULATOR

TRIAL OF "THE PHILOSOPHER"

Chaotic Ending—German Escapes Knoose around the Kneck!

What promised to be the most entertaining trial in Sacramento's short history ended in chaos today, with the accused escaping in an unholy mess of yet-unknown provenance.

A large and well-oiled crowd gathered down at the hanging oak by the river to watch the trial of the German gold miner Marx, colloquially known as "The Philosopher," and best known in these parts for his find of the Chucklehead Nugget. Many thought they might get a look at the Nugget, while others were interested in just how philosophical the German would be with a noose around his neck. Word had it the trial would be right up there with that of Socrates and put Sacramento on the map as the "Athens of the West."

The flower of miner justice was in its fullest bloom —the noose was dangling from the oak before the proceeding began. Accompanied by fiddle music, a crowd including more than a few of the town's business ladies proceeded festively down from the saloons at midday. At the oak stump that marks the heart of the town's "al fresco" courtroom, El Paso Pete stepped forward and volunteered to be the judge. His qualifications, he said, were that "I watched my pappy's trial and hangin' when I was just a young 'un." A black overcoat was produced that, though long, hung well above his honor's knees.

Pete had no trouble summoning a jury of six peers, as he offered to buy a round of whiskey for anyone who would perform his "sibyll" duty. Pete selected six men, all well-known sojourners of our town's fine saloons. The crowd then formed a wide circle around his honor, the esteemed jury, and the accused, and the juggernaut of justice continued its roll.

Judge Pete asked local store owner and mining entrepreneur Mr. Josiah Stanford to state the charges against the accused: destruction of his property (a dam and a hydraulic machine) and—almost as criminal, one gathered from Mr. Stanford's telling—the killing of a man, one Jeremiah Burns. Not one of his men, Mr. Stanford said, and a dangerous outlaw, but a man nevertheless.

Two of Mr. Stanford's "agents," Rusty Comstock and Jeb Miller, then testified how they and others legally built a dam on the river in Chucklehead Canyon; how, in response, the German and his men had attacked them and were expected to attack again; and how Stanford's men turned the tables and moved to head off a new attack, without killing anyone, but that the German and Burns subsequently blew up the dam. The explosion, they said, killed Burns and wrecked the hydraulic machine.

The Philosopher paced morosely around the oak stump where the doomed usually sit. He appeared as much Asiatic as Teutonic. Squat and stocky, bearded and sunburned, he looked like a cross between a sunbaked Swiss gnome and a Volga Tatar. When Judge Pete said it was his turn to have his say, the German stood on the oak stump and spoke to the crowd. He did not kill Burns, he said. He averred that Burns was shot dead by Stanford's men, just before the dam blew up; that he knew in fact of one other man shot dead by Stanford's men; and that a number of Burns's compatriots were surely shot dead by Stanford's men as well and their count ignored. The German admitted that he and Burns ignited a powder keg that wrecked the dam, but, he said, it is Mr. Stanford who has blood on his hands and is responsible for Burns's and others' deaths and the whole chain of events. Stanford, he said, must answer for the theft of water that forced him and the others to defend their rightful claims, and for using a mining machine against men, a machine that threatened to dispossess miners everywhere.

Mr. Stanford objected that he'd heard enough and said he had some questions for the German. A rolled wad of papers in his hand, Stanford approached and cross-examined the accused:

"Mister Marx, they call you 'The Philosopher,' is that right?"

"People have called me many things. But I suppose to some I am a philosopher."

"What would you say is your philosophy?"

"I am for the emancipation of the human consciousness."

Assorted murmurs, grunts, and snorts rose from the crowd. Judge Pete swiveled his fearsome head to quiet them.

"Can you say what that is in plain English?" Stanford asked.

"I am for freedom."

Many in the crowd cheered.

Stanford looked flustered, and circled around the accused as he posed his next question. "Well, Mr. Marx, we are all Americans here—most of us, anyway—so we know a little about freedom. What do you think you can teach us about freedom that we don't already know?"

"Americans think they are free, but they are really not. They suffer from an illusion."

Stanford, not a lawyer, had already violated the first rule of cross-examination: Do not ask a question you do not know the answer to. But he stepped into it farther.

"I'm not sure what you mean. If Judge Pete here wants to pack up and go to Oregon, he's free to do so. That's freedom, isn't it?"

"An animal in a large cage is free to roam about the cage. But he still has a master."

"A master, you say. And who would Pete's master be?"

"The master in America is the same as the master in Europe—the property owner."

Several in the crowd shouted out the rich prices of items in Stanford's store, until Judge Pete threatened "contemptation" for the next one to speak up.

Stanford: "Mr. Marx, you have some queer German ideas about freedom. I have some of them right here in my hand, in your writing. In something you call 'The California

Manifesto.' I can't say I understand the half of it, but the half I do is mighty telling. It seems you want to start trouble, and you think here, California, is the best place to start it. You say there's people out here—you call them the 'underclass'—who should band together and get rid of people like me, and people like good Ben Tucker at the Snake Eyes saloon, people who own some property. Sounds to me a lot like what the Frenchies did to their dukes."

Then, while in peroration, Mr. Stanford slowly marched the circumference of the circle of onlookers. "Now, who do you think these so-called underclass people are? Frenchies? No! You good people around here? Are you an underclass? No! I'll leave it to you to imagine who the underclass are—but I'll tell you right now they ain't going to look like you and me! And this man wants these people to destroy everything! It's right in here! Esteemed gentlemen of the jury! This man is nothing but a bad seed! You heard him—he admits he blew up my dam and wrecked my machine. And he killed a man to boot. If you ask me, he deserves more than a hanging, but that's the best we got for him, so let's give it to him!"

As the crowd cheered, The Philosopher tried to speak, but with a shaking head Judge Pete signaled it was all over. The judge's pointed finger at the jury amounted to his directions to them, and they spontaneously exclaimed The Philosopher to be guilty as charged. In the best tradition of miner justice, the jury then became the assistant hangmen too. The guilty man's hands were again tied, and he was carried over to the hanging oak. Supervised by the local hangman, they hoisted him onto the horse that stood just below the ready noose. In the saddle, The Philosopher, the noose about to be slipped around his neck, did indeed look philosophical, keeping a stoical calm that Seneca would have envied.

However, the hanging was not to be. Just what happened is still unknown. Some report that an Indian or Mexican-looking boy digging in the cemetery caused a commotion. Whatever the cause, the mob around the hanging oak broke into a stampede toward the nearby cemetery, and folks began digging into the empty and occupied ground there with whatever they could find, most with their bare hands. A melee ensued, and in the confusion, The Philosopher disappeared. His whereabouts are currently unknown, as are those of the Nugget he is known for. A search party sponsored by Mr. Stanford has been sent to find him.

SNAKE EYES

10
Prelude to a Hanging

MOVING AS FAST AS WE COULD, ARTURO AND I GOT INTO Sacramento the next day. We were bone tired when we got there, and neither of us had had anything to eat since the night hell broke loose. We arrived about the middle of the afternoon, and the owner of a stable on the edge of town took a pinch of dust to let us both bed down there for the night. For a few extra grains, he threw in a sombrero I spied hanging on the wall. I settled Arturo with some feed and went into town and found a canteen selling pork and beans. I was tired of lugging that bag of dust, but there was no way I could sell it yet, as word would get out and might link me with Karl, making trouble. Fact is, I didn't know how to sell it anyway.

It hadn't been that long since Karl and I had passed through Sacramento, but already the town had changed. It seemed like half the human race was hellbent on striking it rich. There was nearly every specimen of humanity I could imagine coming through there, but they were of two general kinds—the dirty and the dirtier. The dirty were on their way up and in a hurry, and you could see the hope busting out of them. The dirtier ones, the ones coming down, were of two sorts too—the few happy ones who thought the world was a fine place and that it had given them only what they deserved; and the other sort, the downhearted and the melancholic. The happy ones dismissed any notions about luck and believed they were assuming their natural, ordained place in the order of things—on top of the heap. Some of the sad ones were angry and drunk or dangerous or all at once. Most of the sad ones just sat somewhere—in a saloon, if they had any money left, and if not, then by the side of the road—watching the commotion, all but ignored by the happy ones. Nobody paid much attention to me, a boy in a sombrero, even if I was carrying a saddle-bag that obviously had something in it. I guess I didn't fit square into any of these kinds, though I was definitely among the dirtier, and maybe felt as hopeless as some of them did but for other reasons. I felt about as aimless, too, as I had no idea what I could do even if I did learn where they were keeping Karl.

In what passed for the main street in town, there were men and all kinds of four-legged creatures coming and going every which direction—horses, mules, burros, oxen, and even a llama, though I didn't know then what it was called. Staring at it, I almost got run over by two horses pulling a wagonload. To get out of the way, I had to throw myself on a heap of rubbish and so became one of the dirtiest of the dirtier. Those horses came so close I felt their breath on my face. I picked myself up, and just then I saw her—across the road, hurrying along in a red dress and a big yellow hat—Dolores. I nearly hollered and ran after her, but something kept me from it. Rather, I followed her, staying a short way across the road from her until she went into a saloon, the Snake Eyes. As I've said, I'm not fond of them; I'd rather smell a dying horse's breath than the inside of most saloons. Even the best of them stink to high heaven, and this one was hardly among the best. But I had no hesitation going in there to find Dolores.

I went through the swinging doors, and the thing that first caught my eye were two big painted pictures next to each other on the wall—the very same derobed ladies I once saw in Yerba Buena.

There was some gambling going on at a few tables. And then I saw Dolores—in a room full of men all brown and gray, she and another woman in a pink dress stood out like flowers in a dirt patch. They were at a bar in the back of the room, talking to a barman pouring whiskey. It didn't take him long to eye me, as I was giving it to him. I say I had no hesitation going in there, but once through the doors I didn't go any farther. I was amazed to see her at all—stupefied body and soul by her being in that saloon. Then the man pouring whiskey said something to her, and she came toward me. She seemed glad to see me, I thought, and at the same time, we both knew it wasn't right.

"Sixto," she said. "What are you doing here?"

I wanted to know the very same thing, but all I could get out was, "Did you get my letters?"

She said no, she hadn't gotten any of my letters, other than the one I'd left at the house in Yerba Buena. She looked back at the barman and said, "Sixto, I can't talk right now. But come tonight, at sunset—up the stairs in back. There'll be a white flower on the door."

I nodded I would, and then walked out of that place in such a fog I nearly stepped in front of another rolling wagon. I had questions that I think I half knew the answer to and wasn't sure I wanted to know the other half. I went back to the stable and slept in some straw, and when I woke it was almost sunset. I washed my face, trying to clean up a little, then made my way back to the saloon. My stomach felt like it had a cannonball sitting in it.

Even though I did not know much about the ways of the world, especially the ways of men and women, by that time I wasn't totally ignorant. I'd been ignorant enough not to know about the "house" in Yerba Buena, but since I'd left there, I'd heard a few things from miners. Enough to know that the men in that saloon were not going to be satisfied with a smile and some talk. If talking was enough, they could talk to the naked ladies in the painted pictures; come to think of it, one or two of the fellows in the saloon might have been doing that. But most would want more. Knowing that much was what was sitting heavy inside me, and by the time I got to the saloon, I was mighty worked up and ready to give Dolores a piece or two of my mind.

Up the back stairs of the saloon, I found a white flower pinned to one of the doors. Dolores peeked out when I knocked, and she let me in. I could tell she, too, had things on her mind she wanted to say. The room was smaller than the one she had in Yerba Buena. There was a bed, a small bureau with a mirror and a lamp, a nail on the back of the door where she hung her hat, and a trunk in a corner. The bed took up much of the room.

I went and stood in the corner by the trunk.

Dolores sat on her bed. "Won't you sit with me, Sixto?" she said.

I said no, thank you. The room had smells at odds—a perfume of some kind, rose water, but laced through it what you might call miners' musk—a mix of smoke, sweat, wet gravel, and bad breath.

"You wrote some letters to me?" she said.

"Yes."

"That's nice. I'm sure I would have liked them."

"You came right here?" I asked. "From the *convento*?"

"That . . ." she said, "was not a convento, Sixto. You know that now, yes?" She had not looked me straight in the eye since I'd come in, but now she did. "You're angry, aren't you Sixto? You're hurt?"

In my entire life, no one had ever asked me such a thing as that— how I was feeling about anything. What I felt had never mattered to anyone, not even Padre Arturo. I said yes, I was.

Dolores started to cry then, quietly, something I'd never seen her do before. She hadn't cried even when she'd told me about her parents drowning. "I'm not as free as you are, Sixto. You're a man now, and you can do what you want. You can go where you want. It's different for me."

I'm not sure how much I had really learned about freedom from Karl, but he had surely made me think about it. I wanted to tell her that no, I was not that free, or at least I didn't feel like it. But I could see that she was right, that even I was freer than she was.

"But here?" I said.

"Oh, Sixto, I can't explain it. Everything has been so hard. But that's the way it is. This is where I am right now."

It wasn't easy for me to accept it, but what she was saying rang true—she was trying to make her way in a world where she didn't have many choices. I'd always thought that her world was an easy one, but with her parents dead and no other family to turn to, it couldn't be. If I didn't know where to go or what to do, how could I expect her to? She had to feel penned up like a steer in a corral. But one thing I did know something about was forgiveness. The padres had taught me that. I was not the one who had the right to judge; only God had the right to do that. I saw that as much as I wanted to be angry, I couldn't. I loved her, and so I could forgive her.

"I know, Dolores," I said. "I know."

"No, Sixto, you don't."

"Then I don't have to know," I said. "All I know is I love you."

She stood up and gave me a look fiercer than any yankee ever gave me. "Love, Sixto?"

"I've always loved you, Dolores. Ever since I came to your family."

"I always thought that was puppy love," she said. "Because you were alone in the world."

"But I'm free now, like you said. And I'm a man. I can take you away from here."

With a sad smile, she said, "To where, Sixto? Where would we go?"

It was a good question. Then, right there, I thought about Karl drawing the world in the sand and saying it's a big place, and I remembered the big ships that used to come to Monterey from across the ocean, from Hawaii and the other islands.

"Hawaii," I said.

"Hawaii?" she said. "It takes money to go there. And what would we do there? Work on a sugar plantation?"

"We can get the money," I said. "We could buy a farm there."

She smiled the same sad smile. "You're going to find gold, right?"

"Yes," I said. "I will."

Something was keeping me from coming out and telling her that I had the gold right there in my bag. I guess I didn't yet trust her or myself enough.

"Yes," she said. "Everyone is going to find gold. We'll all be rich."

"I will find it," I said. "Because I love you."

"Come here, Sixto," she said.

I went to her, and she took my hands, and I sat beside her on the bed. She looked straight into my eyes and, taking my head in her hands, she kissed me on the forehead, just like she did in Yerba Buena, only longer. And then she kissed me on the lips, like she did long before, in Monterey. Then there was some more of that, and one thing led to another. In my eyes, we were married that day. On the way to her room, I was one of the saddest men in Sacramento, a town full of sad men, and I left it maybe the happiest man in all of California. Dolores was happy, too, more than I'd ever seen her.

Being happy loosened our tongues, and we both nearly talked ourselves out of breath. I told her about my gold, and about Karl, and how half of it was his and that I didn't know what I could do for him but that I was bound to be at his trial and what came after, if that was how it was going to be, because he'd fought a duel for me and because he was my compadre. She'd heard Karl's trial was on for the next day, down at the hanging oak by the river. We talked about Hawaii and how big our ranch there would be, and the cows and horses we'd have, and though I had never tasted a pineapple, that would be what we would grow because she had tasted one and wanted to have all she could eat.

Dolores would have gone away with me that night, but she understood that I had to stay for the trial. I didn't like the prospect, but I said if it came to the worst for Karl, she and I could leave the next night. She promised to tell the saloon that night that she'd come down with the cholera and had a fever. I might have stayed the night, but with her supposed to being "sick," and with other rooms near her, it was too risky. And to be honest, I didn't want to spend more time in that room than necessary. I stayed as late as we thought I could, and then I made my way back to the stable, which seemed to me like a palace that night. Truth is I liked sleeping in a stable more than a bed, though I already had the notion that sharing a bed with Dolores was going to change that.

11
A Hummingbird
and a Crow

THE NEXT MORNING WAS WARM AND CLEAR, A BEAUTIFUL day. But from the moment I woke up, it was like I had two birds at odds inside of me—a happy hummingbird beating fast around my heart and drawing sweet nectar from it, and at the same time a black crow perched on it and pecking away at the dread. I went into town with Arturo, as I'd paid for the stable for only one night. Dolores had told me where the jail was, or what passed for a jail, but it made no sense me going there, as they might well have locked me up too.

I wandered down to the river, where Dolores said the trial would be. The spot was a flat riverbank upstream from the boat dock, with two big oaks some sixty or seventy paces apart and a stump between them. The stump was the open-air courtroom, and one of the oaks was a convenient hanging one, Spanish moss drooping from its branches like the souls of the dead that had been strung up there.

Hours before the trial, the hangman was already there—a man who took his work seriously. I watched him toss the noose end of a thick rope over a branch of the oak, then lead his horse under it. Thin as a politician's promise, he was a tall bag of skin and bones in dirty gray miner's trousers, a black shirt, and black wide-brimmed hat. Here was the bird eating at my heart. In fact, in a large way, he looked like a bird. His eyes, not so much on his face as at the side of his head, were twin *mal ojos*. Settling his horse under the noose, he turned those *ojos* on me. I gazed at the river for a while until I thought it was safe to look back again, and saw him still fussing with the rope.

Under the other oak were a dozen or so mounds of dirt, some fresher than others. This was a cemetery, most everyone in it, I guessed, having made the short trip over from the hanging oak. A few of the graves were unmarked; others had small wooden crosses. A couple had large rocks for headstones, with rough writing scratched into them. One of the rocks read:

Tom Walters
Horse Thief
Ain't no gold where he is
No horses neither

Poor Tom's pile of dirt was so fresh it still had a shovel stuck in it. Even a horse thief, I thought, deserved some of the respect for the dead, so I took the shovel out.

"You can dig it anywhere," the hangman shouted, coming toward me. It took me a moment to understand what he meant—he thought I was a gravedigger—and then, just like curtains opening on a stage and you suddenly see the whole thing, a scheme came to me, all in one piece. It was a desperate one, but it was going to be that or standing by and watching Karl swing from the oak.

The hangman stopped near the stump. "It don't matter," he said. "They're all going to wash away in the next flood. You speaka the English?"

I shook my head. His *mal ojos* looked me and Arturo over, and he let out a little hiss that sounded like a gila lizard, then he turned to go back to his tree. Before he got there, I was on Arturo, headed back to the stable. The hangman shouted at me, but I kept riding—after all, I no speaka the English.

Not sure how much time I had, back at the stable I did a few items of brisk business. From the owner I bought a horse, a lanky sorrel mare, and threw Arturo's saddle on her. And I paid him for a month of Arturo's keep. A month was just a guess. I told him that if it got longer than that, I'd make it worth his while when I returned. If my scheme worked, I had no idea how long it would be before I'd be back, and if it didn't work, I was pretty certain I'd get strung up on the hanging oak myself and he would hear about it soon enough. I told him that my sister needed a room and board for a month also, and asked if he and his wife would take her in, and with a little gold dust inducement he said they would. I believed they were decent Christian people and Dolores would be safe there.

I said goodbye to Arturo and went to Dolores's room at the Snake Eyes. On a scrap from the stable owner, I'd written her a note about her going to room with them. I thought that even if she was in her room, I didn't have the time to tell her what was in the works. So I slipped the note under her door and headed for the cemetery.

The hangman was waiting there, sitting by the river and smoking. He gave me and my horse a long look, wondering, I imagine, why I had a horse now instead of a burro, but he let me be and tended his cigarette. I tied my horse up to the cemetery's oak and took up the shovel. And, taking my time, I started digging a grave. Maybe, I thought, my own.

Earlier, that cemetery had seemed to me one of the more forlorn places I had ever seen. But as I was digging away I thought there were certainly worse places to be dead. It was fairly peaceful there by the river. You could hardly hear the racket up in the town. And the dead there weren't alone, like my friend Thomas and all the untold others up in the mountains. I did feel guilty that, if my scheme worked, their peace was going to be thoroughly disturbed. On the other hand, if the hangman was right and they were all going to be washed away in the next flood, their peace was going to be short anyway.

I took my time digging, as there was no use going too deep. After a half hour or so of slow work, I saw and heard the whole circus coming down from the town. Men and women skipping and marching along with a fiddler, it was like a moving fandango. To be sure, most were well lubricated, and with bottles in hand becoming more so. Karl was front and center, a man at each arm bringing him along. His hands were tied in front of him, something I hadn't expected, and that was going to make things a few pinches more difficult if not impossible. He had to be feeling like a calf surrounded by coyotes, but he was keeping a brave face. I was tempted to let him see me, so he'd know he had at least one friend there, but that would have been risking the whole shebang, so I lowered my sombrero and chipped away at the ground.

While the whole caravan was assembling around the oak stump, a man in fancy clothes and a top hat came up to me—Mr. Stanford himself, it turned out. Short and big bellied, his sideburns were thick and bushy as garden hedges. Not too pleased with my progress, he said, "You get that done before sundown or no *dinero. Hoy. Comprende?*"

"*Sí, señor,*" I said. "I finish."

Not quite sure about me, he gave me a once over, then he marched over to play his part in the whole song and dance they were calling a trial.

The mob, the hanging oak, and me formed a kind of triangle. In my line of sight, the legal circus was about thirty paces away and a little off to my left; to the right of it, and beyond it by about another thirty paces, was the hanging oak. Over the babble of the drunks in the circle, I could hear some of what was being said in the charade. I got the sure feeling it was not going to last long, so now was the time to work fast. I spread out some loose dirt to make a patch about the size of four or five blankets. My next move had to be careful. The only person who might pay any attention was the hangman, and he seemed busy still perfecting the height of his rope and steadying his horse. I untied my horse and, using her as a screen, sprinkled a few pinches of gold dust over the dirt patch, just enough to give it a little sparkle here and there. Then I tied my horse with a quick release and made again like I was working, scraping away at the shallow hole.

In the trial I heard Mr. Stanford barking like a dyspeptic pup. When he finished there was a big cheer, and soon after, I watched them hoist Karl up on their shoulders and carry him toward the hanging oak. You could have pretty much cut the bloodlust in the air with a knife. I untied my horse. I had to wait for just the right moment, and I did. Just as they settled Karl on the hangman's horse, I hollered it from the bottom of my lungs: "Gold! Gold!" Waving and pointing all around me, I hollered some more: "Gold! Here! Gold!"

Any other word—other than "whiskey," maybe—would have landed on deaf ears, but there was something about that one that went straight into the soul of every man and woman in that herd. A stampede came at me, and if I had stayed put they'd have trampled me flat as a silver dollar.

Shovel in one hand and saddle horn in the other, I swung up on my horse. I had to cut her right to dodge the stampede, then kicked her into a full run straight for Karl at the oak. The hangman, to his credit, hadn't come running, nor had Mr. Stanford. They were each on a side of the hangman's horse, Mr. Stanford on the left, the hangman on the right with the noose in one hand and his horse's reins in the other, with Karl between them on the horse, its hind end facing me. As I rode toward him, the hangman's *mal ojos* looked to pop out of his head. I threw the shovel not so much at him as to him. He caught it and sensibly let it back him away. Mr. Stanford did not get out of the way. He chose to hit the ground in place, flattening himself as much as a big-bellied man can, and making things harder for me. I had to jump my horse over him and at the same time give the rear of the hangman's horse a slap so hard it might have branded him. Karl told me later that the horse bucked so mighty you could have stacked three sacks of feed between Karl's "arse" and the saddle, but somehow he held on to the horn, hands tied and all. Over my shoulder, looking for Karl, I saw Mr. Stanford pounding the ground with his fist. Karl's horse was following mine, and we were off. I felt bad about all those graves that were getting tore up, but I had to think they wouldn't mind, knowing they'd saved someone's neck and had a little fun at the expense of some of the folks who'd put them there. I hoped when it was all over they'd be put back in their resting places, if Sacramento could be said to have any place at all that could be called restful.

12
Running from the Hunds

WE HIGHTAILED IT STRAIGHT OUT OF TOWN, STOPPING once just long enough for me to get Karl's hands free. Then we headed for the hills, aiming for no particular place. My horse was faster than Karl's. His was a hanging one, maybe coach horse bred, and not the best rider. We hadn't gone very far before Karl was griping that his bottom felt like he'd gone arse-first down a staircase. I thought he might be a little more grateful that he wasn't swinging from the oak. I didn't need him to outright thank me, seeing he'd done nearly as much for me, but a little appreciation would have been nice.

Later, he pulled up on one of the first hills we climbed and looked back toward the town, and I saw he was brooding about something. "My work," he said. "It is lost." I looked back, too, and all I was seeing was lost time. I was sure someone would be coming after us, and soon. We had to keep moving, there was no time to tarry or talk. Exactly where we were going I didn't know, but going was a must, sore arse and all.

We moved on, keeping to a trail, though I knew we'd have to leave it soon. I'd ride ahead, then slow down a little and wait for Karl to catch up, then push on ahead again, trying to set a pace. After a couple hours or more of hard riding, we'd covered a fair amount of ground, and we stopped on a high hill to rest. That's when we first saw them—three riders, still distant, coming over one of the hills behind us. Karl pointed at my saddlebag.

"That is what they want. They wanted to know where it is. They said they'd let me go if I told them. We can leave it here."

Now, Dolores had said she loved me even before she knew I had the gold, but at this point, I had come to have the sure conviction that she and I were not going to make it to Hawaii without it. I didn't have much of a head for money then, but enough to know that our chances of getting to Hawaii without it were slim, and that if we made it there, our chances of making a go of it would be much better with that gold powder in our pockets.

"No," I said, "I need it."

Karl blew his top. "Ha! So it is not so easy to part a fool and his money! Do you want it or your life? Take some and leave the rest!"

"They'll keep coming for us," I said. "Even if we leave all of it, they'll think there's more. And they want our hides too. Not just the gold."

He knew I was right. We were both outlaws now—I was at least a horse thief—and we'd humiliated the boss. If they caught us, we were not going back to Sacramento alive.

Karl got off his horse. "Then you go on," he said. "Leave me behind. I can't keep up with you."

I told him I was not going on without him. Karl was maybe the most bullheaded man I've ever met, but he definitely wasn't stupid. He knew I meant it and that I was right about it not mattering a whit if we left the gold, so he got back on his horse. But where to? The only place we knew how to get to was Chucklehead, and we weren't going back there. With a slow horse, I knew our only chance was to go off trail. I told Karl to follow me, and to my surprise he did, without complaint or cross word.

We set off on a course going northeast from the trail. At first the bushwhacking was fairly smooth, but it got rougher and slower as we went along, and sometimes we had to lead our horses through deep gullies or around them. About a couple hours before sundown, we came to a shallow stream that was smooth bottomed enough to ride in, and we went upstream for a short stretch until it got too rough. We then crossed it and kept going north by northeast, keeping on well after sundown, until we were falling asleep on our horses.

We had no blankets. Even if we'd had a flint, a fire was out of the question. I'd bought a few scraps of jerky from the stable owner, but we had nothing to feed the horses. Neither of them was a backcountry beast, and they were jittery, not liking, I think, what they were smelling up there—coyotes or bobcats or something bigger. The horses weren't the only ones tetchy. After our first stop on the hill, Karl had been in a rare quiet mood. I suppose when your neck has nearly felt the noose, you get to contemplating more than usual. I didn't have much to say either, as I could pretty much feel it around mine too. Horses and humans are both that way sometimes, they just want to be left alone.

Roughing it like that meant for a hard, sleepless night. In the morning it was still dark when we set out. The hills got steeper and the going slower. I'd climb a hill and then wait for Karl to catch up. When the sun came up, I scanned the hills behind us, looking for a dust cloud or the chasers themselves, but I didn't see anything. I started to think that we'd given them the slip. But by midday I saw them, first their dust and then I caught a quick sighting and realized they were much closer than I'd thought they could be, maybe less than half an hour behind us. At that point, some of our bushwhacking had gotten so steep that it was risky for the horses; it didn't help they were getting hungrier and more ornery by the hour. We had no choice but to stay on them and keep pushing ahead as much as we could.

At the bottom of a hill we came to a fair-sized creek. Getting into it, my horse buckled and went down and wouldn't come back up. It was no fault of mine or hers. She'd stepped into a hole, and I heard something snap. I knew she was no good anymore. If I'd had a pistol I'd have put her out of her misery. We left her there in the creek. With only one horse between us, we had to try something, and staying in the creek seemed the best bet to lose the *hunds*, as Karl called them. Upstream it looked to get narrower and rockier. Downstream looked easier going, and there was a bend that would put us out of sight. If we followed the creek far enough downstream, we'd be out of the hills again and could find another horse for me and feed for Karl's. The hounds wouldn't expect that, going back down to the valley.

I led Karl's horse, he walked behind. The creek bed was sandy and mostly clear so you could see the bottom, with good footing, and plenty wide enough we could have ridden two horses side by side, had we had two. We made it around the bend and then another one, and then we heard a pistol shot, upstream. The hounds had mercy enough to shoot my horse, but there wasn't going to be any for us. The pistol shot spurred us. It was a couple hours before sundown, and I thought if we could make it until then and find a trail going down into the valley, and keep going into the night, we could get clear. We went around another bend, but then before even seeing them, I heard their horses splashing in the creek. I figure the direction my horse had been facing might have pointed the way; either that or they saw no tracks on the other side and guessed right.

They couldn't ride hard in that creek; still, they came down on us fast enough. There were three of them, as I'd seen from afar, and I knew them all: Rusty; the bird-eyed hangman; and, not that surprising, El Loco's pal Fernando. Between him and the hangman they could train three *mal ojos* on you at once, enough to stun a steer. There was no use trying to run; they had their pistols out and on us. I guess we amused them, because they were all smiles. It is very odd, someone pointing a pistol at you and at the same time smiling. Even Fernando was smiling, a thing I did not think possible.

So there we were, all in the creek, us and, twenty paces from us, the hounds and their horses, all catching their breath.

"Well, boys," Rusty said, "this is the end of the road."

"I will take that horse," the hangman said. I let the reins go, and the hangman called his horse to him.

Rusty pointed his pistol at my saddlebag. "And if that is what I believe it is, I will take that bag."

I went and handed the bag to Rusty.

He opened it and sifted his fingers in the dust, then waved me away with his pistol.

Karl said, "You have your horse. And the gold. Isn't that enough?"

Fernando and the hangman laughed, and the hangman said, "We got one more piece of business. Why don't we get it over with?"

By nature, I don't think Rusty was as bloodthirsty as the other two, but he likely had his orders. "You got anything to say," he said, "now's the time."

"Let the boy go," Karl said. "He hasn't done anything. Take him back to your friend the Loco," he said to Fernando. "He has more value alive."

That was just like Karl, thinking about "value." Even at a time like that, making an economy argument for me to stay alive.

It looked like Fernando might have even entertained the thought, but the hangman shook his head.

"Ain't done nothin?" he said. "He's a horse thief."

And with that, Fernando seemed to forget any idea of taking me anywhere and looked pleased about it. He hadn't forgotten, I think, the good kick I gave him back in Yerba Buena. Now it was time to get even and more.

Rusty cocked his pistol. "Yep," he said. "I'm afraid he's right."

I closed my eyes and took a deep breath, expecting it was my last. I felt Karl take my hand. Already compadres, to me that sealed us forever. They say a man's past flashes by before he dies, but my thought was for the future, Dolores's, and I said a quick prayer that He would be with her and save her from trouble.

Two shots went off, one after another. I felt nothing, but I'd heard that's how it is—first nothing and then all at once. But I could still feel Karl holding my hand. Only then did I sense that the shots had come from somewhere farther away than Rusty—from up the hill and to my right. I opened my eyes then and saw riders coming down the hill—one of them wearing a black sombrero with a silver band. Murrieta and a few of his men were coming straight for us. Some others were angling off downstream, and more were coming up the stream behind the hounds.

Rusty and the other two holstered their pistols. A gunfight would have been suicide. The hangman started in swearing a blue streak. A *dicho*—a saying—that Pablo had said about Murrieta came to me: "*Cien años de perdon a el que roba el ladron.*" That is, a hundred years of pardon for one who robs a robber.

Murrieta pulled up at the edge of the creek and tipped his sombrero. "We meet again, Sixto de Sangre. And your *tio*. Why don't you come out of the arroyo?"

While his men collected the hounds' pistols and horses—and our bag of dust—we told Murrieta how it was we'd gotten into the fix he'd got us out of. He was amused by how I'd got Karl out of hot water. From that, he knew that others would likely come looking for us once word got back that Rusty and his pals had failed.

How Murrieta came to save our skins was pure chance. One of his men had been in Sacramento and thought—for entertainment, I guess—that he'd take in the trial and hanging, kind of like going to the opera house. He had met the lead singer, so to speak. He saw us make our getaway and followed us even before the hounds set out, and somehow we didn't see him behind us, banditos knowing the trick to keeping out of sight. He went back to Murrieta and the others, and they were all close enough to start tailing the hounds. Their interest, it seemed, in Murrieta's telling of it, was not so much in saving our skins but in grabbing the gold that he had passed up once but wasn't about to again. Still, they had saved our hides. The how or the why they had didn't really matter much at first.

In what felt less an invitation than a directive, Murrieta offered that we should be his "guests" for a while until it was safer for us to go about. We accepted the offer as, having no food and only one horse and a likely bounty on our heads, going from the fire to the frying pan was an improvement. In question was whether any of our gold was still ours.

The hounds did not get dealt with too harshly. Two of Murrieta's men led them off toward the Sacramento trail—Fernando and the hangman doubling up as I, with pleasure, took Fernando's horse.

For four long days we climbed higher and higher into the Sierra with Murrieta and his men. I was wonderstruck by the sights. Later, an old Mountain Miwok would tell me that his people believed those mountains hold up the sky, and I understood why they might think so, the Sierra Nevada as grand as they are. I saw snow and ice, things I'd heard vaqueros talk about and had been doubtful could be real.

We finally came to a small Mountain Miwok village where the people knew Murrieta. It was dark, and we were dead tired. These Miwoks lived in the high mountains in the summer, in the winter going down into the hills only as far as they needed to get below the heavy snow. Many of the younger ones had never seen anyone like Karl before—a white man who wasn't a Californio or Mexican—but the older ones had at least once, an encounter that had scarred them.

As we were Murrieta's guests, we were welcomed enough, such that they had Karl and me bed down on pine branches at the edge of the village. Murrieta and his men made their own camp. That first night in the village, there were things that might have troubled me— if, or how, Dolores and I would ever come together; that there might be someone out there bounty hunting me, ready to take my scalp; that our gold was the price Karl and I were going to have to pay for being delivered from a bullet. Like I say, I could have let these things trouble me that night, but I didn't. The high Sierra was new and strange to me, far from any place I had called home, but at the same time, I felt I belonged there. It was almost as though, as the Miwoks believed, all things there, from a butterfly to a mountain, were alive and could speak to me. Speak in a language I didn't quite understand, though it seemed I had maybe known it once and one day could again. Maybe. That night, tired to the bone, I was happy to just listen, to forget my trouble.

From Karl to Friedrich Engels

July 30, 1849

Dear Friedrich,

I am writing to you on my last piece of paper with drops of ink borrowed from a notorious "bandito"! (A tale I hope to tell you someday.) Do not be surprised if my next letter is on birch bark or dried animal skin stained with berry juice.

I have made a science out of rationally predicting the future course of humankind, but I haven't even been able to foresee what is in store for myself. If you have begun preparations for a journey here, you must stop them and wait for another time, if any. Things have been such that I was forced to flee the Emancipated Socialist Republic of Chucklehead that I briefly had such high hopes for, and I now am in a small Indian village in the highest California mountains. The forces of reaction are everywhere, and I was lucky to escape with my life.

The village here offers a view of a primitive Communism that I have always thought had little to inform us. However, I was wrong, profoundly—and now you'll know just how much I've been through in California, because how many times have you ever heard me say that!

The purest form of Communism is at work here in the village: The people work not for the survival of a "system" but directly for the other human beings they live with. Everyone's welfare is immediately the welfare of all. Private concerns simultaneously articulate the universal common good. And there is no state standing against and opposed to society. The birth of the "Chucklehead Republic" made me rethink the necessity of an industrial society as a precondition for Communism. Now life in this village has taken my thought even further in that direction: The simpler a society is—not more complex as in Germany or England—the greater chance for the success of real Communism. The ideal unit of social life, which these "primitives" instinctively know, is the extended tribe—which is essentially what villages in Europe are. Modern society has become too smart for its own good and needs to recall its roots. I now agree with those who thought Communism doesn't depend on the development of capitalist industry, that it has always been possible—indeed, has existed to an extent we have grossly overlooked—throughout human history.

You know that I had begun working on a thesis, or manifesto. Because of my experience with the miners' republic, I began to rewrite it. However, all of that is now gone, in the hands of a bourgeois storekeeper who was eager, with others, to string me up on a branch of an oak tree. I intend to write a newer version, incorporating my new insights. However, at the moment I am quite occupied with the pine nut harvest!

I am also—how to put it?—amorously engaged with a native woman. You may scoff, but I am—do not take offense—more serious about her than you have been about many of your proletarian paramours. She is younger than I am but wise in the ways of her people, which I am eager to learn. Communication is a problem, but I am fast learning her language—and as you know, love has a language of its own!

Your secularly eternal friend,
Karl

13
Among the Miwoks

AT MOST THERE WERE ABOUT SIXTY TO SEVENTY MIWOKS in the village. The younger ones had no experience of white men other than Murrieta and his band. To them, Karl was like a spirit from another world. For the older ones, white men were real indeed, as the tribe had once had a short but bloody encounter with them. Because of that encounter, Karl, and perhaps even I, would not have been allowed near the village without Murrieta's say-so.

The Miwoks fed us summer seeds and pine nuts, and once in a while a piece of venison or rabbit. Like the Ohlones, the Miwoks ate acorn mush, sometimes with caterpillars or grasshoppers mixed in. The men were very good with a bow and arrows with heads made from sharp black stone. They could hit a rabbit on the run. Once during my stay, I tagged along on a hunt that felled two deer. The whole village celebrated and shared the meat.

The Mountain Miwoks were not like the Ohlones I grew up with around the mission. They had never been to a mission, had never seen a priest. Some, I think, had heard of priests, and what they had heard likely made them glad they had never seen one. They had their own language. I tried some of the Ohlone I knew, but I might as well have talked to stones. Though their food came harder, these Miwoks were healthier and more spirited than the mission Ohlones. I believe the main difference was pride. The Miwoks had it still—it hadn't been wrung out of them like it had the others. Take a man's pride, and you might as well cut his heart out.

Karl had never seen mission Ohlones, but he, too, thought the Mountain Miwoks had what he called "special virtues." He went around the village making observations, as he called them. It was an odd sight, Karl poking his nose into whatever they were doing, and they pretty much ignoring him. He seemed especially keen on divining the "virtues" of Huyana, a young woman who fed us and, to his delight, showed some interest in him, unlike others in the tribe. She was pretty and strong, and Karl perked up when he found out she didn't have a husband. She liked his curly hair and thought nothing about pulling on it and teasing it at any time, which, to my surprise, he let her do. At first, I believe, she wasn't entirely sure he was fully human, having come, as Murrieta told her, from the other side of the world. But she kept coming around, and soon they were getting very friendly with each other.

For the first few days in the village, Murrieta left me and Karl to ourselves to rest up and mend our sore behinds. Murrieta knew these Miwoks well, their way of life and their language. He went hunting with them and took much of his food in the hut of the village chief. I knew what I wanted to do—I'd had enough of digging and wanted to take my share of the gold, go and get Dolores, and then get the two of us to Hawaii. It took some doing, but I worked up the steam to say something to Murrieta about the gold. Not enough steam to outright ask for it, but with a mind to start a parley that could lead to that. I saw my saddlebag just lying there on the ground in his camp. Any one of his men might have got the notion to run off with it. I didn't come out and say that particularly, but I did say it might be wise to keep it somewhere a little more snug and that I'd be happy to do that, to keep it with me. I thought if he was willing to let me be the "custodian," as it were, that would be a step in my direction. I confess it occurred to me that if I screwed up my courage, or my desperation, I'm the one that might have got the notion to run off with it—half of it—some night.

Murrieta just stayed cagey about it. He smiled and said there was no need to worry.

I hadn't yet told Karl anything about finding Dolores in Sacramento or that I wanted to give up digging and go to Hawaii with her. I knew what he thought about love. He would tell me my life should be determined by my head, not my heart. But if we were going to go our separate ways, I owed it to him to let him know my intention. So I told him the whole Hawaii plan, Dolores and all, and, yes, he did tell me that "transient emotion" should not shape my life. This was at the same time he was growing sweet on Huyana, which I could have pointed out to him but didn't. He asked questions about me becoming what he called a "planter," and I could tell he didn't approve. I asked him what he would do on his own, and he said he'd been pondering his future, too, but didn't say any more. I was a little afraid he was going to tell me he would go to Hawaii with me. He was a compadre, but I didn't see the three of us, me and him and Dolores, making that work.

We'd been in the village for several days when it turned hot one day and I went to a spring close by to wash and cool off. I knew that the Miwok women went there to get water, so I didn't strip down. I washed as much as I could and then soaked my feet. I was the only one there for a while, but then two women came with skins for water. So they would have clean water, I got up and walked on some stones over to a flat rock where I could sit and let my feet dry. As I was walking, one of the women, pointing at my foot, screeched like a red hawk and ran off yowling toward the village. I had no idea what I'd done—foul the water? The other woman then ran off too. I'd had people be curious about my foot before, and sometimes cruel, but I'd never had anyone scream at it. I was sorry I'd scared the women off, but I sat back on the rock to let my offending feet, if they were the culprits, dry out in the sun.

It wasn't long before I saw what looked like the whole village coming to the spring. I had heard of Indians having some pretty powerful taboos, and guessed I was in deep trouble. Maybe polydactyly was a serious offense to the spirit of the spring. Not just the Miwoks were coming but Murrieta and his men, and Karl too. I walked toward them all, ready for chastisement or worse, and then Murrieta held up a hand for me to stop. Dead serious, he came up to me and held out a closed hand. Then he opened it and showed me a piece of broken seashell, half of a small purple spiral.

"Do you know what this is?" he said.

I certainly did. I took off my necklace and fit my piece of shell with his.

"Your mother," he said, "was from this tribe." His face had changed, softened, so that he almost looked like a different man. "You are my son," he said.

If the mountains had stopped holding up the sky right then, I wouldn't have noticed. Behind Murrieta—my father?—I saw the woman who had screamed.

"Is she my mother?" I asked.

"No," he said. "She is your mother's sister. Your mother is not alive. I will tell you about her."

And so he did, later. But first he called me *hijo*, or son, and embraced me. That night, we had as much celebration as could be had in a booze-less Mountain Miwok village. We had what passed for a feast there, the Miwok men danced, and I began to take in what it meant for me to be from that tribe and be the son of Joaquin Murrieta.

Joaquin Murrieta

"I was born in Mexico City. Our family came from Spain more than one hundred years before I was born. They were not counts or other worthless 'nobility' like many who came from there. But they were not peasant soldiers either. Your great-great-great-grandfather was a trader and a clever man, and after thirty years of hard work, he controlled much of the trade between Mexico City and Veracruz, and from there to Spain—hides, spices, gemstones and other things. When I was a boy, we were not as rich as the 'superior' families in Mexico City, but we knew them, and I went to school with their sons. I did not like my life there. It was dull, and things were expected of me that made no sense to me. The only things I liked were horses and hunting. I did not like life in the city and lived for the times we would go to stay at our family rancho. I hope that rancho is still ours and that maybe one day you will go there. I would like very much to die there.

"I had two older brothers, your uncles. They were interested in the family trade and wanted to learn it. I did not care for it at all. So my mother and father said I must become either a priest or a soldier. I didn't care for these, either, and fought with my parents and caused them to worry—what would become of me? The answer they came up with was to send me to California. My father knew a family here who would take me in. But I did not want to be taken in as one of the family. I wanted to be a vaquero on their rancho. The Californios did not live a pampered life, but even theirs—so I thought before I knew anything about it—would be too easy. I wanted to be a true vaquero, to do things that made the blood run in my veins. I was twenty years old when I said goodbye to my family. I didn't know how long I would be in California, and when I left, my mother cried and said it may be years before we would see each other again.

"In that way, I became a vaquero at the Rancho Gonzalez, a half day ride south from the Mission San Juan Bautista. Don Hernando Gonzalez was a good man. Other rancheros respected him, and he was fair and generous to his vaqueros. Our families were friends, but I lived together with the vaqueros in the bunkhouse. I did not want to be treated any differently from them. This was a point of honor for me. I tell you: Don Hernando had a daughter, a very pretty one, and one day he spoke to me, in a roundabout way, about marriage to her. I told him I was grateful for everything he had done for me, but I also told him too, politely, that I couldn't think of marriage yet. What I didn't say was that I didn't want to change my life with my brother vaqueros. That would not have been possible if I became Don Hernando's son-in-law.

"After the *matanza* in the autumn, many vaqueros would make the long journey to go hunting in the Sierra Nevada. We could not all go, as some had to stay behind at the rancho. I had been at the rancho for three years when I first went on one of these hunts. It would be my last time too. On that hunt, all of us were young and afraid of nothing. We rode for many days across the great valley and into the hills. We killed a mountain lion, and grizzly bears, and ate bear and deer meat every night. We were sure of ourselves, but we were foolish and lost track of time. We went farther and farther up into the mountains so that we were very high. Then one morning we were surprised—a snowstorm. Only a few of us had ever seen snow before, high in the mountains in Mexico, and none of us had ever been in such a storm. I had never seen anything like that wind and the cold. The snow so thick in the air and the wind blowing so hard, it was difficult to see very far.

"We weren't sure what to do—if we should build a shelter and wait out the storm or make a run to go below it. Making a shelter in the storm would have been very difficult, and there was a chance we could get trapped and run out of food. We decided to rush down from the mountains the way we had come up, and this was foolish too. We went down the mountain quite far, but it was still snowing,

and I got confused and lost the trail of my *compañeros.* My horse
and I went over a high ledge. I should have died, but I was lucky. I
heard my bones break and I lived. My horse did not. My compañeros
turned back to find me, and it was only with great courage that they
were able to carry me up from there, in a deep arroyo, and the storm
was still fierce. Both of my legs were broken, and my ribs felt like they
were piercing my heart. They tried to take me with them, but it was
slow and I was in great pain, and I lost my awareness.

"My compañeros later told me that my head was split open so that
they could nearly see my brain. I did not have my senses then, but my
compañeros, too, then lost their way in the storm. But by fortune or
God's grace, they came to an Indian camp. The Indians had generous
hearts and gave us shelter for the night. If they had not, we would have
had to gut our horses and sleep in the carcasses or freeze to death. The
next morning, the storm had stopped. My compañeros were afraid I
would die if they tried to move me. They waited a few days for snow to
melt before leaving the camp, but decided that I must stay there and
that one of them, Hector, would stay with me until I healed.

"Those Indians were the Miwoks we are with now. I stayed with
them for almost a year, until I was healed, and then longer, because of
your mother. Hector was with me for many months, but most often it
was your mother who fed me and gave me medicines for healing. Her
name was Taipa, meaning 'to spread wings.' She was very kind and
taught me some of her language. What else can I tell you about her?
I loved her right at the start, before I knew she loved me. In Mexico,
the girls I knew seemed to me foolish. Your mother was young but
wise, like an old man. The people in her tribe respected her. Her
mother and father were dead, and she had a sadness from that, but
she was brave and strong like you. She knew that her people wouldn't
accept me. One of her uncles, Honon, learned about us and tried to
beat her, but I stopped him. He is dead now too. Her sister Galilhai is
her, and your, only Miwok family who is alive.

"In the spring, when I was mostly healed, Hector left, but I stayed
until the autumn when I felt I must go, too, before the winter came

on. I wanted your mother to come with me. My family in Mexico
would not have understood any more than her tribe did, but I didn't
care. I thought we would stay here in California, and I would never go
back to Mexico. I didn't know then that you were inside her. She told
me she could not go with me then. She wouldn't say why, she said
only that I should come back for her in the spring. I tried very hard to
persuade her. I know now that, because of what was coming—you—
she wanted to be with her own people, even if they did not approve.
I loved her, so I promised I would come back in the spring.

"It was a long journey, much of it on foot, but I returned to
Don Hernando's, and he welcomed me. I was strong and ready to
work. My compañeros were happy to see me, and I was happy, too,
knowing that in just a few months I would go to get your mother.
But at the rancho there was a letter for me from Mexico. My father
had died, about three months before, and my mother was asking me
to come home to help her deal with my brothers. They were being
greedy and difficult with her about property and other matters.
Even though I had been away for so long, Don Hernando gave
me his blessing to go. I thought I would be gone for another six
months at most. I stayed in Mexico for nine years. My brothers and
my mother were at war with each other; there were cases in court,
and my mother became ill and begged me not to leave her. I stayed
until she died. After her death, the fighting over the family property
wasn't done—my brothers kept fighting each other—but that meant
nothing to me. I came back to California, to Don Hernando's. He
was in good health still, bless him, and he said I could return to his
rancho. I thanked him, but I said I could not. All I could think of
was finding your mother. In nine years, I had never forgotten her.

"I went, alone, to the mountains. The tribe had moved, and it
took me a long time to find them. And then what I found was death
and grief. Your mother had died only days before I found them.
Others had died with her. The tribe had buried them, and they were
still saying prayers to their spirits. They had been killed by yankees,
two murderers. That was the time when the first bands of yankee

soldiers were coming here, and those men—no, beasts—were probably deserters, hiding in the mountains, lost there. They were not mountain men or trappers. They did not know how to survive without their army food. They came into the village hungry. At first they were peaceful, but they started a fight about food. Honon said they began shooting people as though they were animals. Yankees are not the only men who can be cruel, but I have never seen other men who seem to enjoy killing the way some of them do. And then they call Indians 'savages.'

"I stayed with the tribe until their prayers to the dead were done. These people pray to the spirits of the dead, to ask them to leave in peace. I did not pray for peace. I swore to your mother's spirit and to my God that I would find those yankees and kill them. And then Honon told me about you and gave me the seashell. He said that when your mother became big with you, the women in the tribe would not speak to her or help her in any way, because they knew I was the father. He said he did not beat her, as he once tried when I stopped him, but that he, too, was hard with her and said things. Then one day she went away—where they didn't know. They looked for her but couldn't find her. They tracked her going toward the valley, but they lost the tracks and gave up looking for her. Then some months later, she came back and was big no more. She would not say where she had been or what had happened. Later, she told only her sister a little about you but not where you were. Once, Honon asked her about a child, where it was, and she showed him the seashell and said, "Here. He is here." Honon saw that that shell meant more to her than any other thing in this world. He said she would sit with it and hold it against her cheek and talk to it. She was sad with it, and he wondered if this meant that her child was dead. But, he said, there was something about her sadness that wasn't grief for the dead. She did not pray to your dead spirit.

"I will tell you that I was possessed by revenge. Some men believe we should leave justice to God, or to other men, but I had no faith or patience in either of these ways. Honon went with me to find the yankees. He was a good tracker, but their trail was cold. One of them had left a knife behind, with his name scratched on the handle. And Honon would never forget what they looked like. There were not many yankees in California then, so you would think it not hard to find them, but even so, we searched for those men for almost two years. We went south to Mission San Diego, and almost as far north as the Oregon land. Many times we were close to the sea, and I wondered about you—if you were alive, how I might find you. So I was looking for you, too, not just the yankees. I searched the face of every boy I saw, thinking I would be able to know you.

"We believed we came close to them a few times. We had been to Yerba Buena once already, and then much later we were told they had gone there, maybe to leave on a ship. We hurried to Yerba Buena, as we knew that if they got on a ship we would never find them. But this was before the gold, when there were not so many ships. They were going to have to wait for a ship, which was lucky for us but not for them.

"Yerba Buena was only a small pueblo then, a few adobes and a plaza. Honon and I waited in the plaza. Then Honon saw them, he was certain. We were on our horses and blocked their way. There were a few other men in the plaza then, but this did not matter to us. The yankees demanded to know who we were. I told them my name, and it is possible that the other men in the plaza heard it. I believe that a man about to die deserves to know who is going to kill him. I asked them their names, and they told me—one the same as on the knife. Then I showed them the knife. The other said, 'You lost that'— and then he stopped. I said, 'You left it the day you killed my wife. Now I am going to kill you.' They both laughed, and then they died.

"They are the only men I have ever killed in that way. I have killed others but only to defend myself. The yankees like to tell stories, that I kill men for no reason, that I am an evil man. I have heard that they believe that I killed those men that day only because they were yankees and I was angry about yankees taking land in California. Let them tell their stories. From that day they put my name on a paper to say they would give one hundred dollars to the man who would deliver me to the yankee army. That was before the gold. Now you cannot buy a mule in Sacramento for one hundred dollars! A 'Mexican bandito' was worth less than a mule!

"Honon and I rode back to the mountains. By then we were compañeros, and he wanted me to stay with the tribe. By taking their vengeance they came to see me as one of them. I stayed with them for a while, but I knew I could not keep living with them. I went off to live on my own in the mountains, and in the desert for the winter. Between those places I met men who once were vaqueros, but the ranchos they had lived on were disappearing. Already there were yankees taking land from Californios and sending the vaqueros away. We became brothers. To stay alive we hunted or took a stray cow. Sometimes the Don on a rancho would take us in for a few days. After the gold fever came, it has not troubled us to take a little gold now and then from the yankees, as they were taking many more things. We did not kill any of them in the way the stories say. Those stories are a slander of our people.

"Now, because we have taken some of the yankees' gold, they are offering much more money for me. Not for all of me, only my head. One thousand dollars just for my skull! They have a drawing of my face on a paper and have put it in Yerba Buena, in Monterey, and Sacramento. There are men who would rather hunt for me than for gold. I have seen this paper—it is not a very good likeness. The drawing is much more handsome than I am! They say I am angry about the yankees and their war with Mexico. But they know nothing.

"The Miwoks believe the soul is eternal. Just as the moon dies and comes back to life, so do we. They believe—and I do—that your mother is now in a land where the hunting bows never tire and the arrows never miss. There are forests with streams that roll over golden sand. We will join her there someday, and we will all be young forever."

14
The Deepest Convictions
of the Heart

I NEVER LET IT POSSESS ME—EVEN AS A BOY, I KNEW THIS was a hazard—but in a safe corner of my mind I kept visions of how my mother and I might find each other. These were not elaborate dreams—at the mission there would be a murmur, a bustling of padres, and then Padre Arturo would come to me, beaming, and announce that I had a special visitor. Or Mrs. Morgan would wake me in the stable one morning and tell me my mother was there. But that is as far as these visions went. I would hear she had come, and held some image of what she might look like, but she would never appear.

About my father I never had even these kinds of fantasies. Maybe that was because I knew at least a little about my mother, whereas I knew nothing about him. At most he was an idea, a changeable, shifting one. At times I would look at men like Padre Arturo or Mister Morgan or vaqueros, or even El Loco, and wonder if he was like any of them, if I was like him, but this was only confusing and tiring. More often than not, I could not summon even the idea of a father. There was only a blankness. So I stopped wondering, and over time a complete forgetting set in, a deliberate oblivion.

My father—more than thirty years later I am still struck with wonder when I say those words—was nothing like Mr. Morgan and certainly nothing like El Loco. Padre Arturo was like him in some ways, but he came to disappoint me too. A boy's father may become his hero, but how many a boy first has a hero and then discovers that that hero is his father? I felt a pride I had never felt before, having such a man as my father. For many Californians he was a villain, but I knew the truth of what he did and why, and that most if not all the stories the yankees told about him were not true. The yankees twisted his truth just as they corrupted so many other things. Gold really meant little to him. He did not want to be rich. Nor did he ever want to be famous or notorious. He had wanted peace, and deprived of that, he sought justice; then, forced to live on the run, he did what he had to do to survive.

In the short time we were together, I came to know what kind of man the real flesh and blood Joaquin Murrieta was. He believed what the Miwoks did, that everything around him had a spirit and breathed just as he did. He was always very aware of what was around him. This wasn't just from having to be on his guard against some-one trying for his head. He told me of his love for the desert and the mountains, the mountains most of all, and he knew much about the plants and animals there. In "essence" he was a decent and honest man. He was not a criminal. But he wasn't a saint either. I think he paid a price for being driven by vengeance for so long.

He had a temper. When one of his men got rough with a Miwok woman, he cuffed and kicked the man good. He'd become what he had to be to survive. For that, and for their survival, his men respected him and would do whatever he asked. He did not just give orders; he joked with his men and listened to them. He was the *jefe*, the boss, but they were his compañeros too. And to me he was big hearted and kind. He'd had his sorrows and grief for my mother, but mine were fresh, and he made them his too. It saddened him to hear about my life with the Morgans and El Loco. I had never told anyone about these things in the way I was able to tell him.

I believe he thought I might want to join him and his compadres. Then I told him about Dolores—I left out the saloon part of her life—and he saw that I had other plans. Leaving him so soon after finding him wasn't going to be easy, and he was wise about this. We said that it wouldn't be forever, that there would be a time and place for us again. That he would know his grandchildren. I told him of the plan to go to Hawaii and said he could come there to live with us. That amused him, and I didn't understand why, and I still don't. If it wasn't safe for him to sail from California, he could have gone back to Mexico and sailed from there. This never happened—and I never saw or heard from him again after I left the Miwok village.

My father said my aunt, Galilhai, was much like my mother. They both had strong spirits, were clever like a fox and at times headstrong like a bull. She was happy that I was alive, but I was a stranger, and there was a canyon between us that we would never cross. A few times, I caught her watching me, though the way that she did changed. At first she was afraid of me, as if I were some sort of ghost. I suppose in a way I was, that of my mother. Then slowly I became more real to her, though she never spoke to me directly, always through my father. She took care of me. She fed me, and every night she brought me a bearskin blanket. Once, she used a fish skeleton to comb my hair. She put a white feather in my hair, and that is how I learned that my mother was sometimes called "white hawk," a nickname Honon gave to her. When she and my aunt were girls, they were fighting on top of a high rock. They fell, and my mother kept fighting even during the fall. A white-tailed hawk will do the same thing—fight another one while it's falling, all the way to the ground. I told my father and aunt about my dreams with the white hawk. I thought this was passing strange, but to my aunt it wasn't at all. The Miwoks believed dreams were real, a road to and from where spirits lived, so my dream was no more surprise to her than a sunrise. My father said that my aunt talked to my mother in her dreams and that my mother was happy we had all found each other. I had to wonder if that could be real, if I could dream my way to her as a person, not just as a white bird. I have tried but have never found the way.

Even if I'd wanted, the tribe could not have been home for me, a half Miwok. The men had danced the night I was "found," but it wasn't all for me. They believed that God—the worldmaker, they called Him—came as an eagle and touched all things and gave them life and power; that there was an order to all things, and finding me had mended the order, put it back in harmony. So they danced for that, for restored harmony, as much as for me. Being only something like an honorary Miwok, the few boys in the camp wanted nothing to do with me. Getting a little fussed about by my aunt was about as much entry as I was allowed into the life of the village. Maybe as a very young boy I might have been able to join them. As a young man I could not, and that was fine with me, as I thought the same.

Karl, on the other hand, had a very different time of it in the village. It helped, I think, that my father explained to the Miwoks that Karl was from a "tribe" very different from the yankees who had killed my mother and others. I can't say why his water was thicker than my half blood, other than it was water witched by love into one of the thickest and most potent substances known to man. I'm not sure which came first, his interest in the Miwoks or his love interest in Huyana, who was sweet on him right from the start. It was one of those mysteries of the heart. I guess I've had my own mystery, so I shouldn't wonder. Karl followed Huyana around the camp and started to learn the language. No one told him not to; I guess people generally know when to get out of the way.

It wasn't easy saying goodbye to my father. We didn't know if we would ever see each other again. Though I could have joined his band, he said that running from the law wasn't what he wanted for me. And I was maybe too old to be "fathered" anymore. I had my own plan and my own gold, and he gave me some more. I wondered how much of that might have belonged to the yankees at Chucklehead, but I didn't let that trouble me much. My father said I would need it all to get started in Hawaii, and he was right.

A few days before I left the village, Karl told me he was going to stay and live with the Miwoks. I wasn't surprised. He was happier there than I'd ever seen him. It wasn't just his new love. The mining life hadn't been for him—or me, for that matter. With the Miwoks he found a way of living that made sense to him, that was in line with how he thought we should all live. He set about making his own hut, and it seemed in no time he and Huyana were under the blanket together and married—she had let him eat from her basket, so by Miwok custom they'd tied the knot. Like a Miwok man he pulled up his hair and tied it in a big tuft on top of his head. He took up the bow and arrow like he'd been born to it. He'd go off hunting for the whole day, and when he came back he was a different man than he ever was with me, at peace with himself and the world. Still, he was going to keep writing. He ran out of paper, and my father gave him a few pieces he had. I asked him what he was going to do when he used all that up, and he said he'd scratch away on a deer hide if he had to. He said he no longer had any use for gold and I could have all of the Chucklehead dust—a gift that, to this day, I am unspeakably grateful for.

On the day I left the village, I made my goodbyes. Karl told me I had come far in freeing myself, in fully forming my self-consciousness, and if I kept on that road, that is what I would eventually find: myself. I'd heard a lot of that kind of thing from him, but then and there it made more sense than it ever had, and I thanked him for being a friend and a teacher. What he said was true. I knew myself much better than I did before I met him. That wasn't all his doing, but without him it's doubtful I would have pieced it all together in the way he helped me to.

My goodbye to my aunt was a quiet one—neither of us said anything at all. She put a white feather in my hair and touched my chest, my heart—to say, I understood, that my mother would be traveling with me.

My father didn't seem worried that I was going back to Sacramento where I was a wanted man. He wasn't the worrying kind. I was naive, maybe, but I knew it was what I had to do, and I believed I knew how to do it. He provided me with a different horse and different clothes, and a wide sombrero with a lazy brim that hid much of my face. He went with me for part of the way. The route down was rough, well north of the one we'd come up on. We wanted to make sure we avoided anyone who'd been sent out to replace Rusty and his friends. After three days, we entered the valley early in the morning. It was cool and clear, the kind of California morning that makes you believe it can be the paradise Karl thought it could be, and we said goodbye. Up to that point, my father hadn't, as I said, seemed worried about me. But the moment of goodbye was tough for us both. I did not like having to choose something over him. I knew he didn't like that either, how the course of things had separated us, brought us together, and now was separating us again. I'm pretty sure he was not a believer, but he said, "*Vaya con Dios*"—Go with God—and then I watched him ride back toward the hills.

I took my time getting to Sacramento, as I wanted to get there close to nightfall. It turned out luck was with me on a couple counts. I scouted the stable, hoping it was a church night for the stable man and his wife and they'd be going out, and indeed they did. And Dolores and Arturo were right there and didn't take long to get with the plan and get ready to go. I was already a wanted horse thief, so taking a few of the stable man's clothes for Dolores wasn't going to make me any more of a thief. Arturo had been there about a month, so his keep was paid up. Dolores tucked her hair up under a sombrero, slipped into the stable owner's shirt and trousers, and with some other clothes stuffed around her middle, she passed surprising well as an hombre. We threw a few more of her things into a gunnysack, and just like that, we were on our way out of town, me on Arturo and Dolores on my horse. We rode into the night, following the river as best we could in the dark, until Dolores couldn't go any farther. The next day, we kept close to the river and hailed a boat going down to San Francisco. The boat had no room for a horse or burro, so we set them both free. After all, if I was going to be free, Arturo should be too. It was almost as hard saying goodbye to Arturo as it was to my father. But Arturo seemed to understand the necessity, and, sure enough, when I told him to head south, he trotted straight off in that direction. That way there was plenty of grass and water, and he'd get far enough away from all the crazy gold lust and any miners ready to rope him into their grand plans.

In San Francisco, Dolores and I stayed in my old adobe. Someone— maybe El Loco—had given it a few whacks, but it was still standing. To be safe, Dolores kept up the hombre act, even if she just stepped out of the adobe. We didn't want to take any chances. We were in San Francisco for only two days before we found passage on a Massachusetts schooner bound for Sumatra spice. It was only on our third day at sea that we felt it was safe for her to be herself. By then we could tell the captain was an upright man who ran a tight ship and would have suffered no roguery from his crew. He and they treated her like the lady she was. We got off the boat at the so-called "Big Island" of Hawaii and never left it.

Karl once told me to follow the "deepest conviction" of my heart, but in the same breath he said I should "act for humanity." Dolores and our son and Hawaii became the deepest convictions of my heart. Whether I acted for humanity may not be for me to say, but on our farm the workers earned a good livelihood, were quartered, doctored, and treated fairly, and from what I know about the world, that is more than a lot of men can say.

At first we could not buy a farm, because of the law there, and we worked on a sugar farm and learned a few things. But the law soon changed, and we bought our own land up on the Kohala coast and grew our own sugar. Pineapples, like Dolores had wanted to grow, were not going to make sense; they would rot before they got shipped anywhere. Things were not easy at the start, but sugar prices eventually got very good, and our farm grew. You might even have called it a plantation. We had the means to have a family and had a son we named Joaquin. He now lives in Hawaii, running the business. Dolores got sick two years ago and slowly got worse. Consumption, the doctor said. She died six months ago, and I miss her terribly—I'm still a married man. We buried her at a spot on the farm where you can sometimes see whales jump out of the ocean, something she used to love. I lost interest in the business, and Joaquin was ready to take over. So I came back to San Francisco, at least for a while. And come next summer, I'm going to make a trip into the mountains to look for family and an old friend.

The California Manifesto

The living fossils of old Europe—Pope and Tsar, Metternich and Guizot, the King of Prussia and the Hansa—have there joined together to resist and quash indefinitely the emancipation of the common man and woman. But these powers are impotent in the new land of California. No emperor or church patriarch, no spies of kings nor sour-graped utopian socialists have the reach or power to block the course of history here. Here that emancipation, known in a word as Communism, may find fertile ground and flourish.

America itself is in flux. Already on its eastern coast the scourge of industrialization has begun. But like a gangrenous limb, it may be cut from the body to save the whole. In California may be found that body worth saving and the conditions requisite for a healthy body politic to thrive. Here there are vast spaces of rich land and water for farming, forests and oceans that with proper husbandry will house and feed that body. These material conditions promise success, but it is the existing human conditions that will make good on that promise. From many reaches of the planet have come seekers of fortune, dreamers of the golden dream. Most of them will not realize this golden dream, and even those who do will one day see it for the illusion that it is.

As golden dreamers they were individuals, but bereft of illusion they will see themselves and others for what they were and are, an Underclass long deprived of its freedom and dignity: the poor Kentucky farm boy; the unbonded Chinese; the freed but scorned Negro; the exploited Pacific Islander laborer; the landless Mexican serf; the exiled Frenchman. These and others like them, streaming from the rich and varied springs of the earth, shall combine here and together realize their true human destiny.

In this new land, from the pieces of broken dreams that will give rise to this united Underclass, will come new ways. The old ways of sterile materiality and barren religion will no longer answer, and the mingling of men and women from all over the planet will produce a freedom of the human spirit that in the past has lived only long enough to be strangled in the cradle by princes, potentates, and Popes. This can only happen in a decentralized state, and that can only come into existence where there is currently no state.

Indeed, the existing state of statelessness here—not, as formerly thought, the existence of a proletariat—is the defining precondition for the rise of the Underclass. This statelessness creates a vacuum ready to be filled by new ways of being that look to find the self-realization of the human spirit within the human spirit, not without it. And the vehicle for this self-realization will be Communism—not that Communism formerly envisioned, in which material existence was thought to be the sole determinant—but one with a new vision. That the souls of men and women are dictated by their external circumstances was a revolutionary perspective for the modern age; but while souls are in part molded by their circumstances, they yet have a constant quality that is not touched by material being. This is their essential humanity, and it finds its expression in direct relationship to other humans.

The splendor of California's natural environment will inspire men and women to seek an essential return to Nature, and thus to themselves. In machine-plagued Europe and eastern North America, industrialized men and women have lost this, and it will never be recovered. But here, those who have been divided from their essences may rediscover it. Property relations will be transformed. The middle- and upper-class owners of property, from the shopkeepers to the feudalistic ranchers to the monopolistic traders, must be swept out of the way.

The theory of California Communism may be summed up in a few short sentences: Return to nature. Abolish private property.

Oppose the dominance of the machine. Make human self-consciousness the highest divinity. Practice not the "golden rule" of "those who have the gold rule" but the true one of reciprocal regard. Through these ways will come forth a civil society in which private concerns will simultaneously articulate the universal common good. So far in human history, philosophers have only interpreted the world; through these practices we will change it.

Skeptics and keepers of the status quo will scoff: Your society is a pipe dream, a puff of smoke in a hurricane. But the first forms of this polity have already existed in Indian villages and California mountain gulch republics or communes, and they can proliferate.

In a state of statelessness and decentralization, the structure of such a society will take its shape in these local communes, federated across the land. The native inhabitants of California once knew, before their Spanish corruption, this way of living. There are some who still know. Newcomers to California must have the imagination and capability to govern themselves in the same fashion.

It is only left to them to find the will to do it: Californians unite! Cast off the chains of custom and capitalism! Harness the spirit of your land! Let the winds of freedom blow!

Acknowledgments

I'VE NEVER UNDERSTOOD WHY MOST WRITERS THANK their loved ones at the end of their acknowledgments rather than the beginning. The "best" should come first, not last. And so: Without my wife Katharine (Kathy) Miller's inspiration and help, *Karl Marx and the Lost California Manifesto* would never have seen the light of day. She has been its "agent" and its talented artist, the creator of the black-and-white linocut reliefs that are at the beginning of chapters. These linocuts, requiring many hours of planning, sketching, hand carving, inking, and printing, perfectly illustrate—or so I think, with maybe a little bias—the novel's moods and story. Not only for this book but in every which way, she has been my one constant support for three and a half decades. Thank you, Kathy—with all my love.

I also want to thank Holly Brady for being the sherpa guiding the book to publication; Kim Bookless for her copyediting; and Lorie DeWorken for cover and interior design. Special thanks to my friend Carolyn Godfrey for help with German. And a shout out to the Palo Alto and Stanford University Green libraries for their general collections and access to special collections material.

About the Author

Scott Carlson has been a taxi driver, a short order cook, a hospital orderly, a farmhand, an Army cook, a lawyer, a teacher, a so-far failed screenwriter, a housedad, and a freelance writer—not in that order. He lives in the Bay Area and has never been to Sutter's Mill, ground zero of the California Gold Rush. He has an MA in Creative Writing from New York University.

Author's Note

I F THERE IS A HERO IN THIS TALE IT IS SIXTO, A YOUNG MAN of mixed race raised in a California mission. In placing Sixto front and center, I was quite aware that, as a white man writing in the twenty-first century, my imaginings of a half-Mexican, half-Native American young man's life in 1849 needed to ring true—even in a semi-historical, sometimes parodic novel. I believe that imagining ourselves in the lives of others is precisely what fiction can and should do. I'm hopeful that I succeeded in presenting Sixto's thoughts and feelings in a respectful and insightful light.

The historical context of this novel also required that several characters occasionally use antiquated terms to refer to Native Americans, Spanish speakers, and a black man. Had I not used such terms, I believe the story would have sounded false. By using those words, I do not mean to trivialize in any way just how pervasive and fierce the malevolence of white Americans (perhaps white Europeans less so) was in the 1800s toward all those not white, including Native Americans, African Americans, Mexicans and other Spanish speakers, Chinese, Pacific Islanders, and others. The literature on this topic is extensive and shocking. I hope and believe that accurately portraying how fictional characters in 1849 would have spoken can serve not to reiterate or ratify historical injustice but to give a constructive reminder of it.

I ask readers to also consider that in a *full reading* of my story, the people who are not white, who in this period were unequivocally not just discriminated against but suffered much worse, emerge as some of the best people. Though some of my characters do not treat marginalized people with respect, I believe that when all is said and done, I do.

To write this fictional account, I read extensively about Karl Marx's life and ideas, Native Americans' treatment during the California Mission era, and the California gold rush. A full list of sources can be found in the bibliography below. From my reading I gleaned a good deal of historical fact, but in some places my fiction strays from that fact considerably, and I feel I should say a little about the ways I did or didn't play fast and loose with history.

I have taken the greatest liberties with the life of Karl Marx. For factual background I relied mainly on Sperber's excellent biography, less so on McLellan's. From them and from Marx's writing came the relatively few actual Marx statements in my novel. A fair number of sentences or phrases used in letters from Jenny Marx and Friedrich Engels to Karl also come from these biographies and from Jenny's actual letters (Peters).

It is true that Marx had money troubles for nearly his whole life and was often hounded by creditors. One of his sons did use a cockney accent to chase them off (Sperber, 256). If Friedrich Engels had not bankrolled Marx for many years, he and his family might well have ended up in a poorhouse rather than their very modest digs in London. But as I imagine most readers know, Marx did not travel to California to make his fortune in the gold rush. In fact, he never set foot in the United States, though in 1850 both he and Engels seriously considered traveling across the pond. They were, however, unable to come up with money for the fare (Sperber, 259).

Though never physically in the United States, Marx did have some "presence" here. Beginning in the early 1850s, he wrote hundreds of articles about European news for *The New York Tribune*, then the leading newspaper in the United States (Sperber, 296).

With Marx's "communistic screed" I am guilty of a little anachronism. His *Manifesto of the Communist Party* first appeared in public in February 1848. He would not, then, have been carrying it around and still writing it in 1849 as my novel suggests.

It is almost certainly true that Marx had an illegitimate child by the Marx family's longtime "nanny," Lenchen ("Helene") Demuth. In 1851 (a year or so later than she would in my setting), she gave birth to a son, Freddy, whose paternity was never revealed by Helene. Friedrich Engels "stepped forward" to claim he was Freddy's father (Sperber, 262), but decades later, Engels said Marx had asked him to do so as a way to save Marx's marriage. According to Sperber, there is a "good deal of corroborating evidence"—beyond Engels's statement—that Karl Marx was Freddy's biological father, including Freddy's appearance and allusions to him in letters between Marx and Engels. Further "[c]linching proof" of Marx's paternity appeared in the 1990s in letters the Soviets had hidden in secret archives (Sperber, 262).

One has to wonder if, had Marx gone to California, Prussian agents would have followed him. They seem to have tracked him everywhere else. In a letter to the editor of a newspaper in England, Marx wrote, "Not only are the doors of the house we live in watched by more than dubious-looking individuals, who impertinently take notes when anyone enters or leaves, but we cannot take a single step without being followed by them. We cannot ride an omnibus or enter a café without being honored by the company of at least one of these unknown friends" (Peters, 99).

In a strange twist, the Prussian Minister of the Interior who sent these agents was Jenny Marx's half brother, Ferdinand von Westphalen. In what may be the first instance of the Red Scare, a Prussian agent wrote, "It [Marx's and others' activity in London] is so unusually dangerous for the state, the family and the social order that all governments and every citizen should join forces against this lurking enemy . . ." (Peters, 99).

The image of Karl Marx fighting a duel may seem odd, but in fact, the young Marx fought at least one duel as a university student in 1836. It was fought with "sabers," which was "an old German university tradition, still occasionally practiced today" (Sperber, 38–39). This duel left Marx with a wound above his left eye (McLellan, 17).

I'm fairly certain I have depicted a Karl Marx quite different from the historical one. Though there are indications that, like any human being except perhaps the very worst, he had a sense of humor, he surely was not the near-buffoon I sometimes make him out to be. I do recall reading somewhere about a family heirloom frying pan. I hope that, in his conversations with Sixto, I've presented his thoughts and ideology in a lighthearted yet mostly accurate light.

Mountain-dwelling gold miners sending and receiving letters in 1849 may seem implausible, but in fact, mail service was pretty efficient and well-used. Via the newly established "Panama mail route," a letter could go from New York to San Francisco in thirty days by steamship on the two oceans and overland across Panama. London to New York took about ten days. Relying on these delivery times, I have tried to make the timing of Marx's correspondence with his wife and Engels more or less credible. "Chucklehead" letters to Kentucky or Missouri may have taken an overland route, or sea and then overland, both of which at that time were slower and less reliable than the coast-to-coast route. All the Chucklehead letters are outgoing, so the timing of their delivery is no real matter.

According to Wikipedia, there were steamboats (plural) in San Francisco Bay and up the Sacramento River as early as 1847, though the entry implies there was only one such boat. My educated guess is that if there were any running at all up the river in 1849, they would have been rare. So, while it is possible that Sixto and Marx might have taken a steamboat, it is not likely.

Hydraulic mining such as the machine that blasts Marx and others in Los Infernos is also anachronistic in my story. Hydraulic mining—"hydraulicking"—was eventually widely used but did not begin in earnest until the late 1850s or early 1860s.

Whether Solomon, the African American slave who jumps the boat, is legally free, as he is told by the Boston lawyer, is a slightly tricky question. Solomon's boat ride takes place in April of 1849. Between the time of Mexico's 1848 cession of California to the United States and the adoption of California's constitution in late 1849, it was not always clear what the operative law of the land was. California, never an official US territory, was under American military rule, and at least some Mexican laws appear to have been in effect. Hence, technically, Solomon might have been a free man on the boat, as Mexico had outlawed slavery in the 1830s. On the other hand, during military rule, more than a few white slave "owners" brought their slaves to California with little or no challenge to legality. While many white miners were unhappy about competing with slave labor, it's likely that most didn't oppose it on legal or moral grounds.

Even after California gained statehood, Solomon's status might have been unclear. Although California's constitution proclaimed that "neither slavery nor involuntary servitude, unless for punishment of a crime, shall ever be tolerated," and the state was later admitted to the Union as a "free state," slavery's history in California was "far more complicated" than that (Anderson). An example is the state's passage of a Fugitive Slave Law in 1852 and its upholding by the state's supreme court.

My main source for the legend of Joaquin Murrieta was Ireneo Paz's work. There almost certainly was a real person from whom the legend of Murrieta began and grew, but little to nothing is verifiably known about this person, even whether Joaquin Murrieta was his true name. Distinguishing fact from the much larger myth and legend is too big a task here. Suffice to say the Murrieta story has been compelling enough to inspire retelling in more than a few art forms: Luis Leal's 2001 introduction to Paz's book cites works about Murrieta in biography, myth, narrative fiction, poetry, theater, film, and song. Pablo's campfire story about Murrieta borrows from a few elements common to many Murrieta stories. The later, longer account told by Murrieta himself to Sixto partly echoes Pablo's story but is mostly my invention.

Arnold Rojas's rich and entertaining account of vaquero culture in California is itself a gold mine of overlooked California history.

From Rojas, I learned about vaquero life, about reatas, horses, burros and mules, and the tale-telling of the vaqueros (see, for example, Pablo's stories of Juan Oso, and *el jinete sin cabeza*).

About the Ohlones, I relied mainly on Margolin. For Miwok beliefs and practices, a main online source that I deemed credible at the time I wrote my novel is no longer accessible. One online source that is accessible corroborates some of the Miwok beliefs about death and the afterlife that I used, while another offers some different views. An apparent common problem with these and other online sources is their failure to address the great geographic range of Miwok culture, and the concomitant diversity within it. Wikipedia, for example, provides the geographic boundaries of Miwok "subdivisions" but little about how they differed culturally from one another.

In broad scope, there were Coastal Miwoks, Plains Miwoks (Central Valley), and Sierra Miwoks, and within the Sierra Miwoks there were at least three large geographic groups: the Northern, Central, and Southern. Despite the cultural differences between these groups, most online sources about the Miwoks seem to simply echo each other in generalizations. An example may be the statement that implies all Miwoks believed "Coyote" was the creator of the world. That may not have been the case with Central Sierra Miwoks. Alfred Kroeber was a Berkeley cultural anthropologist who studied the various Miwok in depth, as well as other California Native Americans. According to Kroeber, "In Central California . . . [t]he conception of the creator is often quite lofty, and tricky exploits or defeats are usually not connected with him. Often there is an antithesis between this beneficent and truly divine creator and a second character, usually the Coyote, who in part cooperates with the creator but in part thwarts him . . ." (Kroeber, Religion, 343).

My point is that many online sources tend to simplify. A source will tell you something apparently definitive about a Miwok "land of the dead," or that there was none, but as Kroeber noted, "Ideas as to the world and the existence of the dead vary from tribe to tribe but present nothing specially distinctive" (Kroeber, Religion, 345). And: "The Miwok are said to have held that there was no afterlife; but this is a white man's superstition about them" (Kroeber, Handbook, 452). In sum, I've found nothing in Kroeber's work that contradicts the Miwok beliefs and practices I have presented and had reasonable belief were historically accurate, other than I have admittedly presented only a snapshot of a complex culture.

Borrowings

This novel's story, structure, style and characters are mine. However, as I was weaving my extensive research into the writing of this novel, I generously borrowed material that I believe is either in the public domain or falls within the fair use exceptions to copyright laws. Much of it comes from firsthand accounts by forty-niners in memoirs, journals, and letters. Making creative use of this borrowed material enriched my original story, supplying valuable historical verisimilitude, and for that I'm indebted.

To the extent possible, I've listed my reading in the bibliography below. However, at some point, in a room cleaning, I mistakenly and regrettably tossed out my index-card reading notes. Despite conducting an exhaustive digital and manual search of all of the sources I used in hopes of finding the passages or ideas that I believe are borrowed, some remain unfound. Although some of these passages or ideas might be original, the loss of my notes leaves me uncertain. Thus I'm choosing to list these as borrowings. Should any reader be able to identify the source of an "unknown" borrowed use, I invite them to contact me so that I can acknowledge it in a future version of the book; likewise, if I have failed to note any use, I ask them to please alert me.

Known Sources:

- In chapter 1: The specimen descriptions are from Jordan. I added his name to the museum's.

- In Marx's April 1, 1849, letter to Jenny: Passages related to Neptune, switchel, ship food, cholera remedies, and the ditty are from Walker and Gardiner. Tenerife is from Brand and an unknown source.

Passages related to the captain's conduct, melting tar, a shark, "fat dumpling" and his lashing, storms, a silver lining, and "mad with gold fever" are from unknown sources.

- In chapter 2: "[P]ink-eyed rice rats" and "alley cats" are from Walker. The rest of "rats from all over...the Amazon." is from an unknown source.

- In chapter 2: El Loco was inspired by the Marquis of Pendray, in Richards. Phrases in "His nose...with his claws." are from an unknown source, as may be Loco's "powers" and necklace.

- In chapter 3: The "Two Live Boar Constricters" sign is from Marryat and Cozzens. The "tent" men and their pitch are from an unknown source. "The best reatas...turn black." is from Rojas.

- In the Prussian agents' May 14, 1849, letter to King Frederick: The passage "one great cesspool of *Scheiß*, mud, offal, garbage, and dead beasts." is from Holliday. The *café chantant* and Marx singing the Marseillaise are loosely inspired by Gerstäcker.

- In Marx's May 21, 1849, letter to Engels: "One man...as much!" is from Walker. "To while...any trouble." and "Only to say...the eyes." are from Holliday. "They all believe...of springs." is from an unknown source, as are, likely, a few phrases in "On the boat... piece of the pie." and "There are great...from the American east."

- In chapter 4: Marx's toothache, his gymnastics, and Sixto's description of the village and entry into it were inspired by Gerstäcker; the Mountain Man's "gold lake" story likely by Ritchie, though its phrasing is likely from an unknown source, as is the Mountain Man himself and a few of his locutions. The tooth pulling is mine, except the villagers' aversion to the pulled tooth.

- In Marx's journal entry of May 10, 1849: Much of the structure of the first half of the "Gila Argonaut," and a few lines of dialogue, are from Gardiner. Colton notes a naked thief tied to a tree and tortured by mosquitos; however, some parts of the Argonaut's telling of the story are, I'm sure, from an unknown source(s).

- In chapter 5: "Alborak" is from Gardiner. "A burro...first place." is likely from Rojas.

- In chapter 6: Thomas's experience in the Mexican-American War is inspired by Dantic.

- In Thomas Stilwell's June 14, 1849, letter to his mother: The ox team names are from Hadley.

- In chapter 13: The passage "The Miwoks...young forever." is from a now-inaccessible website.

- The "California Manifesto" is a mash of "Marx-isms" and my invention, except perhaps "the poor...exiled Frenchman."

Unknown Sources:

- In the Prussian agents' April 23, 1849, letter to King Frederick: The passage "Rats are numberless...in the village." Most of the passage "Upon anchoring...bidding vigorously."

- In chapter 2: Phrases in the passage "I believe a burro...he was ready."

- In chapter 3: Phrases in "Padre Arturo...with a bull." The passage "In another box...an old mummy." *Buena suerte* with a burro is likely from Rojas.

- In chapter 5: Most of "Along the trail...fare home." Much of "It is on the verge...of change already." Much of "On the far bank...give her a try." Phrases in "One landed...all right."

- In Marx's journal entry of June 10, 1849: Some of the passage "There is...for directions." The passage "We are encamped...and stay here." "Before the gold...is all men." The passage "judging by...

Brahmins." The passage "but one might...in the canyon." Most of the passage "With four-legged...collapsed on us." The paragraph "We likewise are assaulted by..." The passage "A miner can stake a claim...no trouble." And "democratic equalizer."

- In Thomas's June 14, 1849, letter to his mother: "After...could scratch." "Some...with them."

- In Lucas's (Doc) June 15, 1849, letter to his sister Amelia: [C] ali etc. is from Stillman, as is "destroy...a coyote." The passage "All in all...from it." Most of "They were...Hebrews." The passage "As I said...days' sweat." These passages are likely from multiple sources.

- In Jeremiah Burns's June 15, 1849, letter to his brother Jim: Most of "filled up on whisky...to his foot." "Me and some...out in the creek." "We did not...their own country." The passage "Only a few...reapin it." The passages about holey trousers.

- In Marx's June 12, 1849, letter to Jenny: The passage "A pack of...a saint."

- In chapter 6: Parts of Marx's statements about Americans, "storms," and factories may be from sources other than Marx. Pablo's "tall tales" are from Rojas.

- In Thomas's June 21, 1849, letter to his mother: "Most miners... for practically everything."

- In Lucas's June 24, 1849, letter to his sister Amelia: Most of the passage "Sickness and death...dark portal notwithstanding." Colton notes "the dark portal of the grave."

- In chapter 7: "Six...duty seriously." Burns's statements: "The law...you say?" "All right...not guilty?" Most of "All right...ear too." "Sheriff?...our own." and "Ain't...if you want." Much of the passage "Whipping is cruel...an ear." Burns's "Persians" is likely borrowed.

- In Marx's July 13, 1849, letter to Engels: "But most important... working together."

- In chapter 9: "But they...want them to." Likely, phrases in Marx's "vision" speech up to "will take even that from you."

- In the July 16, 1849, article from *The Sacramento Speculator*: El Paso Pete, his overcoat, his jury selecting and locutions. "The flower...the judge." Much of "As the crowd...hangmen too."

- In chapter 10: The passage "It seemed like half...the happy ones." Miners' musk.

- In chapter 11: Somewhere I read of a hanging interrupted by a scramble for gold. That incident was a real find, not planted as Sixto's is. The passages: "Hours before...hat." "A few of ...into them." "You could...with a knife." and "Any other...silver dollar." Tom Walters's gravestone.

- In chapter 12: "Horses and humans...want to be left alone."

- In chapter 13: "Yankees are...'savages.'"

Bibliography

Anderson, Susan D. "California, a 'Free State' Sanctioned Slavery." February 27, 2020. https://aclunc.org/blog/california-free-state-sanctioned-slavery

Blodgett, Peter J. *Land of Golden Dreams: California in the Gold Rush Decade, 1848–1858*. Huntington Library Press, 1999.

Brammer, Robert. "So, You've Been Challenged to a Duel. What Are the Rules?" *In Custodia Legis: Law Librarians of Congress*. ISSN 2691-6592. June 2, 2016. https://blogs.loc.gov/law/2016/06/so-youve-been-challenged-to-a-duel-what-are-the-rules/.

Brands, H. W. *The age of gold: the California Gold Rush and the new American dream*. Doubleday, 2002.

Carson, James H. *Early recollections of the mines*. 1852. Internet Archive 2025. https://archive.org/details/earlyrecollectio01cars/page/n5/mode/2up

Colton, Walter. *The Land of Gold; or, Three Years in California*. D. W. Evans & Co., 1860. Republished by Project Gutenberg as ebook 69727.

Cozzens, Frederic S. *Sayings, Wise and Otherwise*. American Book Exchange, New York; 1880; pp. 106-108. https://elfinspell.com/CozzensBunkum.html.

Dana, Richard Henry. *Two Years Before the Mast*. Airmont Publishing Company, Inc., 1965.

Dantic, James I. "The Kentucky Volunteer Foot Soldier in the Mexican War: A Social History of Company B, Second Regiment, Kentucky Infantry Volunteers." *The Register of the Kentucky Historical Society* 95, no. 3 (1997): 237–83. http://www.jstor.org/stable/23383895.

De La Perouse, Jean Francois. *Monterey in 1786. Life in a California Mission. The Journals of Jean Francois de La Perouse*. Heyday Books, 1989.

Doten, Alfred. *The Journals of Alfred Doten, 1849–1903*. Edited by Walter Van Tilburg Clark. University of Nevada Press, 1962.

Gardiner, Howard. *In Pursuit of the Golden Dream*. Western Hemisphere, Inc., 1970.

Gerstäcker, Friedrich. *California Gold Mines*. Biobooks, 1946.

Hadley, Craig. *A Nineteenth Century Slang Dictionary*. n.p. https://mess1.homestead.com/nineteenth_century_slang_dictionary.pdf.

Holliday, J. S. *The World Rushed In: The California Gold Rush Experience*. University of Oklahoma Press, 1993.

Johnson, Susan Lee. *Roaring Camp: The Social World of the California Gold Rush*. W. W. Norton & Company, 2001.

Johnson, Theodore T. *Sights in the Gold Region, and Scenes by the Way*. Baker and Scribner, 1849. https://tile.loc.gov/storage-services//service/gdc/calbk/076.pdf.

Jordan, Henry J. *Hand-Book & Descriptive Catalogue of the Pacific Museum of Anatomy and Natural Science, Now Open at the Eureka Theatre*. San Francisco: n.p., 1865. Internet Archive 2025. https://archive.org/details/0221773.nlm.nih.gov.

Kamiya, Gary. "When an outlaw's severed head went on tour in SF." *San Francisco Chronicle*, October 13, 2017. https://www.sfchronicle.com/bayarea/article/When-an-outlaw-s-severed-head-went-on-tour-in-SF-12277208.php.

Kroeber, A. L. *Handbook of the Indians of California*. 1919. https://archive.org/details/handbookofindian00kroe_0/page/n23/mode/2up?view=theater.

Kroeber, A. L. *The Religion of the Indians of California*. 1907. https://archive.org/details/religionofindian00kroerich/page/342/mode/2up?view=theater.

Lord, Israel Shipman Pelton. *At the extremity of civilization: An Illinois physician's journey to California in 1849*. Internet Archive 2025. https://archive.org/details/atextremityofciv0000lord/page/n11/mode/2up.

Margolin, Malcolm. *The Ohlone Way: Indian Life in the San Francisco-Monterey Bay Area*. Heyday Books, 1978.

Marryat, Frank. *Mountains and molehills; Or Recollections of a burnt journal*. United Kingdom: Longman, Brown, Green and Longmans, 1855; Project Gutenberg, 2022. Originally published in the United Kingdom by Longman, Brown, Green and Longmans; republished as Project Gutenberg ebook 69412.

McLellan, David. *Karl Marx: His Life and Thought*. Harper & Row, 1973.

McNeil, Samuel. *McNeil's travels in 1849, to, through and from the gold regions, in California*. Scott & Bascom Printers, 1850. https://tile.loc.gov/storage-services//service/gdc/calbk/081.pdf.

Paz, Ireneo. *Life and Adventures of the Celebrated Bandit Joaquin Murrieta: His Exploits in the State of California*. Translated by Francis P. Belle. Introduction by Luis Leal. Arte Publico Press, 2001.

Peters, Heinz Frederick. *Red Jenny: A Life with Karl Marx*. St. Martin's Press, 1986.

Richards, Rand. *Mud, Blood, and Gold: San Francisco in 1849*. Heritage House Publishers, 2009.

Ritchie, Robert Welles. *The Hell-Roarin' Forty-Niners*. J. H. Sears & Company, Inc., 1928.

Rojas, Arnold. *These Were the Vaqueros*. Alamar Media, Inc., 2010.

Sperber, Jonathan. *Karl Marx: A Nineteenth-Century Life*. Liveright Pub. Corp., 2013.

Stillman, J.D.B. *Seeking the Golden Fleece; A Record of Pioneer Life in California*. Internet Archive 2025. https://archive.org/details/seekinggoldenfl00stilgoog/page/n26/mode/2up

Walker, Dale L. *El Dorado: The California Gold Rush*. A Forge Book, published by Tom Doherty Associates, 2003.